Behind Enemy Lines

Book 3 in the

Combined Operations Series

By

Griff Hosker

Published by Sword Books Ltd 2015
Copyright © Griff Hosker First Edition

A CIP catalogue record for this title is available from the British Library.
Cover by Design for Writers

Part 1

The Channel Islands

Chapter 1

England felt more than chilly to those of us who had survived the rescue of General Carter and my father in North Africa. It had been winter there too but we had not known it. Now, when wind and icy rain driving in from the east we knew that it was winter. Gordy and I had been grateful that the first few days of our demolition course had been indoors. The Nissen hut might have been draughty but it was not as bad as it would have been outside. Jack Johnson, another sergeant in Number Four Commando had been on the course already and he had prepared us for the dullness of the lecturer. As Troop Sergeant Major Dean had told us, "He is not a music hall turn. He is not there to entertain you. Listen and learn. The skills you acquire will come in handy." The commandos and their expertise were all that mattered to the Troop Sergeant Major.

And so, we had. We had listened and we had practised. We had learned how to use the new timers, cord and explosives. We had come a long way since the first days of the war. Boffins were producing new ways for us to kill the enemy each and every day. In our off-duty moments, we huddled around the stove in the barracks and spoke of those we had left behind in North Africa. Old hands and newly volunteered recruits had died. We had achieved our goal and even helped the Green Howards stop a push by the Eyeties and Jerry but there had been a cost. Just six of us now remained from the section which had

3

parachuted behind enemy lines. Our officer, Lieutenant Marsden, was still recovering in hospital. He would be there for a while yet. To be a British Commando was to put your life at risk each time you left on a mission. We did not wage war in the front line. We waged war behind enemy lines.

We got to know some of the others on the course. They were drawn from all of the Commando Troops. One of the sergeants from Number Two Commando came over to cadge a light from Gordy. He saw the fruit salad on my battle dress. Tapping the Military Medal ribbon, he said, "They don't give them out like toffees. You must have been at the sharp end."

I nodded, "A couple of times."

"Can I join you lads? My name is Fred Harris; from Wolverhampton."

"Help yourself. Tom Harsker and Gordy Barker."

Sitting down he took a long drag on his cigarette. "The reason I ask is that I am from Number Two Commando and I haven't been in action yet. I joined after Dunkirk. Have you lads been in long?"

Gordy threw his stub into the stove and gestured to me, "The Sarge here has been in since before Dunkirk. He was in from the start. We have been in action a few times."

He nodded and pointed to our faces which were brown. "And I see you got some sun. Been in Africa?"

I shook my head, "You will soon learn that we don't talk about where we have been. No offence but that sort of information is, well, secret. What I will say is that when you do go behind the lines, and you will, then all of this training will stand you in good stead but this," I tapped my head, "will be your best weapon."

Gordy nodded his agreement, "The Sarge is right. You have to be able to think on your feet and think quickly."

"Sorry about the questions." He pointed to his own battledress which was bereft of any medal of any kind and his new Commando flash on his shoulder. "I just want to do my bit."

4

"We all do. Don't try to be a hero. We left too many mates behind. Some of them tried to be heroes. There are plenty of Jerries out there who will try to kill you. There is no need to give them a helping hand. This war will go on for some time yet."

We chatted about life in the Commandos rather than specifics and we got on well. Fred Harris was young but he was keen. I wondered had I ever been that keen?

We returned to the Troop as soon as the training was finished. There were many lorries lined up when we arrived at the base. As we passed the Quarter Master's Stores we saw Quarter Master Daddy Grant looking harassed. Daddy had been our sergeant until he had been wounded on a raid in France.

"What's up Daddy?"

"We got orders last night. We have to up sticks and go to Falmouth. Falmouth; it's bloody miles away!" He pointed to the office, "Reg Dean said to report to him as soon as you arrived."

Troop Sergeant Major Dean nodded when we entered. "Glad you got back before we left. We have a new billet in Falmouth. We will be there for some time. Barker, you have been promoted to Lance Sergeant and Curtis to Corporal." He smiled, "I know you are supposed to have a say in the appointment of Corporal but you don't object do you?"

I would never argue with the Troop Sergeant Major. I grinned, "No, Sarn't Major besides Ken would have been my choice too."

"Good. He has the rest of the section and they can organise this little charabanc outing. You two take a lorry and go to Oswestry. Your new lads are there. You can pick up the other replacements too. "He handed me a typed list. "There will be twenty lads altogether. Here is a chit for petrol. We expect you in Falmouth by tomorrow night." My mouth must have dropped open for he laughed, "Aye I know; it's a bloody long way up to Oswestry and then down to Falmouth. That's why there are two of you. One gets his head down while the other drives. Now go, I have plenty to do here as it is."

We were Commandos and the prospect of five hundred miles of driving did not daunt us. We threw our Bergens in the back of the waiting lorry. I saw that it was already fuelled. Gordy said, "I'll take the first stag. You get your head down eh Sarge?"

"I'm not tired yet." The train from Scotland had been an overnight one. We had slept, albeit sitting up, for most of the journey. A Commando could sleep on a clothes line. I watched the land change as we drove. The further north we went the more peaceful we found the land. We saw animals grazing and horses pulling ploughs. It might have been pre-war. And then we neared Wolverhampton and Birmingham. There we saw clear evidence of the bombing raids. Great swathes of both cities had been levelled. We were used to that on the south coast but this was the heart of England. Once through the Midlands we drove through the countryside. We had enough jerrycans of petrol to get us to Oswestry and so we pushed on. We drove the two hundred miles in just under seven hours. I was pleased with the speed but it meant we arrived in late afternoon. Days were short at this time of year.

The duty sergeant looked at our orders. "Do you lads want a billet for the night?"

I shook my head, "No, Sarge, we have our orders. We have to be in Falmouth by tomorrow."

"Bloody hell! That is over three hundred miles and the roads in Cornwall..."

"Aye I know. Any chance of some grub. We haven't eaten all day."

Gordy nodded, "Aye me stomach thinks me throat has been cut!"

"Mess is across the square."

I nodded, "I know, I did my training here."

"I'll have your twenty lads ready as soon as you have finished. Don't expect too much from the canteen, will you? The cooks here change more than the recruits."

I handed him the chit for the petrol. "Could you have the lorry and jerrycans filled up, Sarge? It will save us a job."

"Aye, Robinson, fill up the lorry." He handed me back my chit. "Keep this. You might need it. You won't get to Cornwall on a full tank from here."

As it turned out the food wasn't too bad. I liked corned dog hash. I had never eaten it until I joined whereas to most of the lads it had been a staple. Gordy was less enamoured of the fare. He had grown up with food like this. To me it was still a novelty. It filled a hole. After that and some stodgy pudding we made our way back to the lorry. The twenty recruits were waiting there expectantly. One or two had a sullen look on their face. The prospect of a night in a lorry did not appeal. I decided not to get their names at that moment. I would find out who was who were later. It would be better to listen to them talking in the back as we headed south.

"Right lads, I am Sergeant Harsker and this is Lance Sergeant Barker. We have a three-hundred-mile drive ahead of us so make yourselves comfortable. If you need a pee have one now. The next time we stop will be when we have to change drivers or fill the tank up. Get your gear on board and we leave in five."

I heard the grumbles as soon as I turned to speak with the sergeant. I smiled. I would have been surprised if they hadn't grumbled. I wondered what they would have made of our task when we had left Oswestry. We had been told to make our own way to Poole in Dorset with no transport at all. I shook my head; I was becoming an old soldier already!

"Thanks, Sarge. Anything I should know about these likely lads?"

"No. You know the score. There are some cocky buggers. Some have just cut their mam's apron strings and the rest, well, if they couldn't take a joke they shouldn't have volunteered."

I laughed, "In other words the usual suspects?"

"Got it in one. But if I was you I would keep my eye on the big lad. He is a bit handy with his fists." I saw the man he meant. He pushed the others aside to get the seat closest to the cab; it was the warmest. The sergeant turned to go and then said, "Oh by the way your new officer left this afternoon. He took the train to Falmouth."

"Didn't he know we had a lorry coming?"

"Oh aye, he did. He said he didn't fancy riding in a lorry all that way. He likes his comfort does Captain Grenville." I cocked my head to one side. What did he mean? "Don't worry you will soon find out all there is to know about Captain spit and polish Grenville."

I did not like the implication but then that might have been the fact that I was used to officers like Major Foster and Lieutenant Marsden. Change was always difficult. I clambered behind the wheel and I drove for the first hundred miles or so. Gordy snoozed and I was able to hear the conversations in the back. I could not identify faces and names but it was their tone and what they said which interested me.

"Did you see that fruit salad on the Sarge? He had the MM ribbon on his chest."

"Means nowt, old son. NCOs and officers are all the same. They get the glory and it is poor buggers like us who take all the risks. You look out for number one. That's my motto."

From another part I heard, "Well I am glad the training is done. I want to do my bit. They bombed the 'Pool' the other day. Blew up my dad's old boozer!" I heard the distinctive tones of a Scouser.

"Aye I know. We had it bad enough in Manchester but we heard it was a bad 'un."

"It's all the convoys, see." A sing song Welsh voice chirped in. "Jerry knows we have to get everything by convoy now and Liverpool, well you are the nearest port."

"Aye well I am just glad they sunk the Bismarck! That was a big bugger. It sunk the Hood. My uncle was on the Hood." The Scouser again.

"Well don't get your hopes up boyo. I read as how they built another one just as big, Tirpitz! If she gets out then it will soon be all over."

"You are a right misery guts, Taff. The RAF or the Navy will handle whatever they throw at them. And remember our lot, the Commandos, have been doing their bit. There was that raid in Norway. Very successful so I hear." That was the Mancunian.

Then the second voice I had heard, the disparaging one growled, "Well shut it now ladies. I want to get some shut eye. God knows what they will have us doing when we get where we are going. Why that bloody sergeant couldn't have let us have another night in barracks I'll never know. Probably brown nosing."

There was grumbling and then silence which was soon punctuated by the snuffles, snores, heavy breathing and flatulence of the twenty recruits. I had learned a little, at any rate. It would be interesting to see the commando who had spoken with such derision. They had all obeyed him which meant one of two things: either he was a bully or he had done enough to merit their obedience. From his voice, I suspected the former but I had been wrong before. I was guessing he was the big lad the sergeant had warned me about.

We changed drivers twice more and used the jerrycans to fill up the tank. I awoke as we were heading to Launceston. When we had stopped some of the men in the back had descended to take a leak. It had been hard to see their faces in the dark and we still knew no more about them. I stretched and yawned. My mouth tasted as though I had been eating sawdust all night. We had drunk water from our canteens but I needed tea.

"I fancy a brew."

Gordy shook his head, "You sound like the big bruiser in the back." He gestured with his thumb. "He started shooting his mouth off about how they were entitled to a brew and some food. He reckoned he knew his rights."

I shook my head, "A barrack room lawyer?" Gordy nodded. "We don't often get them in the Commandos."

"Aye I know. The other lads didn't seem bothered but they looked to be a bit wary of him. He is a big lad."

"What happened?"

He laughed, "Nowt. I told him to shut it and he did. He grumbled and whinged for an hour or so and then fell asleep I reckon. Been quiet since Exmouth."

"I just hope he isn't in our section."

"You can sort him out Sarge! You have winning ways!" He laughed.

"I'll take over in a minute. I just need to check the directions."

9

"Don't bother Sarge. It is only an hour or so down the road. I'm not tired."

I nodded my thanks and took out the instructions. This time we would not have to find our own digs. There was a camp we would be using; temporarily at least. I wondered why they had chosen Falmouth. It was about as far west as you could get without falling off the end of England. At least we would not have as many air raids here. The Germans had stopped their daylight bombing but their fleets of bombers spread over the country each night like swarms of bees. Dad had told me how they had honed their bombing skills in the Spanish Civil War. Having rescued Dad from North Africa I now knew that Dad had been up to something in those days. I had thought he had just been a military attaché. Now I knew better. When we had time, I would press him to tell me what really happened all those times he was away from Mum, Mary and me.

The camp had a beautiful although somewhat exposed position high above the port. It was far enough away so that we would not disturb the townsfolk with our flashes and bangs. The rest of the troop had not beaten us by much. I guessed that the last of the lads had arrived shortly before night had fallen the previous day. Boxes were still being unpacked.

Major Foster looked harassed. "Ah, Harsker, welcome to Fort Shambles!"

Reg Dean sniffed, "I think that is a little unfair sir. We only arrived yesterday."

"I know Sarn't Major and I realise you have done your best but the good news is we are here for the duration."

"We have heard that before."

The office orderly said, "Telephone Major Foster."

Troop Sergeant Major Dean shook his head, "Officers! Right Tom, get them out of the lorry eh? Let's see what sort of shower we have."

I went to the rear and dropped the tailgate, "All ashore that's going ashore, my lucky lads! Get your gear and let's have one line."

As they descended I watched, with interest, for the man with the mouth. Having heard Gordy's description I was certain that I would recognise him and I was right. He was enormous. I would have put him at more than six feet two. I had not had a close look in the dark but now I saw why the others deferred to him.

I handed the list to the Troop Sergeant Major. He looked at it and shouted, "Hargreaves, get out here and check the new lads off while I shout out their names."

I saw Ken Curtis wander over. Like Gordy he had new stripes. He saluted, "We have a nice little billet for the new lads Sarge."

Troop Sergeant Major Dean said, "We will get yours out of the way first Sarn't Harsker." He looked down his list, "Crowe, Fletcher, Grimsdale, Groves, Hewitt and Smythe, front and centre!"

The six men snapped forward together. I was pleased that the giant stayed put.

"You six are with your driver, Sergeant Harsker. Take them away, Sergeant."

"Right turn, quick march!"

There was a snort from the line. I was about to respond when Troop Sergeant Major Dean snapped, "Man mountain; unless you have a medical condition, I don't know about keep your thoughts to yourself! I have my eye on you. What is your name?"

"Waller, Sarn't."

"That is Troop Sergeant Major to you, Private Waller. There is a note here about you. You don't like authority, well you and I are going to be best friends, believe you me! I am Sergeant Major Authority in these parts!"

I heard no more as I marched my section off to the barracks. The old hands were waiting for us outside. Gordy shouted, "Halt! About face! Stand at ease."

I stood before them with my hands behind my back. "We have had a long and arduous journey but I am afraid there is no rest for the wicked. Get yourselves squared away and then meet me in the cook tent."

11

They had lined up in alphabetical order and the one I assumed was Crowe said, "Where is that sergeant?"

Gordy looked heavenwards. I smiled, "You are a commando. Let's see how good you are eh? Find it!"

Ken Curtis said, "I'll show you where the sergeants are bunked, Sarn't." He grinned at Gordy, "Moving up in the world eh, Gordy?"

"Lance Sergeant Gordy if you don't mind."

As we headed for the cook tent I saw an officer I didn't recognise. Ken said, "He arrived late last night. Captain Grenville."

"Yeah we heard he was coming. Didn't want to come down in the lorry with us."

Ken nodded, "That makes sense. He has been snapping at lads all morning about salutes, uniform, the usual."

"But Major Foster doesn't bother about that sort of thing."

"I know Sarn't; it maybe it's the new broom syndrome eh?"

I saw, at the headquarters hut, Major Foster at his car. Troop Sergeant Major Dean was leaning in. He saluted and the Major drove off. We were tucking in to some sort of stew when Troop Sergeant Major Dean came over. He sat down with his mug of tea. "That new bloke, Waller, looks to be a handful. He is in Jack Johnson's section. According to Oswestry he is a good commando when it comes to climbing, running, fighting and shooting. The problem is he doesn't get on well with others!"

We all laughed, "We have had tough lads before. He might turn out to be alright. The Major off somewhere?"

"Aye, he'll be in London for three weeks or so. The new officer, Captain Grenville is in command."

"And when do we get Lieutenant Marsden back?"

"Another month at least. There were complications. Anyway, it means you run the section until he gets back." I said nothing but sipped my tea. "You aren't complaining, are you?"

I shook my head, "No, it suits me. It will give us time to knock these six new lads into shape."

He nodded, "You have a month."

12

"A month?"

He laughed, "We are victims of our own success. Everywhere we are being knocked back. The only place where we are winning is behind the enemy lines. The Commandos have to hold the fort until the rest of the army is ready to go back into Europe. There will be no rest for the wicked, old son. You have a month and then we will have a mission behind enemy lines."

Chapter 2

Each day Gordy and I had them up at five o'clock in the morning. The old hands were ready for it. A week of rest had prepared them well. The six new recruits did not know what had hit them. We had them out on the roads for a ten-mile run before breakfast. I confess that I needed the cobwebs blowing away too. It felt good. I used Ken and Gordy at the rear to chivvy them along. I knew the level of training they would have had at Oswestry. They would work to the lowest common denominator. Here I expected them all to achieve the highest of standards. Our experiences behind the lines had taught us that you could never be too fit.

When we reached the camp again the new boys were sweating heavily and their breathing was laboured. This did not bode well. I wondered if the men who had trained them at Oswestry were trying to send them out too quickly. I knew that there were far greater numbers now than there had been. Oswestry was just a small training camp. The largest were up in Scotland. I was quiet throughout breakfast. The fog of smoke and the smell of tobacco drowned out any taste the food might have had at one time. I listened to the conversation from the others. Things were not going well in North Africa. We were retreating again. The Germans we had met and fought were the tip of the force which Hitler had sent to support his Italian allies. Following on from the loss of 'HMS Hood' it created an air of depression.

I stood, "Gordy, get the lads ready to go to the range. Let's see if their marksmanship is any better than their fitness."

"Right Sarge. Where are you off to?"

"I'm off to see Reg Dean."

I knocked on the office door, "Come."

Reg looked up when I entered and, waving a hand to the seat opposite began to fill his pipe. "Right then; what's bothering you?"

"How do you know anything is bothering me?"

14

He laughed, "Because you get on with your job and only ever call in to see me when there is trouble."

"You are right Sarn't Major. How long are we in this camp?"

"Why, what's up with it?"

"Nothing but you and I know that having your own digs and looking after yourself makes better commandos." He nodded, "And the other thing is the gossip. When they are with others then they chatter about anything. They listen to rumours. Too many of the lads look on the glass as half empty. You know I'm not like that. These new lads are not the fittest I have ever seen and all the talk of losing the Hood, being driven back in North Africa, well it's not good for them. I'd like us to have a billet in the town. I would like us all in one set of digs. It worked in Harwich."

"I can see that. Well the Major said it was only temporary. He isn't here but I can't see any problem with following King's Regulations. You take your lads and get them billeted then." He laughed, "You are a crafty bugger! By the time I tell the others your lads will have the best digs in town."

I smiled, "I hadn't thought of that." I affected an innocent look but Reg was right. We would have the best choice.

When I reached the range Gordy and Ken had already begun training. They shook their heads. Gordy said, "Young Crowe here thinks he is Al Capone. He emptied a magazine before we could stop him."

That was wasteful. "Gather them round, Gordy. I have an idea." Once they were gathered I took Crowe's machine gun. "This weapon is better than the Lee Enfield the ordinary squaddies get to use but it has one major drawback. Ammunition. We have to conserve it. Now Private Crowe here has emptied his magazine. We don't do that. Short sharp bursts are what we use. Be mean with your shots. Imagine that you are paying for the bullets. We have one more hour here on the range. The first man to empty his magazine has to reload everyone's magazines." I saw a few sly grins appear on faces. "Oh, and the other rule is you all have to put six consecutive bullets in the bull!" I smiled. "Corporal Curtis, you are the referee."

They all wandered over to begin their firing. Gordy should have come up with an instruction which would have focussed them. I realised I had training to do with my number two as well. I waved him over, "After this training we need to find billets."

"I thought we were staying here."

"It was only temporary. I saw Reg Dean and we are the first to jump ship. The other sections will be told at lunchtime. We have a head start on them."

"It's a good idea. It means we don't have to do sentry duty or dig latrines."

"Actually, Gordy it helps to make for better Commandos."

"You are right." He looked up as we heard the short bursts from the Thompsons. "That was a good idea, Sarge. I should have thought of it."

"We just have to make the training more like a game. It will keep them interested. Oh, and I want us all close together when we are in digs. I want to make them run to the camp each morning as a team. We have to bond the old hands with the new ones."

"Do you think we are going into action again soon?"

"Every time the Major is sent to London we have some mission or other. I can't see them letting us rest on our backsides too long here. Besides the Sergeant Major reckoned by the end of the month at the latest."

"But we have just got back from North Africa!"

"I know but things move on quickly don't they?"

When they had to pick up their kit from their Nissen huts some of them began to grumble. Polly Poulson shook his head. There had been a time when he had been one of the younger commandos and now he had battle scars to show his experience. "If you wanted a barracks and a normal army life then why did you join the commandos?"

Private Fletcher said, "More money!" He was the Scouse voice I had heard in the lorry. He became Scouse to the rest of the section.

16

Ken Curtis rolled his eyes. I shook my head. They would learn or they would be shipped out. I was the arbiter of standards in my section. I made them double time down to Falmouth. There were many boarding houses there. I knew, from experience, that they would be the best place for us to be together. I selected the biggest one which was close to the sea. I knew that the MTBs and MLS I saw bobbing about in the harbour would be our transport to wherever we would be sent.

I realised we had dropped lucky when Mrs Bailey opened the door. Her red hands showed that she was not afraid of hard work and her steely eyes that she ran a tight ship. I introduced myself and explained who we were and what we wanted.

"I thought you lads had a nice camp up on the top?" She had the lovely rolling Cornish accent.

"Yes, ma'am but we are commandos. We pay for our own billets."

Her eyes lit up, "You pay in cash then? Not government script?"

I nodded, "They all have an allowance. So, would you be able to accommodate us? There are thirteen in all."

She nodded, "Ten shillings a week and that includes your laundry and breakfast."

"Make it supper as well and you have a deal."

"I'll need your ration books."

"I'll tell you what. You make out a shopping list and my lads will get you the food you need. How's that? It will save you a job too."

She beamed, "If you blokes don't mind shopping then who am I to argue." She held out her hand, "Mrs Bailey."

I noticed that she didn't give her first name. "And I am Sergeant Tom Harsker. If you have any bother with any of these lads let me know eh?"

She laughed, "I have been a landlady these twenty years since my husband died. Don't you worry Sergeant, I can handle these young lads."

I smiled as she gave them a lecture on what they could and couldn't do in her home. She sounded terrifying but she turned out to have a heart of gold. Over the next few months she became like a mother to us all.

17

We discovered that her husband had come back from the Great War a broken man who had died of his wounds leaving her a young widow. Denied children of her own the young recruits became her surrogate children. They confided in her when they thought that I was too unapproachable. The arrangement worked out better than I could have hoped.

After we had sorted our rooms out I ordered Gordy to run the lads back up the hill. I had told them to leave their tin lids in their rooms for we would not be needing them. I also made them leave their greatcoats there too. They were only of use when you were on guard duty and we would not be doing that any time soon.

As they jogged along the road I said to Mrs Bailey, "You might warn the other landladies that the rest of the Troop will need digs too."

"Thank you Sergeant I appreciate the warning." She smiled, "You seem a bit young to be a sergeant."

"Thank you for the compliment but you grow up quick in this war."

I soon caught up with the others and we picked up the pace. I noticed that we attracted little attention as we ran with Thompsons slung and packs on our backs. This was Britain at war. Most people were just grateful that the Germans had not invaded yet.

We spent the afternoon testing the other skills of the new men. We gave the six of them a head start and told them to hide. Polly, Harry and George enjoyed hunting them. Surprisingly we found two gems amongst them: Reg Smythe and Scouse Fletcher were really good at hiding. It turned out that Scouse had been a poacher and Reg something of a tearaway who had engaged in a little burglary when younger. In peace time, both were reproachable activities; in wartime, they were welcome skills. That afternoon saw the beginning of the transition from recruits to commandos.

We were marching back to camp so that we could report to the duty officer when we encountered Captain Alistair Grenville, temporarily the commanding officer of the Troop. He stepped out from behind a tree close to the entrance of the camp. Gordy and I had seen him in the distance. If he thought he was hiding he made a poor job of it.

"Where have you been Sergeant?"

"Training my new section in the woods yonder, sir."

"And who gave you permission to be off the camp?"

I was briefly stumped for an answer. We did not need permission to train. We used our initiative. "The Troop Sergeant Major knows where we were, sir."

It was a lie but I knew that Reg would back us up.

"And where are your helmets? King's regulations…"

"Sir, we don't wear helmets. This is the Commandos."

"Don't be insolent with me Sergeant. From now on you will all wear helmets. Now double time back to the camp. I will be inspecting your barracks!"

I hid my smile, "Sir, we don't have barracks. We have digs in the town."

"What? Why wasn't I told? Right, Sergeant you and I will go and see the Troop Sergeant Major. I can see that there is too much latitude here and you have taken advantage of the Major's absence! I will soon put a stop to this nonsense."

"Right sir. Lance Sergeant take the men to the armoury and then they will need to get some rations for Mrs Bailey."

Captain Grenville gave an irritated snort and turned to march towards the headquarters. He didn't bother with any preliminaries. He strode in and began without preamble. "Troop Sergeant Major Dean this Sergeant tells me that you have allowed him and his men to take accommodation in the town! Why was I not consulted?"

Reg kept a neutral expression on his face, "It is Standing Orders, sir. The Major always intended for the men to take digs in the town. The camp needed setting up and that is why we used the barracks." He held up a sheet of paper. "It's all here sir!"

Somewhat deflated he rounded on me, "And this sergeant tells me that he doesn't need permission to take his section off training! Is that Standing Orders too?"

"In the absence of the section officer, yes sir. Lieutenant Marsden is still in the hospital. If you like I can have the Sergeant inform you

19

when he takes his men off though, sir. You can do that can't you Sergeant Harsker?"

"Of course, Troop Sergeant Major."

Somewhat mollified he said, "Right well do that and don't forget the helmets next time."

I coughed, "I told Captain Grenville that the Major encouraged us to use our helmet comforters rather than helmets but it seems Captain Grenville wants us to wear helmets, Troop Sergeant Major Dean."

I said it in a reasonable tone for I knew that Reg would back me up.

"You see sir, when we operate behind enemy lines we need to be silent. The helmets are metal. If a Thompson hits one it sounds like a bell going off. Major Foster encourages the lads to use a soft hat to avoid that." He pointed to the sheet of paper he had given the Captain, "Standing orders too, sir."

He was defeated and he knew it. His eyes narrowed, "Well I have got my eye on you, Sergeant Harsker. Just because your officer is indisposed is not a good reason for you to take advantage of his absence."

"No sir, sorry sir." I did not mean my apology but Dad had taught me that martinets like Grenville could be handled better with feigned subservience. From his shiny uniform, I suspected that he had not seen any action. I wondered how he had become a captain in the commandos without combat experience. I put him from my mind as I led my men back to our digs. I had more important things to think about than the feelings of an inexperienced officer.

Over the next few days we gradually inculcated the men into the section. They had to learn everything. On the third day, as we trekked across a ridge line, a couple of Hurricanes flew overhead. The new men all looked up. I shouted, "Halt!" They stood and looked at me expectantly. "Here is another lesson for you. If we are in enemy territory never do that!"

Private Bert Grimsdale said, "Do what, Sarge?"

"Look up when you hear an aeroplane. You keep your face down." I saw the blank looks. "Lowe, tell them."

"If you look up then they have more chance of seeing your white face. Keep still when they fly overhead and keep looking down."

"But what about aircraft identification? Isn't that important, Sarge?"

"No, Private Hewitt. If you were an ARP then it would. What difference does it make what kind of aeroplane it is? We don't pack anti-aircraft guns. A pilot can see more than you think. We have to be invisible."

There were many such lessons. The more we went out, the more we learned. Lowe, Poulson and Gowland were the best teachers for they had learned it the hard way, in combat. By the time the Major returned I was well pleased with their progress. Even Peter Groves had improved. He still needed watching but he was not the gangster with the machine gun that he had been.

We knew something was up as soon as the Major returned. Officers and Troop Sergeant Major Dean were summoned to a meeting and the sergeants were told to be ready for a briefing. We gathered in the Sergeant's Mess. There were just four of us for the Troop was down to four sections at the moment. The rest were at Ringway having their parachute training. Jack said, "Well it won't be you lads who get given this job."

"Why do you say that?"

"You had that North African caper. We have all been sat on our arses since Christmas."

"You know it doesn't work that way. It could be any one of us or all of us who get sent out."

"Mebbe. How are your new lads?"

"Getting better. They think they are trained when they get here but we all know they aren't. How about yours?"

"Alright except for Ted Waller."

"The big lad?"

"Aye, he would be a good commando if he wasn't such a thug. I am not certain he sees the difference between Germans and his mates. He is too handy with his fists. The lads are scared witless of him."

21

"You'll get the better of him though."

"Of course! It is just that I wish I didn't have to."

The three officers came in with Reg Dean. The third officer was a new lieutenant: Lieutenant Green. Major Foster, in contrast to Captain Grenville, grinned at us. We were a team and the major was part of it. "Well chaps it seems that, once again, our specialist services are required." He jokingly wagged a finger in my direction, "I blame you Sergeant Harsker! You make rescuing Generals look so easy that they are sending us off again." He nodded to Reg Dean who took out a map and pinned it to the blackboard which was used by the mess orderlies for the daily menu.

The Major beckoned us forward so the eight of us were in a loose semi-circle. I saw that Captain Grenville did not appreciate the proximity of so many non-commissioned officers.

"As you must have realised with so many of our fellow commandos learning to use parachutes and Lord Lovat and 12 Commando only recently returned from Norway there is a shortage of experienced commandos. Now I know that you all have new recruits and we have two new officers but, be that as it may, we are still experienced enough for this mission." He took his swagger stick and tapped the map. "The Channel Islands. As you know the powers that be decided to make them open to prevent damage to the civilian population. The Germans have begun to build defences to prevent us from taking them back. Here at Les Lands, close to St. Ouen, on Jersey, they are building a gun emplacement. They intend, according to our information, to put four 155 mm guns there. They would have a range of over twenty thousand yards. Our job is to damage the gun emplacements."

Captain Grenville asked, "Why not use the RAF? They could level the whole island if they wanted to."

That in itself proved that he had not done this sort of thing before. Major Foster said, "Civilian casualties. They are using forced labour to build these emplacements and they are housed close by."

Reg Dean said, "And that means you have to go in softly, softly!"

"Quite so, Sarn't Major. Now there is a small bay to the west of the tower. At low tide, there is a ribbon of rocks which makes the approach tricky. The cliffs are not sheer and we shouldn't need ropes but they are tricky. At the top, there are two gun emplacements and a round observation tower. As yet the guns have not been mounted. Our mission is to destroy the three targets. Each target will be assaulted by one section. Sergeant Harsker and Troop Sergeant Major Dean will be the screen preventing the garrison from interfering."

Troop Sergeant Major Dean asked, "How many in the garrison, sir?"

"There are fifty guards for the labour force and another thirty guarding the site itself. The Germans are worried about the resistance attacking them and most of their defences appear to be to the east, the landward side."

"When do we go sir?"

"In two days' time. The tides will be right. We have to be in and out within four hours or we risk the MTBs and launches being grounded on the rocks." He tapped the map again, "It sounds hard but I think we might have a good chance of pulling this off. Six months down the road and they will have put barbed wire all over the cliffs and have machine guns dotted all over the place. It would be good to think we could destroy it but so long as we slow down the progress by at least half a year, then we will have succeeded. Let's get down to the details."

We had one day to practice and to gather all our equipment. I was happy with my section but I knew that some of the other sergeants were worried. At least half of my section had more experience than any other commandos in the whole troop. That gave the new recruits more confidence too.

Chapter 3

We were to travel across the Channel on an ML. The benefits of being so close to the harbour paid off for we had but half a mile to carry our Bergens to the waiting boat. Mrs Bailey let us use her lounge for our briefing. This was our first mission behind German lines and we needed the whole section to be prepared. Troop Sergeant Major Dean joined us and watched as I briefed them. "Empty your battle dress and trouser pockets."

They all did as I asked. The old hands had nothing in them save cigarettes and matches. The new ones had pictures of sweethearts and letters. Grimsdale even had a bill from a grocer.

I nodded, "The cigarettes, pipes and matches are fine. The rest stays here on this table."

"But Sarge! That is a photo of our lass."

"And you need it to remind you what she looks like?"

"No Sarge but…"

"Listen Groves, if we are captured you give your name rank and serial number. Nothing else. We are commandos and the Gestapo and SS would love to get their hands on you. Imagine if they had a letter from your wife. They could use that to break you. You don't need it with you." I pointed to Poulson, Lowe and Gowland. "These three have nothing like that on them. Focus on the mission. Nothing else."

As we headed down the front toward the launch Troop Sergeant Major Dean said, "I hope the other sergeants are as firm."

"They will be, believe me. What made you come on this little jaunt? Not that we don't want you."

"Shortage of officers. Captain Grenville reckoned a section without an officer might not do its duty."

"That is a load of…"

"I know but this is good. I have spent too long behind a desk while you lads go and do your bit. I have been champing at the bit to get back to the war. I don't want putting out to pasture just yet."

We marched the men down to the waiting launches.

I recognised Bill Leslie as we approached the boats. He was on MTB 371. He gave me a cheery wave. "Watch your wallets lads! Army is here!"

"Just get us there in one piece eh, old son?"

"We always do! Mountbatten's taxi service that's us."

Captain Grenville and Fred Briggs' section appeared behind us. "Get a move on Harsker. We have to board too."

I saw Bill roll his eyes. I explained, "Sorry, sir. You are in good hands here. This is a good crew."

I saw the crew smile and nod. Captain Grenville snapped, "No more than they should be. We are all on the same side you know." He led his men on board 371. Poor Bill would be stuck with him.

Some people just didn't get it. The Troop Sergeant Major said, "I can see now why they were so keen to get shot of him from the Guards."

"The Guards?"

"Aye he transferred. He wanted action he said. Major Foster told me. Apparently, he is well connected."

"Stick that on his gravestone then."

"That's a bit harsh Tom."

"I'm sorry Sarn't Major, but the day you think you are better than someone else is a sad one. Without these navy lads, we would be up the creek without a paddle. I know how valuable they are." I shook my head. People like Grenville annoyed me. They were snobs who thought they were better than everybody else. "Rights lads, follow me. There is our launch."

We were waved aboard our launch. "Perhaps Captain Grenville will realise that after this mission. He hasn't done it before has he?"

"Perhaps not, Sergeant Major."

The older hands showed the new lads where to stow their bags. We had learned through experience how to keep our Bergens out of the way

25

of sailors who were used to their tiny home. We were temporary passengers. We left three hours before dusk. It would take six or seven hours to reach Jersey. For the daylight hours, we would have the cover of three Hurricanes who would fly above us and protect us from enemy attack. We were still stowing our Bergens when we felt the launch slip away from the harbour. Unlike Poole and Southampton, as soon as we left the coast we felt the swells coming in from the Atlantic. I smiled when I saw three of the new boys race to the stern to empty the contents of their stomachs. Even Reg Dean looked a little green.

He shook his head, "This is the first time I have been on one of these. Is it like this the whole way?"

"It will get worse in the middle section especially as we won't have an horizon there. You get used to it."

One of the hands came aft, "Anyone fancy some cocoa?"

Gordy nodded, "Stoker's cocoa?"

I said, "Just straight cocoa, thanks. We'll save the other for the journey back."

He disappeared and the Troop Sergeant Major asked, "Stoker's cocoa?"

"Cocoa laced with rum. Very nice too but not before action."

We watched the sun set and the Hurricanes waggle their wings as they headed for home. I pointed up, "That's our guardian angels gone. Now let's hope there are no E-Boats out there."

The young Lieutenant who commanded the launch said, "Amen to that, Sergeant."

We slowed down to eight knots as we approached the island. Major Foster's boat led and we were tail end Charlie. I did not envy the crews of the four boats for they would have to wait for us and they would be within range of the German guns.

The Lieutenant said, "Better get your men ready Troop Sergeant Major. We land in thirty minutes."

We went below decks. Gordy rubbed his hands, "Right lads get yourselves blacked up. It's Al Jolson time!"

26

Gordy always managed to make me smile. His humour was invaluable just before we went into action. It relaxed everyone. My old hands had made sure that every magazine had been loaded by hand and the guns cleaned. We had no demolition charges but we had extra Mills bombs and magazines. We hoped we could get away without being spotted but I was not confident. We had too many new men. Mistakes happened.

We took only three Bergens ashore with us. Polly, Harry and George carried all the spare ammunition and grenades. My webbing was festooned with them but they had the spares. Reg nodded and I led the men on deck. Gordy took half down the starboard side while I took the other half down the port. I could see the island ahead. There were breakers showing where the savage rocks waited to tear the guts out of an unwary captain and his ship.

Once we had passed the spit of land the water became calmer and the Lieutenant edged us closer to the launches ahead. In the small bay, we had the room to land together. It was important to move quickly up the cliff. As soon as I saw the beach I jumped into the sea. I managed to land six feet from the bows and the water came up to my waist. I forced myself through the surf to the shingle, stones and sand. I cocked my Thompson and peered up at the cliffs. The Major had been right, they were not steep. We would not need ropes. We would use hand signals only. The Troop Sergeant Major ran alongside me and tapped me on my shoulder. I ran to the foot of the cliff. We were in the centre. The Major would take the tower to my left and the other two teams would deal with the emplacements on my right.

I put on my safety and slung my machine gun around my back. The first part was easy and I virtually walked up the shallow slope. It was when I was a third of the way up that I saw the problem. The slope was not steep but the surface, was covered in light sand and slippery shingle It could prove to be treacherous. It had not shown up in the aerial photographs. We would just have to deal with it. I turned and made the signal for follow my line. It was here that the rubber soled shoes would

27

come into their own. They gave a better feel to the ground beneath our feet.

I glanced up the dark slope. The shadows could prove to be deadly allies of the Germans. There could be loose rocks hidden from sight. I moved to my right. Moving diagonally across the slope was safer. I saw a rock to my left and I grabbed it. It allowed me to climb back up to the slope to my left. We were making progress although not as much as we had planned when we had first viewed the site. Above me I saw the gap between the tower and the emplacements. That was our route. I could not worry about the other three sections. My section had to be in place and protect them while they laid their charges.

Suddenly I was aware of a shadow above me. It was a sentry. I had to think fast. If he glanced down he would see us, raise the alarm and then all would be lost. I moved as fast as I dared. I drew my dagger as I went. I had no Bergen to slow me down and I never took my eyes from his back. Then I heard a grating noise as one of our commandos slid and fell a couple of feet down the slope. The sentry heard it and turned. He was six feet from me and I saw his face as he saw me. I sprang forward with my dagger held before me. Even as his mouth opened to scream my dagger hit his throat and my weight knocked him to the ground. Blood erupted all over my arm and face but he made no sound save the thud of his body hitting the ground.

I was on my feet in an instant. I sheathed my dagger, grabbed my Thompson and had it cocked in one swift movement. My breathing was laboured and I forced myself to slow it down so that I could hear. There was silence. I looked to the right and saw the new Lieutenant and his section as they approached the emplacement. To my left were Gordy and Polly. I waved them forward as Reg tapped my shoulder. We moved down the slope towards the huts. I saw, a hundred yards away, the wire fence around the workers' huts. I caught a glimpse of the two Germans from the glowing butts of the cigarettes. I turned and, seeing Ken and Harry gestured towards the sentries.

They slipped silently towards them as I located the guard hut. I saw the slight glow from the door. I waved an arm so that the rest of my section would follow me. I heard the sound of voices from within. From the size of the hut I guessed that there would be, perhaps twenty men inside. There were two doors. I pointed to the rear door and Gordy took Crowe and Scouse Fletcher. Reg was with me and we moved to the front entrance. I had to improvise a plan. When I reached the door, I waved to my section to spread out in a half circle and then mimed to the Troop Sergeant Major that I was going to go inside. He gave me a questioning look. I nodded firmly and he shrugged.

I nodded to George Lowe to open the door. He held it and used three fingers to count down. As soon as the door opened I stepped inside and said, in German, "No one move or you will be shot." I was lucky. There were four men seated around the table which was close to the door. They had cups in their hands. My Thompson was inches from the head of the nearest one. Reg was next to the one at the far side and, before anyone could move the rest of my section were in covering the rest.

George had the Bergen with the rope and the lengths of cord. "Get them all tied up." We had practised this many times but this would be the first time that we would employ the strategies taught to us. The number of guns pointing at them cowed the Germans. All was going well. I watched with pride as all fourteen men in the hut were securely bound. I was just about to leave when I heard a shot.

Troop Sergeant Major Dean shouted, "Outside!"

We raced outside. Harry and Ken were there. Ken said, "It wasn't us. It came from the gun emplacements."

Troop Sergeant Major Dean said, "It makes no difference anyway. The cat is out of the bag now!" He pointed and I saw Germans running up the slope from the huts which contained the compound guards.

"Spread out and keep low. Wait until I give the command and then short sharp bursts. Right Crowe?"

The lad from Manchester nodded, "Right Sarge! I ain't filling no more magazines that's for sure." Reg and I took the centre of the line. Gordy was at the extreme left and Ken the right. I saw the Germans running blindly up the hill. We were crouched with darkened faces. We

29

were as close to invisible as it was possible to get. The Germans were so focussed on their footing that they made the cardinal error of failing to look up. I waited until they were thirty yards from us and then I shouted, "Fire!"

The thirteen Tommy guns fired as one. The air was filled with the smell of cordite and the sound of screaming Germans. They were scythed down. The survivors turned tail and ran. Reg said, "You hold here while I go and find out the SP."

As he ran off I shouted, "Gordy, Ken take half the section back to the top of the ridge form a line there." I saw that I had Polly, Harry, Scouse Fletcher, Bert Grimsdale and Alan Crowe. "You new lads are doing well. When we fall back go as a pair. Scouse, you go with me. Back, then cover. Right?"

"Right Sarge."

I knew that the other teams would need time to set their charges. We had to buy them that time. I had no doubt that they would have sent for reinforcements. I worked out that we had fifteen minutes at most. Jersey was small. Nowhere was more than fifteen minutes away. Our elevated position meant I could see lights in the distance. When I saw five pairs approaching I knew that we were in trouble. They were vehicles and were coming from the main garrison. I shouted. "Reinforcements on the way, sir!"

"Fall back in five, Harsker!" It was Troop Sergeant Major Dean's voice I heard.

The men who had taken shelter when we had scythed down their comrades now began firing blindly up the slope. "Gowland and Poulson, start lobbing grenades. Keep their heads down."

"Right Sarge."

I turned to the three new boys who were all close to me. "Take out a grenade and pull the pin. When I say then lob them as high in the air as you can manage. We want an air burst. When you have thrown them run as fast as you can up the slope to the others."

"Right Sarge."

They all answered me but I could hear fear in their voices. "You are doing fine. Keep calm and do what I say. We'll get out of this."

Harry and Polly's grenades began to go off and the firing below us ceased. I heard the noise of German trucks as they ground up the road. Behind me I heard Reg Dean, "Right Tom, get out of there!"

Bert turned to move. "Wait until I tell you. Right?"

"Sorry Sarge!"

"Harry, Polly fall back and join Gordy!"

"Right Sarge."

"Ready. Throw!" I pulled back my arm and threw as high as I could. The other three did the same. "Now run back to the ridge!"

As they ran I gave a long burst with my Thompson. Below me I saw the four grenades go off. The explosions illuminated the charging reinforcements. The blast knocked them to the ground and the wave of concussive air hit me too. I turned and ran. I heard the sound of heavy machine guns as the reinforcements cleared where we had been. I reached the ridge and dropped down next to Gordy and the Troop Sergeant Major.

Reg Dean patted me on the back, "Well done. Five more minutes and we can leave."

"Gordy, Ken, set booby traps." I turned and saw the German sentry I had killed. I took his two potato mashers and tore the laces from his boots. I improvised a booby trap. I put one German grenade next to his outstretched arm and tied it to a second some three feet away. I spread some sand and stones on the laces.

"Here they come Sarge and they are mob handed."

"Everyone, throw one grenade each and then give a burst from your Thompson. As soon as you have fired get down the cliff."

I heard a cry from my right as someone was hit by the blind German firing. Major Foster yelled, "Fall back! Fire in the hole!"

I hurled my grenade. I had emptied my magazine and so, as the other Thompsons fired I took out my Colt and aimed at the figures illuminated by the explosions. The slope meant that we achieved a

31

greater range with our grenades than we might have expected. I hit one officer and a sergeant before my pistol clicked on empty.

Gordy was by my side, "Come on Tom! There's just us left!"

I turned and ran down the slope. It was harder going down than I might have expected. It was Gordy, however, who lost his footing when the first of the demolition charges went off. He tumbled over and I saw him hit a rock. He lay still. I ran down to him and hoisted him over my shoulder. I grabbed his Thompson too. It would not do to leave that for the Germans. Luckily, I was on the gentler part otherwise I might have fallen as well. I heard machine guns from the cliff and then the crack of grenades as they triggered the booby traps. Rocks showered me and splinters of stone too. The Germans were firing blind. They could not see us.

I found it hard to breathe as I laboured towards the water. Gordy was no lightweight. I saw the MLs bows. It was with some relief that I felt the icy blast of the sea and then hands were reaching down to pull Gordy from my shoulder. Once he was on board Scouse and Grimsdale hauled me up. Scouse said, "I thought we were a pair Sarge! What happened?"

I rolled on to my back and sucked in air. "The usual, Scouse, things didn't go as planned! Get used to it, they never do."

I saw his face, grinning above me as the whole of the cliff above us erupted violently as the last of the charges went off and destroyed the gun emplacements. Even as I was being pulled aboard the launch was reversing out of the bay and heading back to Blighty.

Chapter 4

We were not out of the woods yet. Gordy said, "Sarge, Reg Smythe is wounded. A bullet to the arm. We have no Bill Becket anymore."

Bill Becket had been our first aider. He had died in North Africa. Reg Dean said, "As I recall from his docket Hewitt has St. John's ambulance experience."

"Hewitt, see to Smythe. Use your first aid kit." There was no argument. The young commando just nodded and headed below deck. "Troop Sergeant Major, we had better keep a good watch with the navy lads. These MLs are lightly armed. Our Thompsons come in handy."

Nodding Reg said, "I am glad I came on this little jaunt but the Captain was wrong. You could have handled this yourself."

I shrugged, "I didn't mind. There is always someone to blame if it goes wrong."

"And I don't believe that for an instant. You would never blame anyone for a mistake you made. You should be an officer."

I shook my head. "I tried Officer Training Course. I didn't like the blokes who were training. They were too much like Captain Grenville for my liking."

"They aren't all like that and I am certain you wouldn't be. Give it some thought. I know the Major has talked about recommending you for promotion."

I pointed to the coastline we had just left. The sky was growing lighter. "We will have to wait until we get back to Blighty. We have six hours of open sea and I am pretty sure that Jerry will not be happy about our handiwork." We could see the fires still burning on the cliff top. Although there had been no ammunition there the three buildings had had enough flammable material to make them go up like Roman Candles.

The Killick came around with mugs of cocoa. He winked as he handed them out. "Stoker's cocoa."

Troop Sergeant Major Dean nodded appreciatively as he sipped his. "This is a bit of alright!"

"Navy looks after you. I'll pop below and see Smythe while it is quiet."

The wounded commando was lying on the mess table. He looked a little pale but he was awake and smoking a cigarette. Hewitt was finishing bandaging it. "How is he?"

"I found an exit wound, Sarge, so the bullet passed right through. I don't think it hit the bone. He would be in agony if it had."

Smythe grumbled, "It still hurts like buggery!"

"You have to be alive to feel pain. You'll live. Think of the stories you can tell about how you were wounded on a commando raid eh?"

He smiled, "I hadn't thought of that."

I turned to Hewitt, "Good job. From now on you are the section medic. I will get you a proper kit."

"But Sarge I was just in St. John's ambulance. I only did it so that I could get in the Boro games for nowt!"

Hewitt came from the north east and was a Middlesbrough fan. He and Scouse had had plenty of arguments with Crowe who supported Manchester United. "It doesn't matter why you got into it; it is a valuable skill. You are it."

I went back on deck. The sky was even lighter now and I could see the other boats. Bill Leslie's MTB was behind us and the other led our little flotilla. I looked at the sky. It was empty now but I had no doubt that there would be German aeroplanes seeking us out soon enough. The motor launch's Hotchkiss and twin .303 guns were our only defence. I finished my cocoa and then changed my magazine. Gordy, Ken and my other experienced men did the same.

"Everyone, change to a fresh magazine."

Peter Groves said, "But we are on our way home!"

Gordy snorted, "Well just in case Jerry decides he hasn't had enough of your company do as the sergeant says eh, Grovesy? Just humour me!"

We were two hours from Jersey when the search plane appeared. It was twin engined and kept going in and out of the clouds. I had no idea exactly what kind it was, probably a Henschel. It made little difference. We were spotted. I saw our young naval lieutenant go on the radio and a few minutes later we began to speed up. The launch was capable of twenty knots and we felt the difference as we began to bounce across the swell from the west.

I had to shout to make myself heard above the sound of the engines, "Jerry will be here soon enough. Bullets can go through the decks so we might as well stay here and take our medicine. Have your guns ready but don't fire until Lance Sergeant Barker or I give the order. We have done this before. If you are ordered to fire just aim in front of the aeroplane and, Crowe, this time you can empty your magazine!"

"Thanks very much Sarge!"

It was not aeroplanes which found us; it was a pair of E-Boats. We had met these before. They were heavily armed and extremely dangerous. They came from the west and their powerful engines soon brought them within sight of us. We could run but we could not escape. The aeroplane which had been spotting now dived down to attack us. It was a Henschel 129 and it had not only two machine guns and two cannons but bombs as well. It flew along our line so that it could engage us all in turn. Our young lieutenant swung the launch from side to side to put him off his aim but he was so fast that he had to hit one of us.

I braced myself against the bridge and held my Thompson against my shoulder. The twin engined aeroplane would be flying at over two hundred miles an hour. It would be over us and gone in a heartbeat. I heard the pom-pom on the MTB as it hurled its shells at the aeroplane. The .303s chattered too. Our Hotchkiss was slow firing but the gunner gave it his best shot.

"Ready! Fire!" The deck erupted as ten Thompsons let loose with a barrage of .45 slugs. I knew from my dad that it was terrifying to fly

35

through such a storm of lead. He began to pull up and I saw, as he flew overhead his bombs as they fell from the sky. They did not hit us but I saw them explode in the water close to the stern of the launch ahead of us. The propellers came out of the water as the explosives tore into the hull. It came down and stopped. It was dead in the water. I saw commandos in the sea. Lieutenant Green was still on the deck which was now canted to one side as it took on water.

Our young lieutenant slowed us down and shouted, "Get those men on board, as quick as you can!"

The leading MTB wheeled around to come to the aid of the second MTB. We would not be able to out run the E-Boats. We would have to fight them. The alternative was to leave the men on the other launch to their fate. I went to the side. I saw Horace Maguire, the section sergeant, he was face down in the water. I dropped my Thompson and jumped in. The icy sea was a shock. I came up and put my left hand under his chin to force his head up. I then sculled back to the launch. I heard Troop Sergeant Major Dean's voice. "Just four feet to go. Keep coming." I could hear the guns as the MTBs and E-Boats began to duel. In the sky, I saw that the Henschel was flying low and smoking. He would be lucky to get home. Then I heard, "Grab this, Tom." I felt something hit my right shoulder and I reached up and grabbed the wooden pole. I was hauled up still holding the unconscious Horace. We flopped on the deck like a pair of stranded fish.

Hewitt was there. He said, "I did some work at the baths, Sarge. Let's see if I can remember how to resuscitate."

I got to my feet. Reg threw a blanket over me, "You are a mad bugger and no mistake." He pointed aft, the MTBs were beating a retreat. One of them was smoking. "It looks like we are losing this one."

Just then the launch leapt forward as the lieutenant gunned the motor. "Change your magazines, lads. We'll need them again in a minute."

We were now overcrowded. As we headed north and west I saw bodies bobbing in the sea behind us. We had not escaped unscathed. I glanced down at Horace, "How is he Hewitt?"

"Alive Sarge!"

"Good lad, get him below decks, will you?"

Troop Sergeant Major Dean bellowed, "All wounded commandos get below decks. You are neither use nor ornament on the deck and you will only get in the way."

I loaded my last magazine and watched as the two MTBs drew close to us. We had more chance if we had all three boats together. We could combine our fire power.

The Killick hurried by with more magazines for the .303s. "Number One has radioed for air support. You pongoes just keep your heads down!"

Reg Dean snorted in derision, "I'll keep my head down when I am dead! Ready with your guns lads. Let's show these sailors that they have commandos on board!"

There was a ragged cheer. We were down but not out. I could see that Major Foster's boat was labouring. The gunner on the Hotchkiss at our stern took his chance and began firing at the bridge of the leading E-Boat. Sometimes you get a break and he did. The shells tore into the bridge. They must have hit the coxswain for it suddenly swerved to starboard. Major Foster and the commandos of Jack Johnson's section let fly with their Thompsons. The second MTB began to fire at the stricken E-Boat. When smoke began to pour from it we all cheered. The flight of Hurricanes which zoomed low and strafed the two Germans brought the conflict to an end. When the damaged E-Boat sank the survivors swam to the second E-Boat which beat a hasty retreat back to the Channel Islands. The Hurricanes emptied their magazines and then waggled their wings as they headed home.

Bert Grimsdale said, "Bloody Brylcreem Boys! Back home to bacon and eggs. There's the life for you!"

This kind of attitude made me cross. "Private, you don't have the first idea what you are talking about. It was lads like that who stopped the Luftwaffe in forty! They can have all the bacon and eggs they like as far as I am concerned. They have earned it!"

The former poacher was taken aback by my verbal attack, "Sorry Sarge. You are right."

"Stand by at the stern there, we will take Mr Horrocks' boat in tow and well done Able Seaman Hogan! Double tot for you tonight. That was damned fine shooting!"

The gunner was cheered by commandos and crew alike. He had been lucky but he had saved us that was certain. With the MTB attached by a rope we had a slow eight knot journey back to Falmouth. Two survivors from the other motor launch died and I knew that if we did not reach port soon then there were at least two more who might go the same way. One of those who was badly wounded was Lieutenant Green. He had a wound to his head. Neither the SBO nor Hewitt could say for certain what his wound was. His life was in the hands of God now.

I was tapped on the shoulder by Horace, "I hear I owe my life to you." He nodded to Troop Sergeant Major Dean. "Reg told me. Thanks, but you took a huge risk."

"We look after our own Horace, you know that."

"Aye. What a cock up. I mean we get down with barely a wound and then we lose, well God knows how many."

"It is luck. You can plan all you like but there are some events you can't plan for. We acquitted ourselves well." A thought struck me; a memory of the raid. "What happened on the cliff top? Who fired the shot? A German?"

He shook his head, "Nah, the new officer, Captain Grenville. He thought he saw someone moving and he fired his pistol."

"There was no one there?"

"There was a sheep. Poor bloody thing jumped off the cliff. The daft bugger couldn't even hit that. I am not impressed with him."

Once again, we had the Hurricanes above us for the last half of the journey. They had flown back to their field and rearmed. I was constantly having to explain to soldiers that fighters did not carry huge amounts of ammunition. I sat with Reg Dean and Horace as we watched the south coast of England grow closer.

"How many men do you reckon we lost Sarn't Major?"

"Have to wait until we get back to Blighty, Horace, but a fair few. I saw Commandos in the water when your launch went down and I dread to think what the MTBs will be like. They took a fair old pounding. Why?"

"It just strikes me there is a limit to the number of men who can fight in the commandos. I mean anybody can join the army but it takes special skills to do what we do."

"There's plenty, don't you worry."

I agreed with Horace. The Captain and Waller were two examples of those who seemed to have the necessary skills but there was something lacking. Each time we lost a commando it set us back. I was just grateful that I had only had one of my men winged.

The Killick came along with cocoa, "Jimmy the One says there is an ambulance waiting in Falmouth. Your officer will be taken away as soon as we arrive."

"Ta."

"You lads did alright. We have had some who think they are passengers on the Queen bloody Mary."

I laughed, "It's not our first time."

"I know. You are Tom Harsker aren't you?" I nodded. "Aye Billy Leslie told us about you. He said you could handle yourself. He was right. It takes either a nutter or a brave man to dive into the sea with his boots and gear on."

We saw the doctor and the medics as we pulled in to the jetty. The wounded were all whisked off. Troop Sergeant Major Dean was right Major Foster's MTB had many casualties. Even the Major was wounded. Jack Johnson had survived and his man mountain, Private Waller, too. The rest of his section were either dead or wounded. He shook his head in disbelief as the ambulances took away all but him and Waller.

"You get back to your digs Waller. I'll see you at the camp 0800 hours. Have a lie in."

Waller shook his head at the attempt at humour, "Right Sarge."

39

"Of all the men to survive it had to be him! He is the most unpleasant commando I have ever met."

"He's getting no better then?"

"Worse if anything. Mind you he has got guts. He stood at the stern and blasted away with his Thompson. He doesn't bother about his mates."

Reg asked, "Perhaps we ought to ship him out."

"I can't think of a reason. He just doesn't fit."

The last MTB tied up and Captain Grenville and Fred Briggs' section disembarked. There were just six of them. I saw four bodies covered in blankets by the stern rail. The Captain came over to Troop Sergeant Major Dean. "Where is Major Foster?"

"Taken to hospital. Just a scratch but he will be away for a day or two."

"Right, carry on Troop Sergeant Major." He strode off without even looking back.

Corporal Baines came over to us. "Fred bought it, Sarn't Major."

I couldn't help directing my gaze to the rigid back of the captain who walked away without a care in the world.

"How?"

"It was the last attack. Fred had our section add their fire to the MTB. Those E-Boats are bastards! He was encouraging the lads when he had his head taken off by a German cannon."

"Where was the Captain?"

There was a pause. "He was below decks. He told Fred that he was a commando and not a sailor." He pointed to the MTB where I saw Bill Leslie being reprimanded. "Your mate Bill said we were all in the same boat and he should do his bit." He shook his head, "When the fighting was over Captain Grenville insisted that he be reprimanded. He has lost his Leading Seaman badge. He is back to Ordinary Seaman and he has fourteen days loss of privileges." I felt my fists clenching. Bill had said what he had done because of me. He had lost two promotions. It was like me being reduced to a private.

40

Reg said quietly, "You can do nowt about it son. He's an officer. Your mate knew that when he opened his mouth. You know there's no point in arguing with an officer. They always win." He turned to Harry Baines, "You take charge of the section until I can sort something out."

"Right Sarn't Major."

"And don't forget to write a report for the Major." He winked and Harry nodded. As he left Reg said, "There's more than one way to skin a cat. If Mr Grenville likes to do things by the book then let's use it eh? Tomorrow morning, nine o'clock in my office with your reports too."

"Right Troop Sergeant Major."

"And Tom."

"Yes, Sarn't Major?"

"Thanks for keeping an eye out for me. You are a good lad."

That compliment made my day. I could take the Grenvilles of this world all week long and twice on Sundays so long as I had men like Reg Dean and his ilk on my side. "Right lads, back to the digs. Scouse bring Smythe's gear and gun."

"Righto Sarge."

Their spirits were down as we marched back along the front. "Come on Lance Sergeant, a song to help us march."

He began singing one they would all know and I noticed that their step became just that bit sprightlier.

Bless 'em all,
Bless 'em all.
The long and the short and the tall,
Bless all those Sergeants and WO1's,
Bless all those Corporals and their bleedin' sons,
Cos' we're saying goodbye to 'em all.
And back to their Billets they crawl,
You'll get no promotion this side of the ocean,
So cheer up my lads bless 'em all

Mrs Bailey heard us singing as we were approaching and was at the door waiting for us with a smile on her face. We had not told her we were going behind enemy lines but she was no fool and our preparations

41

had led her to only one conclusion. She frowned as they all passed her, saluting as they did so. "Where's Reg, Sergeant?"

"He took a bullet in his arm." Her hand went to her mouth. "Don't worry, Mrs Bailey, he'll be right as rain in a few days." She nodded. I added quietly, "We are soldiers and we will get hurt. Some of the other sections had men killed. We were lucky."

I saw her welling up, "It's a shame. You young lads having to fight these nasty Germans. It's like the Great War all over again!"

I felt sad for the woman. She was reliving her time almost twenty years earlier when her husband had been, like my dad, on the western front. She must have seen many young men go to war and either not come home or, like her husband, come home broken.

Chapter 5

I arrived at the camp early for I wanted to write my own report. I was never certain who would actually read them but I was diligent and I did them. When I reached the office Troop Sergeant Major Dean was smoking his pipe and reading through his own paperwork. He gestured to the chair.

"You know, Tom, I am not certain I can go back to a life behind a desk. I reckon I will have a word with Major Foster. I am Troop Sergeant Major I should be sharing the risks with you lads."

"You'll get no arguments from me."

"In the meantime, we need to do something about Fred Briggs' section."

"What about Corporal Baines?"

"He's like Ken Curtis, he was only recently promoted. You won't like it but I am going to give Gordy a chance with them. He impressed me on the operation. When the Major comes back he can make a decision but Gordy has the right personality."

I nodded, "You are right; he is a perfect choice. I can't think of a better sergeant. He will be a good leader for the section and, you were correct, I am not happy about losing him but we do what we do for the service eh? Will you tell him?"

"It would be for the best and it might be a bit easier too." He picked up a clipboard, "This is for Captain Grenville; it is not me asking. Give him your plan for the week. And we have had orders from Headquarters to send the new chaps for parachute training. I will send your lads and the new ones from Briggs' section."

"Good. They will enjoy that."

"What are your plans for your section today?" He nodded towards the clipboard.

I groaned inwardly. The Captain was in charge again until the Major was fit. "I guess we will do some cliff and rope work. We nearly came a cropper the other night. Their accuracy is fine and we have their fitness in hand. They are turning out to be a good bunch."

"Excellent and Lieutenant Marsden is back next Monday."

"Thank the Lord for that! He can deal with Mr Grenville."

"Send Gordy to me at ten. That will give me the chance to catch up with this paperwork. It soon mounts up."

I stood, put on my beret and saluted. As I opened the door I saw Captain Grenville standing there. I saluted. He looked right through me. It was as though I didn't even exist. I stood aside and he entered. I had put him from my mind before I reached the cook house where I knew I would find my section. It would not do to let him get under my skin.

They were all waiting and, in contrast to the other sections, looked happy. The other three sections had the haunted look of those who have seen their best friends die. I had been through that on the retreat to Dunkirk. It stayed with you for a long time.

"Right, my lovely lads. I thought we would do a bit of rope work today. George, go and get us some rope from the stores."

"Righto Sarge."

"Gordy, Troop Sergeant Major Dean wants to see you. Ten o'clock."

He had a worried look on his face. "What did I do wrong Sarge?"

"You aren't in bother. Just see him eh? And Lieutenant Marsden is due back on Monday."

The old hands gave a cheer. The new boys had yet to meet him. When George arrived back with the ropes I led the section out. "I'll meet you lads at the cliff."

"Which one are we using Sarge?" Gordy had a worried look on his face. Being summoned to the Troop Sergeant Major's office was daunting.

"The one to the west. "

There were a number of cliffs and rock climbs for us to use. The one I had chosen would allow us to use belays. I wanted them working with each other. They had to be able to trust every man in the section. As Gordy would testify you never knew when you needed a mate to get you out of a tight situation. We had made progress but if I was losing Gordy then I was losing the heart of the section. I needed them to become closer.

Gordy had not returned by twelve. "Right lads, that was a good session. We will head back to camp and try some unarmed combat this afternoon." Just then a cheery Gordy arrived, "Well?"

"Thanks, Sarge. Troop Sergeant Major Dean told me what you said. I have learned a lot with you."

Ken and the other old hands looking confused, "We are losing Gordy. He is taking over Fred Briggs' section."

They were more than happy for him. "Drinks are on you tonight Sergeant Barker!"

"And for once I will be happy to pay."

The walking wounded trickled back over the next few days. Major Foster was the first to return, complete with sling and scarred face. His smile soon disappeared when Troop Sergeant Major Dean gave him his reports. Major Foster was a good officer and a gentleman. We understood that he had words with Captain Grenville but they were in private. Reg Smythe returned a day later. Like the Major the doctor had advised longer to recuperate but Reg was keen to rejoin us. Finally, on Monday, Lieutenant Marsden returned. He had a slight limp; if you did not know him you would never have known but the wound had been life threatening. Like Major Foster, he fully endorsed Gordy's promotion and it was made permanent. I had lost my number two. Ken would be just as good, in his own way but Gordy's humour was irreplaceable.

Over the next couple of weeks bandages disappeared and replacements arrived. Two more sections returned from detached duty and our decision to get such good digs proved to be amongst the best I ever made. The other sections were spread all over the town. We were central and together. It made us a tighter team. Our new members returned from their training in Manchester complete with wings. They all looked to have grown up while learning to be paratroopers at Ringway.

Towards the middle of summer, we knew that something was being planned. We had visits from high ranking officers. Lord Lovat made a visit and even Admiral Lord Mountbatten who was now in charge of Combined Operations. There were, however, other officers who arrived. They had no unit insignia which made me wonder about them. Dad had often spoken of officers who went behind enemy lines. Some called them spies while others used the term intelligence officers. The end product was the same.

Two days after the last of these had visited us I was summoned by Major Foster. There was just Lieutenant Marsden in the office and Reg Dean had placed a guard at the door.

I was waved to a seat, "Sorry about the dramatic nature of this, Tom, but this is fairly secret and we have to make sure we maintain our security."

"Right sir." I was intrigued. I remembered the brass who had visited. What could this mean?

The Major took out a map. "This is Guernsey. The Germans have captured the head of the resistance in the Channel Islands. He is a man called Maurice Dimmery. We found out he was captured six days ago but it wasn't until today that we found out where he was being held." He jabbed a finger at a small spot some two miles from the centre of St. Peter Port. They have him held here in an old manor house. Our job, your job, is to get in and rescue him."

"Aren't we too late sir? I mean the Gestapo and SS are good. If they have had him for a week then he will be broken already."

The Major looked at Lieutenant Marsden. I can't tell you how we know this, because I haven't been told but I have it on the best authority that Berlin is sending interrogators over to the island but they won't be there until the middle of next week. Apparently making him wait and worry is a technique the Gestapo are fond of. We have three days to get in and get him out."

"Parachute?"

"Not this time. The islands are so small and the air defence so good that it is just too risky. You and Lieutenant Marsden and three of your

46

men will go by submarine. You will be landed and then the submarine will lie off shore for twenty-four hours to allow you to get in, rescue Maurice Dimmery and get back to the submarine."

"Right sir. Do you mind me asking, why me?"

"Your skills with the French and German languages and, more importantly since you rescued the captives from North Africa your name is often spoken of. Brass know you can think on your feet and you work well with Lieutenant Marsden here. You are seen as a winning team. We need winning teams."

"Right sir."

Lieutenant Marsden asked, "Who do you have in mind to come with us?"

"Ken Curtis and Polly Poulson. They have the most experience. We need that."

"Good. While you are gone Troop Sergeant Major Dean will take over your section. We don't want speculation about this. Now time is of the essence. You leave within the hour. A car will take you to Southampton where 'H.M.S. Sunfish' is waiting for you. It will take all day to get to Guernsey. You will land after dark and then the 'Sunfish' will charge her batteries and then pick you up. The Lieutenant has all the signals and codes. We have to get him out. If you fail then the RAF will bomb the house. They will flatten it completely. You four are the only chance this man has. The 'Sunfish's' commander has orders to wait just one hour for you. if you haven't returned then the order will be given and the bombers will go in. And if you are inside... "

"Right sir. I'll go and get the lads."

"I will wait here, Tom." Lieutenant Marsden grinned, "We will succeed. I can feel it in my bones!"

He had more confidence than I did. Reg Dean was waiting for me. "I know you are off somewhere but they won't tell me where. I will come with you. Otherwise little lips will flap eh?"

I nodded, "I am glad you are looking after the lads."

"It's the least I could do. And listen, you watch yourself. You are not Superman, you know!"

The section was in the armoury. "Curtis, Poulson get your gear. Wait outside for me."

The two of them knew me well enough to just nod and leave. Scouse Fletcher said, "Where are yer off to Sarge?"

Troop Sergeant Major Dean snapped, "That is bugger all to do with you Fletcher but you and I will get to know each other well over the next few days. I am going to be your sergeant." He gave an evil grin. "Won't that be lovely?"

As I left he winked.

I caught up with the other two. Lieutenant Marsden waved us towards the lorry. We threw our Bergens in the back and jumped on board. The Lieutenant sat with us and the lorry set off east towards Southampton.

"What's going on, Sarge?"

The Lieutenant put his finger to his lips and moved us down to the tailgate where the road noise would disguise our words. He was seated next to Ken and I was next to Polly. He said, "You brief Poulson, quietly eh? Loose lips and all that. I'll tell Curtis."

I explained to Polly what we would be about. His eyes widened, "A submarine?"

I smiled, "Yeah we get about a bit, don't we?"

Once briefed I went through my Bergen to make sure that I had all that I required. One thing I had taught my section was to keep their equipment ready to be used at a moment's notice. I had eight grenades and two Thompson magazines. I had six clips for my Colt and four for my Luger. My Luger was in the bag along with my sap, the blackjack I had found to be a useful weapon. I had a canteen but I would need to refill it with clean water before we boarded the submarine. My emergency rations were there too: my salt, porridge, dried food and Kendal Mint Cake. Finally, there was my toggle rope, lengths of cord and waterproof cape.

Satisfied I put it down. "Sir?"

"Yes, Harsker?"

"I am not certain we need to take our Tommy guns." I saw him frown. "If we open fire then we are going to be in trouble. Better to have a weapon which fires single shots. We use Thompsons and they will know that there are Commandos."

"I see what you mean but I would like to have one. Poulson, you bring yours."

"Right sir."

I must have dozed off for Polly suddenly shook me awake. "Here we are Sarge, Southampton."

We descended and the Lieutenant said, "Carter, there are three Thompsons in the back. Have them put in the armoury when you get back."

"Righto sir and good luck lads… wherever you are going."

We entered the docks. The Lieutenant had the necessary papers. The Redcap said, "There is a jeep for you." He grinned, "It will be a tight fit!"

He was right. With our Bergens and the driver we hung over the side of the little vehicle. We bounced down the cobbles to the far end of the port. There were three S-Class submarines there and a sub lieutenant waiting for us. He waved us to the forward hatch. 'HMS Sunfish', you must be Lieutenant Marsden?" The Lieutenant nodded. "Right sir, if you could get your chaps down the forward hatch away from prying eyes we can get under way."

There was a tap next to the submarine. "Sir, if we fill up our canteens here…"

"Good idea."

We began to fill them up while the sub lieutenant looked nervously around as though he expected Germans to suddenly appear. I smiled. He looked to be about eighteen. I suspected this was his first mission.

Lieutenant Marsden led us below into the stygian, red lit depths of the submarine. It was truly like going into hell. Poulson clattered his head off the bulkhead and a rating chuckled, "You pongoes will have to get used to ducking! By the time you leave us you'll look like Quasi-bloody-modo! The bells, Esmeralda!"

49

The sub lieutenant snapped, "Thank you Hutton! This is not a music hall you know!"

There seemed to be no room at all to move. We reached a curtain which the sub lieutenant drew back. "This is the officers' mess. You can use this while we head east." He must have seen our faces. "I know it is a bit cramped, still you won't be here for long. The captain will pop along and see you when we get under way."

We put our Bergens on the tiny table and squeezed around it. I was aware of the highly unpleasant smell of fuel, battery acid and stale cabbage. The smell made me want to vomit and we were not even under way. The Lieutenant cocked his head to one side, "Cosy!"

We heard a voice from the tannoy, "All hands to stations! Prepare to leave harbour."

"Bloody hell sir, they don't hang about do they?"

"No Poulson; they do not. I suspect they are in a hurry."

I could see the nervousness on all their faces. "Sir, why don't we go over the maps. You never know. We might become separated."

"Good idea Harsker." Although the red light made it hard we soon became accustomed to it. "We land here on the southern tip of the island. This little peninsula is called Icart. There are no houses nearby. There is a small hamlet called La Villette here." He pointed to some houses about a mile from the beach but there are thick woods so we have cover. The house is here, close to the edge of the woods they call Les Nicolles. The house stands by itself in its own grounds. It is the only one. It belonged to some lord or other who left when the war began. It has a lodge and extensive grounds." He pointed to a spot just half a mile from the beach. "There is an old tower here. It is medieval but we can use it for shelter."

Ken nodded, "Looks fairly straightforward sir."

"It would be Curtis if it wasn't for this." He pointed to a place just five hundred yards from the target. "This is the German airfield. It used to be the island's main airport. There will be guards and aeroplanes. It is another reason why they have used this house. It is secluded but there is help close by. If we have to use guns then German soldiers will be there so fast it doesn't bear thinking about."

"When will the sub be back for us?"

"That is what I want to check with the captain."

We became engrossed by the maps as we all memorised them. We would not have the luxury of time when on the island. If danger came the maps would need to be in our heads. One thing was clear; we had to head south. West took us to the airport and east to the capital, St Peter Port.

An hour after we had left the harbour the captain, Lieutenant Archibald Conklin, came to see us. He too was young. "Sorry I wasn't here to greet you chaps. Busy getting the old tin can out to sea eh."

"Sir, how deep are we?"

The Lieutenant laughed at Polly's question. "We are still on the surface. We travel faster that way. It is getting dark and we have a destroyer as an escort. By the time he leaves us it should be dark and we will trim to keep our profile as small as possible. I hope to get to within five miles of our destination on the surface. We will then go under and approach the beach underwater. My chaps will give you a taxi ride ashore and then we will pop off and hide."

He made it sound easy but I knew it would not be. He had to wait close enough to get in quickly to pick us up and deep enough so that over flying aeroplanes could not see him.

"What time is the pick up?"

"It will have to be after dark. We will have been under during daylight and so we will surface and head in to charge our batteries. We should be there by ten. We have to leave by three. That gives you a five-hour window. I can wait a little longer for you. An hour is too short a time frame eh?" His smile left his face as he said, "It you aren't back by five past three then I use my radio to send a signal home and the bombers will come. You know that don't you?" Lieutenant Marsden and I nodded. "Still you should be out by then. I will have a good man watching the landing site. You signal and we will there lickety split!"

"Good. Have you done this sort of thing often, Captain?"

He smiled, "Good gracious no. You are the first of the cloak and dagger chaps. The whole crew is excited to have commandos on board. We have all heard about you. Have you done much of this sort of thing?"

We nodded, "We have but this is the first time we have been in a submarine." Lieutenant Marsden shook his head. "I have no idea how you do it."

"You get used to it. Well I'll pop back to the conning tower. If you need anything just give a shout. Oh, the heads are a bit tricky. Ask the CPO if you need to use them."

After he had gone Ken said, "Heads?"

"Aye, Ken; the toilets."

Ken shook his head, "I'll hold it, Sarge. If this is a mess then God knows how big the bog is!"

It might have been my imagination but the air began to feel heavy and I longed to be on deck. When we travelled on MLs I was never below deck. I was not claustrophobic but if I was a submariner then I would soon become one. To take my mind off the atmosphere I questioned the lieutenant.

"What do we know about this chap we have to rescue?"

"What do you mean?"

"His age for a start. If we have to run will he slow us up? What does he look like?"

"Good point. He is forty years old and is a teacher. As far as I can discover he is single. He wears glasses and is slightly balding. His build is described as medium."

"No photograph then?"

"No, I am afraid not. The other members of the resistance wanted to have a go at rescuing him but Intelligence persuaded them to let us have the operation. They didn't tell them about the bombing raid."

I could see that, with the airfield being so close, the wrecked house would appear as collateral damage. "And what is the plan, sir?"

"Scout out the building tonight and then lay low during the day. If we can get to the house before dusk then we can attack then. The Germans are predictable about meal times."

The Lieutenant was right. It was how we had rescued the general, his staff and my dad; we had struck while most of the guards were eating. The difference this time was that we only had four of us. The number was right. The submarine couldn't accommodate anymore and a larger number would be harder to hide. It would not be an easy lift.

We were brought food and tea. Both tasted oily. The rating who brought them shrugged, "You get used to it, chum." I ate because I knew I needed to not because I wanted to.

When we heard the tannoy next my heart sank. "All hands, diving stations!"

Watertight doors were slammed shut. The submarine became even more coffin like. Ratings rushed by to go to their stations. After the initial noise and the clanging doors there was a slow hiss, like a beach ball being deflated and then there was silence. I noticed my ears hurting. The rating who was watching the panel near us said, "Hold your nose and blow or chew something."

Holding the nose worked, "Thanks."

He said, like the other rating, "You get used to it."

I think they were both wrong. I would never get used to this mole like existence. I know we only had a couple of hours to go and the longest part of the journey had been endured but the last part seemed interminable. There were occasional noises from the hull; some were alarming creaks. I preferred the dangers of an aeroplane to this.

Lieutenant Conklin came forrard, "Well chaps, we are approaching the bay. Best get your gear together. You will go out of the forward hatch. We have a dingy. The lads will paddle you ashore. Who is your signaller?"

Ken said, "Me sir."

"Right, preface your message with 'Sunfish'. Just a little precaution." He cocked his head to one side. "If you are captured and they make you signal us without the prefix 'Sunfish' then we will know and we won't surface,"

Ken said, "I wouldn't talk, sir."

"I know but we have lost submarines before because the beach was compromised."

I nodded, "He's right Ken. It makes sense. And it doesn't hurt to be careful."

He said, "Now it is close to dawn now so we will have to be quick when we rise. And I think you lads will have to be fairly quick and get to ground." He smiled, "But you know what you are about eh?"

"Yes Lieutenant."

I had no need to check my guns; I had done that before. We blackened our faces and hands and followed the two ratings to the forward torpedo room. It seemed an age before the message was passed down to open the hatch. Polly was too keen to be out and received a dousing as the seawater from the hatch cascaded on him. It made the torpedo men smile. They had half inflated the dingy and they dragged that out first. They took the air line and then we followed. It was pitch black and there was no moon. We moved down the deck out of their way. I saw that the machine guns had been fitted to the conning tower rail and lookouts scanned the shore. All that we could see was a black lump.

We heard a whispered, "Ready lads!" as the inflated dingy was lowered over the side.

The dingy was held close to the bow and we gingerly descended. One false move could tip us all over. There were two spare paddles and I handed one to Ken and we helped the two ratings to paddle us to the distant bay. We heard the surf as it slithered and hissed along the shingle. Polly and the Lieutenant leapt ashore. Ken and I laid our paddles down and jumped into the surf too. I waved to the ratings who quickly paddled back to the waiting submarine. They would move away from the island to recharge their batteries and then sneak back before dawn. We had the easier task.

There was a gentle climb from the beach to the tower which was visible from the water. We moved quickly but carefully, watching all the time for any sentries. Mercifully there were none. The four of us moved swiftly and silently. We reached the wrecked tower and threw ourselves within its bramble covered interior. We took off our Bergens and hid them beneath the prickly bushes. Satisfied that they were hidden the Lieutenant led us north west along the trail towards the wood of Les Nicolles.

Quickly we crossed the two apologies for roads which led to the beach and headed across the open fields. They were tiny roads. I doubted that a lorry would fit down them. There were sheep there and they scurried out of our way. I could smell the smoke from houses to our right. They would belong to islanders but we could not risk involving them. We were on our own and had to get in and out unseen. We dived for cover as a vehicle drove by. It had to be German; there was a curfew. We could tell, from the sound, the proximity of the road. Once the night became silent again we rose and approached the road. We did not leave the safety of the woods but lay down to watch.

It was a proper manor with a walled entrance and a gate. We saw two German sentries seated around a brazier. They were close enough for me to hear their conversation. It was just soldier talk: they complained about their Feldwebel and the food. They bemoaned their duty and the fact that the beer was poor. After an hour, a Feldwebel came by and they snapped to attention. He reprimanded them for both being seated and pointed out that only one should sit and the other should patrol around the perimeter. He said it should be every fifteen minutes. If they failed to do so they would be given field punishment. He tapped one on the shoulder with his stick and they went off around the outside. The Feldwebel was showing him what to do. I looked at my watch as they did so. This would be a good opportunity to see how long it took. It was ten minutes. The Feldwebel left them after he had finished his patrol and told them they should repeat in fifteen minutes. He then returned inside. As he went through the gates, which were not locked, I saw that there appeared to be no guards on the inside. That made sense. There was a high wall all around.

The Lieutenant looked at his watched and, tapping it, gestured for us to move away. It would be dawn in less than an hour. The journey back was as incident free as the one there had been. Once inside our tower we ate some rations and drank some water. Neither was needed but we had learned to eat and drink when we could. We spoke, in whispers.

"What did that sergeant say, Tom?"

"He told them off for not patrolling. I think we can count on the fact that they are likely to do so tomorrow. I reckon that is our chance. It gives us ten minutes to get one. Two of us can wait around the back and get the other."

"Aye Sarge. It looked to me like there were woods to the east of the house too."

"Then we just have to get inside, overcome the rest of the guards, find the prisoner and escape without anyone being the wiser."

"Sergeant Harsker, you make it sound impossible."

"No sir but I am a realist and I would prefer to assess all the problems before we get inside."

"What do you think then?"

"We have the advantage that this will be an English designed house. There will be an entrance hall, a couple of sitting rooms on either side. The dining room will be on the west and the kitchen on the east. I am guessing there will be a library or billiard room; something like that. There will be up to ten bedrooms upstairs. I am guessing they will be for the guards. If this is Gestapo or SS they will have their own cook. There can only be a maximum of twenty people in the house and as the officers will have their own rooms and, probably the sergeants too, then it is more likely to be twelve to fourteen. There will be two on duty and a duty sergeant. Inside, I am guessing a third guard for the prisoner."

"Well-reasoned but where will the prisoner be?"

"Cellar. It looks to be an old house and the cellar will probably run the length of it. Part will be the wine cellar and they will have their prisoner, probably shackled, to the wall."

The Lieutenant smacked his head, "God I am a fool! I forget bolt cutters!"

The three of us grinned, dived into our Bergens and each took out our home-made ones. "One of these should do the trick, sir."

He laughed. "Are you saying we get in and out without them knowing we have been there?"

"I reckon it is our best chance. We take out four guards, one by one. If we can't do that silently then we ought to join the tank corps where we can make as much noise as we like. It took fifteen minutes to get to the house that means fifteen minutes to escape. Ken can hurry on ahead and signal the sub so that the dingy is there by the time we reach the beach."

"But that means we have to time it so that we started our attack after nine thirty."

"Make it later sir, it will be darker. They have more chance of being asleep and the sub should be there. We have until three, remember?"

"Good, so all we need is to evade detection until then."

"Yes sir, we each take a two hour stag. As soon as dusk arrives we are up and about ready to get to the woods." We prepared our beds. It would be a cold night.

Chapter 6

The Lieutenant insisted upon the first duty. I rigged up my oilskin cape above me and made a tent under the brambles and rocks. I was almost certain that I would be invisible. I quickly fell asleep. The Lieutenant woke me. He said nothing but gave me the sign for all clear. I drank some water and spat it out. It was as close to cleaning my teeth as I would get. I could still taste the oily submarine in my mouth. I wondered if I would ever get rid of the taste.

I crept to the entrance. It was still dark, but only just. I risked leaving the tower for a pee. Steam rose showing how cold it was outside. I peered into the bay which was still dark. I could hear the early gulls as they called and swooped over the water. The sound of the surf was reassuring. I went back into the tower and lay in the entrance. The best way to watch was to lie still and to listen. You could hear more than you could see.

I didn't bother to look at my watch. That merely made the time go more slowly. Instead I concentrated on listening to the sounds of the woods and the houses waking up. There were people within five hundred yards of us. From the state of the interior of the tower no one came here save to bramble in the late autumn. The fruit was still green, small and hard. I managed to hear vehicles as they started to use the roads. In the distance, I heard the sound of aeroplane engines as they were fired. I saw the sea change from dark grey to grey and then, as the sun peered, a sort of bluey grey. It was then that I checked my watch. My two hours had ended five minutes earlier. I went inside and tapped Polly. His eyes widened and then he relaxed as he recognised me. I made the sign for safe and then remade my cocoon. I was asleep almost instantly.

We were all awake by four o'clock in the afternoon. We had had disturbed sleep but we had all slept long enough. We ate more tasteless rations, drank water and waited for dark. We could not speak and we could not go outside for our ablutions. We had to wait for the dark.

Night and the dark were our friends. The sun was our enemy. It was a bizarre world in which we lived. We had become used to the aeroplanes flying in and out of the airport. They were mainly Henschel 129s and Messerschmitt 110s. We had glimpsed them through the bramble bushes as they came overhead. It showed us the proximity of the airfield. If things went wrong they would do so in a big way.

Once night fell we all felt a huge sense of relief. I don't know how the others felt but to me it was like being a criminal, a burglar. We had 'cased' the joint and now we would be breaking in. The difference was that we intended to use deadly force. We donned our bags and checked all our weapons. This time we would need to take our Bergens with us.

The Lieutenant gave us our last instructions before we left our sanctuary. "We need to slow down any pursuit. I will keep watch while you chaps lay booby traps close to the path we use. When we overcome the guards we need to make the house the German's enemy."

"Right sir."

"Tom, you need to lead. You speak German and your language skills might just make the enemy slow to react."

"Yes sir."

"Curtis, you and Poulson take care of the patrolling guard. Take him on the patrol which is closest to eleven as you can."

"Right sir."

"Right let's go. It's ten o'clock. I want to break in at eleven thirty. Fifteen minutes to effect the rescue and back here for twelve. We should have three hours to spare."

As we moved through the woods we heard noise from the house to our right. It sounded like some sort of party. Perhaps the noise might disguise any noise we made when we fled. As we made our way through the woods we were even quieter than we had been the previous night. We knew where the enemy was this time. We could smell their cigarette smoke. Once again, they were close together around the brazier. The Feldwebel would not be happy. While the Lieutenant kept watch we used Mills bombs and the cord to make tripwires along the path leading

59

through the woods. We just laid three. Hopefully they would trigger one and then waste time looking for many more. We just had to delay them.

Then we rejoined the Lieutenant to wait. We watched as the German guards finished their cigarettes and one of them left to patrol the perimeter. Polly and Ken prepared to move off. The guard had only been gone for three minutes when the Feldwebel arrived. "Ah, you are obeying orders. That is good. The Gestapo are flying in later tonight from Berlin. Send for me as soon as they arrive. They are important men."

"Yes Feldwebel. Does that mean the prisoner will be leaving?"

"The Gestapo are a law unto themselves. I think we are here for some time. When Manfred returns tell him. I will be in my room."

He seemed satisfied and returned indoors. I dare not tell the others that we had less than a few hours to affect our rescue. If we spoke then the guard might hear us. I looked at my watch. It was ten thirty. When the guard returned Ken and Polly slipped silently off and headed east to wait for the guard on his next patrol. The two guards lit cigarettes and then began talking about the Feldwebel. They did not like him. We watched, a few minutes later as one of the Germans stood to start his patrol. That gave us ten minutes at the most.

I waited until the German sentry was looking east and I ran across the road. My rubber soled shoes were silent. By the time he looked west again I was lying in the shelter of the wall under a jungle of nasturtiums. He stared at the wood. I wondered if he had seen the Lieutenant for he was at the exact spot where the German looked. I crawled closer to the German. I had three minutes left. If Ken and Polly took care of the other guard I would have longer but the sentry who was now ten feet from me would be suspicious of any delay. Suddenly the sentry stood. He still stared at the woods. He brought his gun up and slid the bolt back. Had he seen the Lieutenant? I was on my feet in an instant. Even as the German took a step forwards I pulled back hard on his coal scuttle helmet and ripped my dagger across his throat.

The Lieutenant sprinted across the road as I rolled the body under the nasturtiums. I took his potato mashers and jammed them inside my

60

battle dress. I sheathed my dagger and took out my Luger. A moment later Ken and Polly arrived. They nodded and we went in through the gate. We went fast and we went low. We could see lights in the upstairs rooms. I fought the urge to check my watch. It had to be about eleven. We had not seen any men returning from a night's drinking and we were gambling that they would be in the mansion and preparing for bed.

The Lieutenant waved Ken and Polly around to the back door. We went to the front door. I was just about to open when I heard a German voice from inside. "I will check on those lazy swine outside and then I am turning in. See you in the morning Gerhardt."

I heard something mumbled which suggested the speaker was some way away. I waved the Lieutenant to the other side of the door. A shaft of light shone on the path. I waited until the Feldwebel had closed the door before I put my arm around his neck in the Japanese stranglehold. I used the Luger behind his neck to add extra pressure. He was a big man and he struggled but he eventually went limp. I dropped him to the ground and quickly bound his arms and legs together behind him. I rammed his cap in his mouth and used cord to tie it in place. While the Lieutenant kept watch on the door I dragged him to the wall and laid him beneath a bush. With his grey uniform, he would be hard to spot. Just then I heard the roar of a Junkers transport. Someone was landing and they were landing late. Could this be the Gestapo?"

The Lieutenant had his hand on the front door. I listened and could hear nothing. I nodded and he opened it. Stepping inside we quickly scanned the interior. We could see nothing but upstairs we could hear voices. I turned, with Luger pointed as I sensed a movement from our right. It was Ken and Polly. They held up their hands in apology and made the sign for all clear. The Lieutenant pointed to the left. There was a short corridor and I could see a shaft of light from stairs leading down. I moved forward.

When I reached the opening, I looked down the stairs. I could see nothing but I heard someone humming. That must be Gerhardt. I began to move down the stairs. I knew that the odds were one of the stairs would creak no matter how careful I was. I was lucky. It was towards the bottom when one creaked.

"Is that you Steppi?"

I continued down laughing, "No you fool, it is me Hans!"

"Hans?" I could hear the suspicion in his voice but by then I was at the bottom of the stairs with my gun pointed at him.

"Hands up and you will not be hurt!"

"Kommando!"

I nodded, "And you know that we mean business."

The Lieutenant had appeared behind me. He said, quietly, "Curtis, tie him up." I saw that the key to the cell was obligingly hanging up on a hook. I saw the racks of wine to my left and right. "Poulson, open the door. Harsker, keep watch at the top of the stairs. Your German might come in handy again."

"Sir, we have less time than you think. The Feldwebel said the Gestapo were coming tonight and I just heard a transport land."

"Right. We work quickly then. Let's get the prisoner out and to the beach. Harsker you will be the rear-guard. Do you want the Thompson?"

"No sir. I have a Luger as well as my pistol. If I use the Luger it might confuse them."

I went up the stairs as quickly as I could. I took out the two potato mashers and, after breaking the porcelain tops, attached one to the inside handle of the door. I tied a cord to the other one. When the others arrived, I would rig a booby trap on the door. I heard something being dragged below me and then a door shutting. Ken came up the stairs. I pointed to the front door. He nodded and opened it. The Lieutenant led Maurice, the resistance leader. He looked to be in a bad way. He had been beaten. He would slow us up. I pointed to the front door. He and Ken put their arms underneath the Channel Islander's arms and helped him down the path. Polly raced up. He had the key in his hand. I pointed to the front door and then as he followed the others I finished rigging the booby trap.

I closed the front door. The others had disappeared. I hurried across the road. I soon caught up with them. We did not follow the same path we had taken to get there. We went down the road. The Lieutenant hoped it would confuse them. Maurice was in a bad way and we were not moving as swiftly as we had expected. It would take twice as long to reach the beach and the submarine. I heard the sound of a vehicle coming down the road and we quickly headed in to the woods. It did not pass us and I wondered if it had gone to the house. Was that the Gestapo?

Polly took over from Ken who raced ahead to signal the submarine. I hung back in case we were being followed. We were just passing the house with the party when I heard the dull crump from behind us. Someone had triggered the booby trap. It had served its purpose. We now knew there would be pursuit. Polly and the Lieutenant could go no faster. I waited in the dark. I heard in the distance the sound of loud voices and from the airfield, the sound of klaxons. Men were being mobilised.

In my head, I visualised the others as they passed the tower. Ken would be at the beach and he would be signalling. The submarine would surface and then the crew would have to paddle to shore. I would need to leave in ten minutes. I did not have ten minutes. I heard another crump and then shouts as the first of the booby traps in the woods was set off. Then I heard the bark of dogs. Where had they come from? I considered another booby trap but there was a house nearby. I did not want to involve civilians. I turned and headed for the tower.

As I ran I heard whistles, shouts and barks as pursuit was organised. A second crump was reassuring. I saw it becoming lighter ahead and knew that was the sea. A sense I did not know I possessed made me turn. I saw, twenty yards away, an Alsatian, a German guard dog. I barely had time to raise my Luger and fire three bullets. The savage dog was thrown to the ground but my shots would have drawn the pursuers like a beacon.

I turned and ran the last two hundred yards to the beach. I saw the low silhouette of the submarine and the dingy. It was sixty yards away. "Poulson bring your Tommy gun and come with me!" I turned and ran

63

up the slope to the tower. "Cover the path. They are on the way." I took two grenades and a cord. I strung the cord across the path.

Suddenly Poulson's gun chattered and I heard the sound of breaking branches and cries as he hit someone. I took out another grenade. "One more blind burst and then run back to the beach. I'll be right behind." He fired and ran. I counted to five and then hurled another grenade high into the air. I turn and ran. I heard the sound of bullets cracking off the tower. They had set up a heavy machine gun.

I heard Ken's voice, "Sarge! Come on!"

I saw that they had loaded the dingy. "Go! I will swim if I have to!"

I knew how long it would take to paddle the two hundred yards to the submarine and with the Germans behind I did not want us to be sitting ducks. I turned and saw two Germans running towards me. I levelled my Luger and fired two shots at one and then my last two at the other. I hit the first one who fell to the ground. The other dived for cover. I ran and hurled myself into the sea. It was hard trying to wade through the surf but the sailors slowed up their paddling. I was almost blinded by the flash from Poulson's machine gun as he sprayed the beach. Ken and the Lieutenant hauled me aboard. One of the ratings said, "We brought more paddles!"

I grabbed a paddle and we paddled for all we were worth. I was at the rear and as the odd man had to alternate my strokes to make sure we were going straight. The extra paddles made us move much faster. I saw the flash from the twin machine guns on the submarine as they added their fire to Poulson's. It would keep the German's heads down. We bumped into the hull of the boat and many willing hands pulled us aboard.

I Heard Lieutenant Conklin's voice, "Leave the dingy, Cartwright, get everyone below decks! Clear the bridge! Prepare for emergency dive!"

I was pushed unceremoniously into the packed forward torpedo room. The two ratings hurtled after me as I heard the cover on the tannoy. "Dive! Dive! Dive!"

The two ratings barely managed to shut the hatch before the watertight doors were slammed and I felt the submarine start to move. It was so fast that some water came in before they had sealed it. Bullets clanged alarmingly from the hull. We were jammed tightly into the torpedo room. Lieutenant Marsden said, "Everyone all right? Any wounds?"

"No, sir."

"How are you sir?" I saw Lieutenant Marsden speaking with the rescued resistance leader.

He smiled weakly, "Better for having escaped. Thank you, gentlemen. I thought I would end my days in that cellar." He shook his head. "You know the Gestapo were coming for me?"

"That is why we came, sir. We couldn't let that happen."

"I tried to be strong and I told them nothing but I know that I would have broken." He shrugged apologetically, "I was a teacher! I am not a hero like you fellows."

One of the torpedo men said, "He is right you know. We couldn't even begin to do what you lads do."

Ken said, "You are the heroes. We get to fight back! You have to spend your days in a steel coffin!"

I shook off my Bergen and placed it on the oily floor. It made a seat. I leaned against the torpedo and closed my eyes. Once the bubbles of our descent stopped it all became peaceful. Even the smell seemed a little less nauseous. Perhaps I would sleep all the way back.

Suddenly the tannoy sounded, "Rig for depth charges! Silent procedures."

Polly asked, "What does that mean?"

The leading hand began to tie a rag around his ears. "That means, my old cock, that Jerry is up top and he is going to drop depth charges. If I were you I would put something over my ears. The concussion is something wicked!"

I reached into my Bergen and took out my spare socks. I pulled my comforter over my ears and jammed the socks inside the hat. I saw

Maurice looking for something. "Sir, if you use your jacket and tie it around your head with your tie."

"Thank you, sergeant. It appears I am ill prepared for an attack under water. This will be a novel experience for me."

"And for us."

The socks and hat dampened the sound a little. More importantly they stopped the concussive effect. I was not prepared for the first explosion when it came. It was not so much the explosion which was a dull sound seemingly far away that hurt us, it was the waves of concussion which followed. Even with the socks it still felt painful. I followed the example of the leading seaman and placed my hands over my ears as well. That helped and the second depth charge was not as painful. I knew that we could expect no help from the RAF this time. It was night time. Cynically I realised that it did not matter to those who had sent us what happened now. If the submarine sank the Germans would still be denied their information. Lieutenant Conklin had told us that five of the S Class submarines had all been sunk in the first two years of the war. We were expendable.

There was a lull and I wondered if we had escaped. Polly went to speak but the leading hand put his fingers up to silence him. Suddenly there were six explosions in seemingly rapid succession. There was a flickering of the lights and then it all went dark. My claustrophobic fears surfaced. If the batteries died we would sink like a stone! Dim emergency lights came on and I breathed a sigh of relief. Had we been able to talk it would have helped but we had to remain silent. Each man was alone with his thoughts and his fears.

There was another gap between explosions and concussion. None of us thought that it had ended. I worked out that the ships who were hunting us were doing sweeps. I did not know exactly how they were finding us. It was probably some underwater Radar, a little like our ASDIC. The next pattern made the whole boat shake and one of the pipes running the length of the torpedo room burst, showering us with a liquid. One of the hands leapt to his feet and dexterously turned a spanner to stop it. We had two more attacks and then I felt us sinking. The pressure on my ears grew. The pain increased but the effects of the depth charges diminished. We heard them explode but they did not hurt as much.

Suddenly we hit something. It was the bottom of the ocean. The 'Sunfish' leaned over and then stopped. I saw the ratings all lie down. Again, I worked out that we had descended to the bottom to sit out the attack. We were trapped on the seabed. I copied the ratings and rested my head on my Bergen. Before I used it as a pillow I took out my canteen and had a good swig. Dehydration would be as much of a problem as anything else. I looked at my watch. It was less than an hour since we had descended and the attack had begun. I wondered if the batteries were fully charged. We would find out eventually. The life of the batteries would determine when we would surface.

I stared at the top of the submarine and pictured the ships above us. They would be like circling wolves around an injured animal. We would have to move eventually. Would they wait us out? Gradually the depth charges stopped. I prayed they had run out but I knew that would not be the case. We were too close to St. Peter Port. They would send for more. When daylight arrived, I had no doubt that they would use aeroplanes to drop more charges on us. The Channel was suddenly not as deep as I might have liked.

An hour later I heard the faint hum of the electric motors starting up. I felt us begin to rise and, I suspected, move. The ratings sat up and I saw some of them removing their rags from around their heads. I left my socks in place. I was taking no chances. We kept rising. I desperately wanted to speak but I was used to obeying orders. The last order was for silent procedure. I almost jumped out of my skin when the watertight door was opened and the young midshipman stood there. He came over to Lieutenant Marsden. I leaned in to listen as he spoke.

"The captain is taking us up to periscope depth. He is going to try the radio to get some air support."

The Lieutenant nodded, "Thanks for the information. Have we suffered much damage?"

"Some of the batteries were hit and we have men with burns but if we can surface we can use our engines."

He left us and the door shut ominously once more. Any happy thoughts we might have harboured were shattered when we heard bullets hitting metal. We were being fired upon. We began to descend again. For the next hour, we suffered more attacks. Even worse the air appeared to be getting fouler. Maurice, the resistance leader, began coughing. Lieutenant Marsden gave him some water. The attacks continued relentlessly. There appeared to be fewer charges but it was a shorter gap between them. How could this little submarine take so much punishment?

We were taken by surprise when we heard the tannoy, "We are surfacing. Gun crews prepare."

The leading hand said, "You lads should get ready to bail out. If we are going to the surface we are in trouble."

I hated this. We were helpless. I wanted to be able to join the crew and fight back. We were out of our natural environment. The pressure on my ears diminished rapidly as we rose. I took my socks and put them back in the Bergen. As we ascended I reloaded the Luger. It would not do much damage to a warship but I would feel better firing it. I wondered when the watertight doors would be opened. I didn't like the idea of being stuck here behind a sealed door.

Once again, we heard bullets striking the hull of the sub and then I heard the machine guns on the conning tower fire. We were all thrown from our feet as something, probably a shell, hit the water close to the side and the submarine lurched at an angle of forty-five degrees. Polly smacked his head off a pipe and began to bleed. Even worse we started to take on water.

The leading hand ran to the voice pipe, "Bridge. Forward torpedo room. We have been hit and we are taking on water."

I saw the ratings as they jammed jumpers into the damaged section to try to stem the flow of water. The watertight door opened and a Petty Officer ran. "Harris get the hatch open and these commandos on deck. You lads better put on life jackets!"

"But, Chief, what about the Germans?"

68

The Petty Officer ignored the rating. "When you get out go over the starboard side. The armed trawlers are on the port side. You will be safer in the water than in here."

We hurriedly put on the lifejackets as the hatch was opened. We were soaked by the water flooding in. Ken bravely clambered out first. I think he expected the rattle of bullets. I followed him. I glanced to the left and saw the trawlers. They were a mile away and one was closer than the other. Even as I watched a shell came from the forward gun and splashed into the sea behind me. The gun crew of the 'Sunfish' fired in return. It missed.

I reached down to pull Maurice up. "Ken get in the water. Keep hold of this chap."

"I can swim, sergeant."

"Very good, sir, but until we get you back to Blighty we will wrap you in cotton wool."

Ken dropped over the side. Another shell fell. This one was closer and was on the port side. They were straddling. The next one would hit the sub. "Over you go."

As he disappeared I pulled the bleeding Poulson up and unceremoniously dumped him over the starboard side. "Get a move on, sir!"

"Jump, Harsker, I will follow." Lieutenant Marsden was struggling to get out of the hatch wearing his life jacket.

I jumped into the sea beside the other three. The sea had mixed with oil from the damaged sub. It tasted disgusting. I realised it was daylight. I could not see any land. Lieutenant Marsden landed next to me. I checked that the resistance leader was in good hands and then I paddled round to the bow. I saw, as I reached the domed bow, another shell hit the water and make a water spout. This one was remarkably close to the sub. A tower of water rose high and showered the conning tower. The sub lurched alarmingly. I knew we could not last much longer.

I saw that the leading trawler was just half a mile away and was almost firing along open sights. Suddenly I saw twin waterspouts on

69

either side of the trawler. That couldn't be us, we only had one gun. Then I heard the roar of aero engines and, looking up I saw a flight of Blenheims. They were an outdated aeroplane but more than up to the task of seeing off a couple of armed trawlers. Their machine guns shredded the wheelhouse of the leading trawler. I saw the second one heel to port as she headed away. Then there was an almighty explosion as the trawler was hit. I had seen no bombs fall and I wondered what on earth it was.

I paddled back to the others, "What in earth is going on Sergeant?"

"One of the trawlers has been blown up and the other has high tailed it home. There are three Blenheims as guardian angels. We are safe! We have made it!"

The Leading Hand leaned over the side, a big grin on his face, "If you lads would come back on the deck we have made alternative arrangements for you." He pulled me aboard and as I stood on the deck he pointed behind him, "'H.M.S. Cleveland', a Hunt class destroyer!"

I saw the sleek shape of the destroyer as it raced towards us. This was truly combined operations; the air force and navy had been involved as well as us and I was thankful that the young lieutenant had managed to contact base.

Chapter 7

A scrambling net was rigged over the side of the destroyer and we clambered on board. The injured ratings were also transferred to the destroyer's sick bay. While the tow line was being attached we were taken to the officers' mess. Maurice was whisked away to the sick bay. I saw that Polly had wiped away the blood from his head. He would not want to be taken to a hospital. He was a commando. A bump on the head was nothing. Sub Lieutenant Jennings and two ratings wrapped blankets around us while the mess orderly poured us tots of rum.

Lieutenant Marsden drank the rum gratefully, "Thanks Sub, you arrived in the nick of time."

"Yes, it looked a little hairy. The trawler was lucky with its first hit. I am afraid the captain will have to take it easy going back. We don't want to lose the 'Sunfish' on the last leg. You chaps settle down here." He grinned, "On the QT we heard that everyone is pleased with your success. I envy you. Life on the 'Cleveland' is dull by comparison."

Ken said, "Aye sir but considerably safer."

When we were alone I said, "That was the most frightening experience of my life. I wouldn't want to do that any time soon."

Even Lieutenant Marsden had been shaken by the experience. "You are right, Tom. I know submariners get extra pay but they earn every penny of it."

The slow tow meant we reached Southampton well after dark. Intelligence officers waited for Maurice but he insisted on shaking us all by the hand. "But for you four commandos I would be a dead man. I owe my life to you and I will always be grateful."

He was spirited away and we never saw him again. After the war I discovered that the Channel Island resistance had suffered many casualties. I was just happy that we had saved at least one. Lieutenant Conklin was one of the last to leave the submarine. Lieutenant Marsden strode over to him. "Thanks awfully for what you did. We are grateful that you got us back safely."

He grinned, "We were delighted to be of service. It was a little exciting, wasn't it? If we hadn't had so many batteries damaged we might have escaped them without sending for help. Still we got back a little quicker. There is nothing like a Hunt class destroyer to put the willies up Jerry. Good luck to you chaps. I'll have to run. We need to find out where they can repair the old girl."

We might have hoped that Intelligence would have provided a lorry for us but they had their prize and we were forgotten. We went to the officer commanding the docks. Like us he was surprised that we had been ignored. "I have no vehicles available until tomorrow. You'll have to spend the night here."

I did not relish the prospect of a night in Southampton. The air raids there were legendary. "Sir, if you give us four chits we can take the train back to Falmouth."

"Are you certain?" He looked at the Lieutenant who nodded. "Very well then. Sergeant have four railway warrants made out for these chaps eh?"

Ken looked at Polly's head as we headed west on the Great Western train. We were all tired and dirty. I know that I felt drained. Normally, after a mission I was buzzing but the voyage on the 'Sunfish' had been traumatic. We travelled in silence; each of us lost in his own thoughts. The rhythm of the carriage meant I was soon asleep. Ken woke me up, "Next stop Falmouth, Sarge."

The Lieutenant and Poulson were still asleep. "We'll give them another ten minutes." He lit a cigarette. "You and Polly did well, Ken."

He shook his head, "I reckon I need to learn German. You have used it a couple of times. If you hadn't discovered that the Gestapo were on their way we might have been caught with our trousers down. Their arrival must have triggered the booby traps."

"I think you are right."

"Anyway, Sarge, how about starting those German lessons again?"

When I had been corporal Daddy Grant had had me teach the lads a few phrases in French and German. Since I had been promoted I had been too preoccupied. "A good idea and I should have thought of this myself. We'll start today."

We shook the other two awake as we hissed into Falmouth. As we left the station the Lieutenant said, "You chaps get off to your digs. My motor is at my billet. I will pop up to the camp and report to the Major. I daresay they will be worried."

"Right sir."

Mrs Bailey was using a stone on the step. She saw the dressing on Polly's head and her hand went to her mouth, "Whatever has happened? The other lads said you were off somewhere." She put a maternal hand on Polly's face. "I have hot water on. You lads have a bath; you smell of oil and I don't know what. If you leave your uniforms out then I will wash them." She shooed us inside. Mrs Bailey was a force of nature.

I piled my clothes next to my bed and went to take my bath. One of the advantages of digs over a barracks was that we could personalise it more. Mum had given me a bath robe for Christmas and it was a luxury. Had I worn it in a barracks my life would have been a misery but here I could indulge myself. It was only when I came back from my bath, smelling clean and freshly shaven that I realised what Mrs Bailey had meant. My clothes smelled of oil, mildew, sea water and blood. I was not surprised that we had had a compartment all to ourselves on the train. We stank!

Mrs Bailey kept a neat and tidy little bed and breakfast. Her linen was crisp and white. She had brought out her best china for the three of us. She put the pot of tea on the table. "I baked some scones. There's not much sugar in them but the jam is bramble from before the war. That will sweeten them up."

"Thanks Mrs B."

She smiled at Polly, "You are too young to be fighting in this war!"

She didn't know that Polly had slit a man's throat less than two days earlier. He might have had a baby face but he was a killer. "My mum uses carrots to sweeten cakes Mrs Bailey."

73

"Does she Sergeant Harsker? I have never tried that but it sounds like a good idea. And they will help you lads see better in the dark. I have some growing. I will try to get a recipe for that."

I smiled for the reference to carrots making it easier to see in the dark was good Government propaganda. To deceive the Germans about aerial radar the story had been spread that night fighter pilots were fed carrots. I knew this because Dad had told me of the radar. I didn't doubt that carrots were good for you but I doubted they improved night vision.

After a mission, there is nothing like a night in a comfortable bed with clean, crisp linen. I slept like a baby but I was up early. I rose before Mrs Bailey. I made a pot of tea and lit the fire. I had my first cup and toasted some bread. I had just finished my second cup when Mrs Bailey came down in her dressing gown.

"Sergeant Harsker, if you had said that you wanted to be up early I would have had breakfast ready for you."

"Don't worry, Mrs Bailey, it was no problem and it will save you the trouble of lighting the fire." I poured her a cup of tea.

As she stirred in the half a teaspoon of sugar she took she said, "Your boys were worried about you. They said you were off somewhere dangerous." She held up her hand, "They didn't tell me where but I knew it was somewhere dangerous. They are good boys, Sergeant," her eyes began to well up with tears, "you will look after them, won't you? I know they think the world of you and would do anything for you but they deserve to have families, children. They should survive this horrible war. Too many have died already."

"Don't worry Mrs Bailey. I intend to see that all of them survive. This country needs young men like them."

She smiled, "Good."

I ran through the dark streets towards the camp. It was not yet dawn and the streets were empty save for the milkmen and their horse and carts. I needed the run. When I led the men, I had to be fitter than they were. It came with the stripes. The Lieutenant could watch us but I had to lead when we trained. I guessed that we would be training now for a while. We had had two missions in quick succession. I knew that we were too valuable to be wasted. We had proved ourselves as a Troop. When we were next used it would be something big. We would have to be ready.

I was half way up the hill when I overtook Jack Johnson who was marching to the camp. "You are up early Jack."

"Could say the same about you."

"You know what it is like after a mission. You are on edge."

"Aye, we heard you had had a little trip. France?"

"Nah, Channel Islands again. We went in by submarine and you can keep those steel coffins for me. How is your section going?"

"The new replacements are good lads. It would be perfect except for that big bugger, Waller."

"Still causing trouble?"

He nodded, "But I am going to break him. You know me Tom. I don't do Kings regulations but I will with this one. If he wants to be a smart arse and a barrack room lawyer then I will show him. It is why I am going in early I want to have a chat with Reg Deane about him."

"I thought he was running my section."

"Oh, he is but he still meets with Horace and me before breakfast. The Major thinks this is his Troop, Troop Sergeant Major Dean knows it is his."

"Anything on the horizon then?"

"The Major wants us practising demolition charges. He has found an old tin mine not far away. It is played out and the owner is an old spinster. Her fiancé died in the Great War and she wants to do her bit. She says we can blow it all up if we like."

"Excellent. Real buildings are always better than ones the engineers build for us."

"And even better it is ten miles away so we will get a twenty-mile run in each day."

When we reached the camp Reg Dean was in the office with Horace and they were smoking. The Troop Sergeant Major grinned when he saw me, "The wanderer returns. I thought you might have been away longer."

75

I shook my head, "We had just one night over there and then another on the sub."

They all leaned forward, their interest aroused, "How was it?"

"The worst experience of my life, Horace. We were depth charged. You feel bloody helpless lying on the bottom of the sea expecting to be drowned or blown up at any minute."

Reg nodded, "I can see that. Did you get the job done?"

He was careful not to ask me what the job was. If the Major had wanted them to know he would have told them. "We did and we all got back safely. Poulson banged his head but that was on the sub."

"Now you are back we can start the training at the mine."

Just then Gordy walked in. He shook his head, "I can see that the new boy will have to get up a little earlier." He held his hand out to me. "Good to see you back, Tom."

"And it is a relief to be back." He cocked his head quizzically. "I was just telling the lads that a submarine is now my idea of hell!"

As we were all there, Troop Sergeant Major Dean outlined the Major's plans for us. "This will take us three months. If we are given jobs in the middle then so be it but Major Foster seems to think that the other Troops will be blooded. He wants us to be experts at climbing and blowing up buildings."

Jack Johnson nodded, "Good, that will give us a chance to knock some of these new lads into shape."

"You mean Waller?"

"I do."

The Sergeant Major tapped a manila envelope, "It is easy enough to ship him out. He is a bad 'un."

"I know Sarn't Major but I would feel I had let the commandos down. I have never failed to turn anyone into a decent soldier yet."

"Well we will watch your back. He is a nasty piece of work."

When the Major came in he confirmed our orders. We would begin the next morning. Our sections had to be at the camp for seven. He wanted us to take under two hours to get to the mine. Eventually we would have it in an hour and a half. Our aim was to make our Troop the fittest and the best trained in the service. When the others left he gestured for me to join him in his office.

"Well done, Tom. Lieutenant Marsden told me what you did over there. That was smart thinking. He's recommended you for officer training."

I shook my head, "I am sorry, sir, but that would be three months of my life and the war wasted. I want to keep fighting Jerry. The chap we rescued showed me that what we do is important."

"The war will still go on without you, Tom. You know that."

"Of course, I do and I would be lying if I said I didn't want more responsibility but I am happy at the moment. Lieutenant Marsden is a good officer." When I said it, I was thinking of Captain Grenville. If he were my direct superior then I might change my mind. So long as I had Lieutenant Marsden as an intermediary then I was satisfied.

"Very well. You should know that his report cites all three of you for a medal."

"In which case, he should get one too sir. He did as much as we did."

He gave me a shrewd look, "Perhaps."

We spent the day preparing the men. We went to Quartermaster Daddy Grant to gather our ropes and demolition charges. As we would not be needing them for some time we stored our Thompsons and Colts in the armoury. It was safer that way. We always worried when we carried in England that they might fall into the wrong hands. Not everyone in England was fighting the same war. There were Irish Nationalists who would love to get their hands on two automatic weapons and the criminals who had managed to avoid conscription. They still ran their nefarious operations and sold things on the black market. It annoyed me to think that criminals were benefitting from the war supplying those with too much money the things that they couldn't get.

The four sections were all on parade at 0700 hours. All, that is, except for Private Waller who was late. Jack was fuming. He tore a strip off him in front of everyone. I saw the Troop Sergeant Major nodding his approval. "And, Private Waller, you are on jankers for the next week! When we get to the mines you are going to dig the latrines for the Troop."

The rest of his section and those he had bullied looked especially pleased.

We set off with Major Foster setting the pace. He was a fit man and we used the light infantry march. We alternated quick time with double time. I smiled as I saw that Captain Grenville was struggling to keep up. He was not as fit as any of the rest of us. The Guards prepared you for ceremonial; the commandos prepared you for war.

The mine was on a remote hillside. There were plenty of buildings and broken machinery. It looked perfect. We had a variety of things and materials to blow up. It was important that we knew how much explosive to use. The winding gear was still in place above one of the shafts. There were other shafts which had been boarded over. It looked perfect. We spent the first day preparing the site. Each night four men under the command of a corporal would spend the night on guard. It meant we could leave the explosives and equipment there. Private Waller spent the day digging latrines. I saw the dirty looks he threw Jack Johnson's way. It did not bother the most experienced sergeant in the Troop.

Horace's corporal drew the first night shift. We had tents for them and they seemed quite happy to be there. As we doubled back to the camp Waller kept grumbling. Eventually Jack and Troop Sergeant Major Dean pulled him from the column and took him to one side. We continued back.

When Jack and Troop Sergeant Major Dean arrived, they stood in front of the giant. Troop Sergeant Major Dean said, "Tomorrow, Waller, you will report here, to me, at 0630 hours. Understood?"

"Yes, Troop Sergeant Major!" Waller saluted and then stormed off back to his billet in the town.

Major Foster joined the sergeants and Lieutenant Marsden. Captain Grenville was conspicuous by his absence. We had finished for the day and so there was no reason why he should have stayed but the rest of us were a team. It seemed we had two men in the Troop who stood out like sore thumbs. One was an officer and one a private. They were both problems, in their own ways.

"What do you reckon about Waller, Sarn't Major?"

"Sorry sir; I don't like to give up but he is a lost cause. You can see it in his eyes. He doesn't like authority and he is a thug." He shook his head. "If he wore a black Waffen SS uniform then it would make sense. He would fit right in with that lot."

Lieutenant Marsden said, "I say, Sarn't Major, that is a little strong."

"It might be, sir, but it is true."

"Right, I will get his transfer arranged tomorrow."

Jack shuffled uncomfortably in his seat and said, "Sir, can you give me a week?"

"Are you sure? He is a bad apple. You don't want him spoiling the others, do you?"

"That's the point sir; I think the other lads are good lads. Between us we might show him the error of his ways."

The Major nodded, "Today is Monday. You have until Thursday night. If the Troop Sergeant Major is not happy by then he goes."

"Right sir. Leave it with me."

After we had finished at the camp I left with Jack and Horace to go back to town. "I think Reg and the Major are right, Jack. How can you change him?"

"You gave me the idea this morning Tom."

"Did I? How?"

"When we met up and walked to the camp. We just chatted like mates, didn't we?"

"We are mates."

"I know. Well, tomorrow I will wait close to Waller's digs and just chat to him while we walk to the camp. I'll find out what football team he likes; the kind of music and comedians he favours. I have tried the hard man approach and it doesn't work. I'll try the matey one. Instead of picking on him like he thinks I do, I will make him feel special eh?" He shrugged. "If it doesn't work then I have failed."

Horace snorted, "No, Jack. It is Waller who is a failure. You have to face it there are some bad 'uns. He is one." Shaking his head, he laughed, "I bet you would have tried to make a decent soldier out of Adolf too!"

I left Mrs Bailey's a little later the next day. I wanted to allow Jack the opportunity to have his chat.

Jack was outside the office smoking a cigarette. "Did it work?"

"I am not certain. He spent half the journey just not talking. Eventually he opened up a bit but he just doesn't like anybody. He is a loner. Reg might be right but at least I have made the effort.

I forgot about our bad apple once we reached the camp. Each section had the task of blowing up one part of the complex. We were just using two-pound charges. The Major wanted us to see how to damage something with a small charge. Rather than have them all blow up at once we would set our charges and then retire. We would set them off one by one. It was safer and we could judge the effect better. My section had part of a conveyor used to move the tin ore to a hopper. Jack's section would destroy the hopper.

Ken was our demolitions expert and I watched him explain to the new men how to set the charges quickly but efficiently. We were all concentrating so hard that we jumped when we heard a shout from Jack Johnson's section. Private Dixon came flying through the air and he was followed by Private Waller who kicked him hard in the head. The rest of the section restrained him. I ran over with the officers and the other sergeants. Jack shook his head.

"What happened Sergeant Johnson?"

The section medic was tending to the unconscious private. "We gave Private Waller the job of attaching the wires. Private Dixon said he was doing it wrong and he hit him and then kicked him."

Waller shouted, "It was not wrong! I was doing it right."

Horace Maguire went to the hopper and examined the wiring. "Dixon was right. This would never have gone off in a month of Sundays."

"I have had enough of this outfit. Major Foster I demand a transfer!"

The Major said, "I am sorry Waller. It is too late for that. You have assaulted a commando. This means a court martial and the glasshouse."

He struggled to escape the men who restrained him. "You can't do that!"

"It is your own fault and if you continue to make a nuisance of yourself then it will just increase the sentence. Sergeant Johnson, let your corporal take over while you escort Private Waller back to the camp."

"Yes sir."

"If you don't mind Major Foster I will go along with Sergeant Johnson. I am not certain that Private Waller has calmed down enough yet." I saw Red Dean's eyes narrow. He did not trust Waller.

Waller suddenly feigned a smile and became still. "I am all right Sarn't Major. Trust me I am calm now. I can see the error of my ways."

"Nevertheless, you will have an escort."

The two of them marched him off down the hill. I did not envy them their task. We went back to our tasks. Waller's mistakes and his outburst meant there was a long delay but eventually we all retired a safe distance and the four charges set off. I felt sorry for Gordy. This was his first opportunity to impress and his charge had only half destroyed the tool store. I could see his anger. While my section went to look at the results of our handiwork I went to speak to him.

"You look a little angry, old son."

"I told them what to do and they got it wrong!"

"Then it is your fault."

"What?" He looked like I had slapped his face.

"If you had told them properly then they would have got it right. You know that."

He opened his mouth as though he was going to argue with me. Then he nodded. "You are right. I wanted to be the first to finish and I

81

rushed my explanation. I'll get it right next time." He looked down at his boots. "Perhaps I am not cut out to be a leader."

"Of course, you are. We all make mistakes. Just be grateful that you made it here on the training ground. We have weeks here yet. Take it steady and you will be fine."

"Thanks, Tom."

The Major decided to double down to the camp as it was a little later than we would have liked. Two miles from the camp was a bend in the road and a small copse. Gordy's section was leading and he suddenly stopped and shouted. I ran, with Major Foster, to join him. We saw, sticking out from under the bush two pairs of feet. Gordy was already moving the bush. As he did so we saw an unconscious Jack Johnson and Troop Sergeant Major bleeding from his side and his hand. Of Private Waller, there was no sign! They had been attacked and it did not take Sherlock Holmes to work out who had done it

Chapter 8

"Hewitt!"

"Yes Sarge."

"Troop Sergeant Major Dean has been stabbed."

Hewitt had grown in confidence since I had made him our medic and he quickly took out his bag. The Major was with the Troop Sergeant Major. "Sergeant Barker, take your section and get to the camp. I want an ambulance as soon as. We will bring the two of them to the camp. It is only two miles."

"Yes sir. Right lads! Run!"

"Sergeant Maguire. Have your section pick up Sergeant Johnson and carry him to the camp."

Lieutenant Marsden said, "But he has a head wound."

"If you look at his face you can see that he has had his jaw broken. That damned animal did this."

Private Hewitt looked up from Sergeant Major Dean. "I have stopped the bleeding sir but I will need to keep the pressure on. If the other lads pick him up we can make it to the camp."

"Right. Captain Grenville, you go back to the camp and wait for the ambulance."

"What will you do sir?"

"The three of us will try to apprehend this man. He is a danger to others not just commandos. Anyone who can overpower these two needs to be approached with care."

The Captain nodded, "Right you men," he pointed to six men standing close to Reg, "On three, lift. One, two, lift."

Major Foster turned to me. "Where do you reckon he would go?"

"He is not stupid, sir. I think he would get off the road as soon as he could. Too many opportunities for him to be seen. I think he would look for transport." I pointed to the left. "There See that farm over there?

83

When we came up I am sure I saw an old farm lorry there when we passed it. It isn't now."

"Then let's go." He unholstered his Colt. Unlike the sergeants the officers had retained their hand weapons.

We ran up the track which led to the farmhouse. I was not hopeful. Waller had had more than two hour's start on us. He would not be anywhere close. The gaping door was ominous. As we entered the hall we saw an old man. He was bleeding from the nose and was lying against the stairs. When he saw our uniforms, he recoiled.

"Don't worry, sir. We are not here to harm you. Did you see a huge man dressed like us?"

"Aye the bastard was stealing my lorry. When I shouted at him he came and hit me." He wiped the blood from his nose. "Next time I take my shotgun!"

"I am sorry for the attack on you. The man is a deserter. What is the licence plate and make of your vehicle? We will tell the police."

"DAF 319; it is a Bean New Era truck. He won't get far. There's hardly any petrol in it. I couldn't get any."

"Are you all right sir?"

"I served in the Great War; of course, I am all right. Get the bugger and give him a good hiding for me, will you?"

"We will, sir. Believe you me."

We ran down the track and back to the road. We caught up with the men carrying our injured sergeants just four hundred yards from the camp. There was an ambulance there already.

Major Foster said, "Have the men get their guns. I will ring the police. Waller is our problem. We will catch him."

We dumped our bags in the stores and went to the armoury for our guns. When we assembled the Major had finished on the telephone. "They have found the abandoned lorry. It is near a village called Burras." He pointed to the two lorries we had. "I want the whole Troop. We will hunt this animal down. We can't let him loose on the civilian population."

I went with Lieutenant Marsden and Major Foster. I drove. It was only half a dozen mile to Burras. Now that he was on foot Waller couldn't get very far; not without stealing another vehicle. As he had discovered to his cost few vehicles had fuel these days. When we reached the village, there was an ancient policeman standing next to the vehicle. "One of the locals said that they saw a giant running west. I don't know where he is going. There's nothing but fields until Crowan and the only vehicles they have there is Harry George's tractor."

The Major said, "I think he is panicking." He pointed to the rear of our lorry. "There is some petrol in there. Could you get the vehicle back to the farmer?"

"Old Fred White?" The Major nodded, "Aye, he's a good old stick."

The Major saw Captain Grenville's lorry pull up. "Everyone out of the lorries. We go on foot. He is heading across country. I want us to operate as four sections. Captain Grenville you take Lieutenant Marsden and Sergeant Johnson's section. I will go with Sergeant Barker. Lieutenant Green go with Sergeant Maguire. Keep two hundred yards between each section and if you see any tracks then give a shout."

"What do we do if we find him?"

Lieutenant Marsden's question was a good one. "Take him if you can but I want no one to take any chances. He has burned his bridges. I want him taken or dead!"

I knew my section. "Polly take the left and Ken the right. Harry and George in the middle with me. The rest of you fill in the gaps. Ten yards between each man." I had my Thompson slung over my shoulder. I would use the Colt. We began to trot west. He had a head start but not as much as he had had before. Then we had not known where he was heading. I knew he could turn off the track but I doubted that he would. He would try to put as much daylight between us as he could. He was a fit lad and he would run and run. Darkness began to fall and I prayed that the Major would not call off the search. Waller was a good commando but he was a big man. He would not find it easy to hide. We kept going. There were many false alarms.

85

At the back of my mind was the thought that he would need food and water. He could keep going but without food and water he would make bad decisions and mistakes. We had passed Crowan and were approaching Leedstown when I heard a shot and a shout from the right. That was where Jack Johnson's section was. I ran towards the noise. The field through which we ran had been recently ploughed. My men waited for me to reach Ken Curtis. "Did you see anything?"

"I saw a flash just yonder."

"Keep the lads low and follow me."

I ran half crouched with my Colt cocked and ready. I saw Waller. He had Captain Grenville. I could see that the captain's head was bleeding. They were in front of a tree and Waller had the Captain's Colt to his temple.

"Take another step and he is dead."

"Drop it Waller! We have you surrounded."

"Is that you Harsker? You must be mental! If I surrender it is the hangman for me. I might as well shoot this bastard. So, don't push me."

"Waller, I am giving you one chance to surrender."

He suddenly fired two shots blindly. I heard a shout as he hit someone. Waller laughed, "I hope that was you, Harsker."

I levelled the Colt. Waller had placed his head as close as he could get to the Captain's. "Last chance Waller!"

"Bugger…"

That was all he got. I fired two quick shots and the side of his skull exploded showering Captain Grenville in blood, bones and brains. Waller's body fell to the ground. He was dead. I found that my hand was shaking. This was the first time I had shot someone who was not in enemy uniform. Everyone seemed frozen in time. Suddenly the silence was shattered by Captain Grenville's voice, screaming, "You damned fool Harsker! You could have shot me!"

Major Foster's voice, in contrast was calm, "But he didn't. Good shot Harsker. Who is injured?"

"Private Briggs sir. His arm was clipped."

"Get him some medical attention eh? Sergeant Maguire, have six men pick up Waller's body. We'll take it back to Burras. Well done men. If he had escaped this might have become ugly."

We turned and headed back to Burras. Lieutenant Marsden walked next to me. "Will I be in bother for this, sir?"

"Bother, Harsker?"

"I shot a British soldier!"

"You shot a dangerous criminal who had already tried to kill four people. There will be an enquiry but I think the enquiry will concentrate on what led up to this. You had nothing to do with any of that."

I lowered my voice, "And what about Captain Grenville? He seemed awfully upset."

"I am certain that the captain will thank you once he has calmed down. It must have been a shock to him. You did well Tom. You have nothing with which to reproach yourself."

The policeman was still at Burras trying to start the old lorry. He seemed relieved when we arrived. Major Foster handled the whole situation as though he was born to it. "Sergeant Barker see if you can get the truck started. We have shot the deserter, Constable. He tried to shoot one of my officers. We will take the body back with us. This is a military matter now."

The Constable seemed relieved, "Thank you Major. I could do without the paperwork and folks hereabouts will be glad that the danger is passed. It is bad enough worrying about German soldiers attacking us without our own lads doing it." Although there was no malice in his words they struck to the heart of me. He was right and this should not have happened.

We had a late start the following day. The Major told us all to get in by eleven. I was still up early. I had found sleep difficult. My dreams were haunted by Waller's face exploding before me. It was the first killing which had bothered me. I went down to the harbour to watch the waves. The sea had a soothing effect on me. Perhaps that was why I had found the submarine so hard to take. I could not see the sea. It helped to clear my head and I headed back to the camp.

87

The Major and Lieutenant Marsden were in the office. "Ah Harsker, glad you came in early. Headquarters want a witness statement from you. Fill in all the details you can about the events leading up to the incident and including the moment you were forced to shoot him." He smiled, "By the way they were two damned fine shots!"

"Right sir. How are Jack and the Troop Sergeant Major?"

"The hospital telephoned. Troop Sergeant Major Dean is still critical but Sergeant Johnson has had his jaw wired and he is being released later on today. If you take the lorry down at two o'clock he should be ready after the doctor's rounds."

"Right sir. And Captain Grenville?"

The two officers looked at each other, "Er Captain Grenville is on leave. We all felt that he needed some time after the traumatic events of last night."

I wrote my report. I didn't know it at the time, none of us did, but Captain Grenville asked for and was granted a transfer to another Troop. It was felt it was in the best interest of the whole service. I for one was happy. He had affected the whole Troop adversely.

Gordy came with me to pick up Jack from the hospital. His face looked swollen and painful. He could not speak and the doctor told us that he had to have rest for at least a fortnight. Jack's eyes told me that was one order he would be disobeying. We had a list of instructions for our own doctor and medics. Promising that we would obey we took Jack to the lorry. He sat in the front between Gordy and me.

Gordy told him what had happened and when he said I had shot Waller Jack patted my knee in gratitude. Jack had a notepad and pencil with him and he wrote down what he wanted to say. Gordy read it out.

"Waller suddenly doubled up as though he was in pain on the way down the hill. When Jack went to help him, he was hit in the face and that is all he remembers."

I nodded, "We didn't take Waller's dagger from him. It is not hard to work out the rest. We know that Waller was fast. Even if Reg was expecting something he would expect to be thumped and not knifed. He had cuts to his hands. They sound like defensive wounds to me. I hope Reg is all right. The Troop needs him."

Gordy said, "I reckon he will be more embarrassed than anything else."

"I think you are right."

The excitement of the previous day had upset our plans. We were now an officer, a Troop Sergeant Major and a sergeant down. The Major wrote that day off. He sent half a section to relieve the sentries at the mine. He called in the officers and all the NCOs to his office. "We have some serious work to do. Waller's action has the potential to destroy this Troop. You chaps have to make sure it doesn't."

Gordy said, "Sir I think it is the opposite. The lads are angry with Waller. I think they think the privates have let us down. That's what my section said on the way back yesterday. They are determined to be even better in the future."

"Gordy may be right, sir. If we look too deeply into this it may cause us problems. I mean, we are a tighter unit now, no disrespect to Captain Grenville, but as long as he isn't here that bit of grit is not gumming up the works is it, sir?"

"I am not certain that Captain Grenville would appreciate being called a bit of grit, Sergeant Harsker."

"Sorry sir, I was out of line. But all I wanted to say was that we just need to train as though yesterday didn't happen."

Everyone, including Jack nodded. I saw the pain it caused Jack. He would never forget the previous day.

We were back at the mine the next day. The shifts of sentries had tidied up the mine site. Commandos were, by their nature, tidy soldiers. We left no trail unless we had to. The Major had decided that we would plan and practise assaulting the mine as though it was in enemy hands. We were each given a section to attack. The first time we did it the men were in high spirits for the attack went well.

The Major gathered us around. "Excellent men. I wish that every attack went that way. I think we would all fancy attacking an enemy target with no sentries." I saw the crestfallen looks on their faces.

"Sergeant Harsker have your section pick up some staves." There had been some barrels which we had blown up. The sentries had placed the surviving staves in a pile.

"Right lads, you heard the Major." As I picked up a stave I found myself intrigued. What was the Major planning?

"Sergeant Harsker, you and your section are the German guards. Feel free to use your staves on anyone you see. If you are hit by a stave it counts as a bullet! You are dead!"

Ken and the others grinned. This was like the games of cowboys and Indians we had all played as kids. We were the cowboys and the rest were the Indians. While the rest of the Troop disappeared I said, "Right lads, in pairs. Ken, you take the west, Polly, the east, Harry the south and I will take the north. Scouse, you are with me. Remember they know we saw the first attack. This one will be different."

Fletcher had a grin on his face. I shook my head. "Don't get cocky! They will use all the tricks we know to get through to the targets. Stand with your back to something. Watch for distractions."

To be fair to the rest of the sections it was not a realistic test. It was daylight and we knew they were coming. Even so they did their best. The staves meant we could not strike at distance. There was plenty of cover for them apart from the last thirty yards. That was where we had to watch. I caught a movement out of the corner of my eye to the right. I said quietly, "Someone coming from the right. Don't turn. Watch to your left. They may try from two directions at once."

I did not envy those who were attacking us. They had to reach us before we could swing our staves. Rather than turning to my right I swivelled my eyes. I saw the comforter in the bushes just ten yards away. I knew what they would try. There would be a distraction to my front and then whoever it was to my right would rush me. Sure enough, I heard noise from my front; it was the sound of a foot on rocks. I was swinging my stave even before I turned. It smacked into the shoulder of Private Ryan. I turned to my front and was just in time to poke Horace Maguire in the chest. He grinned as he stopped, "You have eyes in the back of your head!"

There was a yelp from my left as Scouse Fletcher brought his stave around to hit Corporal Price.

"Don't get too confident Fletcher. There are another seven out there."

However, that was, largely, the end of the attack. Bereft of their two leaders the rest of the section tried a brave charge. They were easily sent packing by just the two of us. The Major blew his whistle and I turned. The others had taken George and Reg but we had inflicted more casualties. We gathered around to discuss the attack and to learn from it.

"Now we learned a great deal from that. Sergeant Maguire's section; you went to pieces when you lost your sergeant and corporal. Rank means nothing in the commandos. Remember that."

Private Golightly said, "But sir, it was daylight. We stood no chance."

"Sergeant Barker's section managed to incapacitate two of the guards. It is harder but we are all about finding solutions to impossible problems."

"And the other point is that if we had been Germans with real guns and not staves then when Private Ryan was fired upon the alarm would have been given. We all need ways to kill silently at distance."

Ken said, "Sarge, I have an idea." He took out his toggle rope and started to make the knot at each end larger. He stood ten yards from the winding gear and threw it. The rope whirled and wrapped itself around one of the metal struts.

Everyone applauded. Lieutenant Marsden became excited. "It is like a bola. The South American Indians used them. If we had wooden balls we could make them. They are a silent way of incapacitating a man."

And so, another weapon was created. We all made our own bola and practised with them. Some became more proficient than others but it gave us a silent edge.

We trooped back to camp in high spirits. Or, at least most of us were in high spirits. Poor Jack Johnson was on a liquid diet and it did not sit well with him. However, when we heard that Reg Dean was on the mend the morale of the whole Troop improved. I know not why but we had more focus to our training. It was almost as though we were trying to be the best for the Troop Sergeant Major.

Two weeks after the attack I was summoned to the office by the Major. "Two things. Harsker, you have been exonerated of any blame and Captain Grenville has left the Troop."

"Thank you, sir. I was worried."

"Well I can tell you now that Captain Grenville made a complaint about you. He said you put his life in danger. He wanted you reduced to the ranks." I remembered Bill Leslie. Captain Grenville was a vindictive man. "Thank God that Lord Lovat was on the board. He dismissed it out of hand. Now we can get back to what we do best."

"Will there be any more missions before Christmas, sir?"

"Hard to say. I know some of the other Troops have got their feet wet. It may well be our turn soon. The thing of it is that there are some in London who are keen to start a second front. They see us as an assault force."

"But we aren't sir! We are like a scalpel. We make sharp incisive attacks and get out before anyone knows. It would be a waste of all our training."

"I agree with you but now that Italy is wavering there are talks about an attack in Italy."

"But what about North Africa? The last I read Rommel was almost in Alexandria."

"I know. All I am saying is that we need to be ready to go into action at a moment's notice."

By the time November had been and gone we had, effectively, demolished the whole of the mine complex. The scrap metal was taken off to be made into Matildas and the stones and bricks were used to fill up some of the mines. We were ready for action. Major Foster was a great student of human nature. The whole Troop was given two weeks leave. It would not take us up to Christmas but all of us would enjoy the celebration no matter when it was. When we returned on December the twelfth Jack and Reg would be back with us and we would have a full complement once more.

Chapter 9

Mum was delighted that I was coming home for Dad was also due back. When I telephoned the house to tell her she almost wept for joy. "The whole family together! I have had my Christmas present already!"

As I headed north on the train I saw the effects of twenty-six months of war. There were many burned out buildings and vast swathes of towns had been levelled first by German bombers and then by civil defence workers as they cleared dangerous buildings. Every house we passed had tape on the windows and every person had the haunted and thin look of someone who has suffered each and every day. The people on the train, too, appeared depressed and downhearted. Bombing and rationing were not good bedfellows. The war was becoming a battle of wills between the civilians of Britain and Germany. Who was tougher?

Dad was waiting for me at the station. I had no idea how he knew which train I would be on. I had not planned my route, I had taken the first train for each leg.

He embraced me, "Welcome home, son!" The hug was held longer than we did in the days before the war. Each time you said goodbye you thought it might be the last and each time you said hello you were grateful that you were both still alive. We threw my Bergen in the boot and I clambered into the car. As we roared off down the country lane he asked, "How are your section?" He knew them from the rescue.

"Oh, they are fine. They are champing at the bit to be off again. Training and preparation are not their strong suits."

"Nor, I suspect, yours."

"I have just travelled all the way from Cornwall, Dad and it seems to me that the people are in danger of losing the will to fight."

"Don't underestimate the British spirit, son. I spend most of my time in London now and they are having it tougher than anyone. The Blitz would have beaten down most nations already but they are standing up to the enemy and defying him. But I think your underlying message is right, we need to beat them before they beat us."

The house was in the distance, "Well I am doing my bit!"

"I know old son but no talk of war while you are on leave eh? Your poor Mum and Mary worry about us all the time. Keep it light and keep it jolly. I know you can do that."

"Of course. To be honest it will be a relief not to talk about it."

As soon as the car pulled through the gates mum and Mary ran out; Mum was crying. I know they were tears of joy but they always seemed so incongruous. After she had hugged me and almost stopped me breathing she held me at arm's length. "The Military Medal! Well done you! My son, the war hero!"

I shook my head, "I was just lucky that was all."

She laughed, "Sounds just like your Dad talking. He was as modest too. Come on in and get out of the cold."

Mrs Bailey's bed and breakfast was a lovely house but it was not a home; it was not my home and the minute I stepped through the door I knew that was where I was. I came home so rarely that it was an absolute treat. I knew that my family was lucky. The house in the countryside meant it was unlikely to be bombed and with a huge garden mum and Mary could grow more vegetables than most people. Mum had written that they also had chickens and I heard them clucking outside.

We had always brought back wine from our holiday home in France and Dad had a good selection. He brought up two decent, dusty clarets from the cellar for our dinner. We had a pheasant stew; meat was in short supply but a couple of young farmers were sweet on Mary and there was always plenty of game. It was a delightful diversion from the dangers of the war. All thoughts of the submarine and Waller's attempted murders faded. Dad and I just listened to Mum's tales of the village and country life. It was as far removed from our own world as it was possible. For that reason, it was the best thing we could hear. It was the reason we were fighting the war; to preserve our way of life.

When I woke, the next morning, I felt the effects of the wine, port and brandy we had consumed. I thought I would not need to eat for a week but Mum's chickens meant fresh eggs for breakfast and they helped to calm my stomach.

"Tell you what, son, what say we take a couple of guns and see what we can get from the woods for our larder?"

Mum seemed happy. "And I can get your uniform washed and cleaned." I felt half-naked in my civilian clothes but I also felt like a different person.

"Great idea."

We were both good shots but even if we failed to hit anything it would not matter. I knew why Dad had suggested this; he wanted to chat. We said little until we reached the woods. "Fred Lythe reckoned there were some pheasants over by Badger's Brook."

"Fine. Let's try there."

We were both good stalkers and we settled down close to the bubbling brook which ran through the wood. We were patient and after an hour were rewarded by two plump pheasant, a male and female. They began grazing. We were up wind of them and they were just forty yards away. We knew without speaking which each of us would take. Dad would go for the male on his side. I would take the female on mine We were using small bore rifles. A shotgun made too much mess. I took a bead on the head. I followed her movements and got into her rhythm. I squeezed gently. Almost in the same instant Dad fired. They both fell dead.

"Good shot!" We went to retrieve our birds. They were both plump. The animals did not know there was a war on.

While I tied their heads together and hung them over a branch Dad got his pipe going. I was always tempted to take up the pipe. What stopped me was the fact that I knew it was addictive. If I didn't start, I would never have to give up.

"So, what's been going on?"

Dad was the only person in whom I could totally confide. His security clearance was the highest that there was. And so, I told him of the two raids in the Channel Islands and my experience in the sub.

"Thank the lord I have never had to go down in one of those things. I like the open air and open sky."

I nodded, "They are tough, the lads who man them, and they rarely even manage to sink any ships. They have all the danger and none of the rewards."

"You think what you do is rewarding?"

"When we rescued the resistance leader I did. And destroying those gun emplacements will save lives. Yes, it is rewarding."

My tone might have seemed aggressive for he smiled and held up his hands. "You'll get no argument from me. If you and your section hadn't rescued me I would now be a guest of the Gestapo."

I nodded and then told him about Captain Grenville and Waller.

He came over to me and put his arm around my shoulders. "That must have been hard; shooting one of your own men."

I nodded, "It was shooting someone in the same uniform and Jack had thought he could save him. Even as I pulled the trigger I wondered if we had done enough."

"From what you told me, you had. We have no time in this was to molly coddle men. Waller was a casualty of war. If there hadn't been a war you can bet your life that he would have been in prison. His sort always ends up there." He tapped out his pipe, "That is where these woolly-minded liberals go wrong. There are some people who can't be helped. And as your Troop Sergeant Major and Sergeant found out, innocent people can get hurt by them." He stood, "Come on, what say we call in the Golden Sun for a couple of pints before dinner?"

"Excellent."

And that was the end of our war talk. By common agreement we talked of anything but the war. It was easier than we thought. Sadly, the leave flew by far too quickly. Dad and I went to the pub a couple of times and we had a fine Christmas dinner. We spent nights playing card and board games and listening to the radio. The four of us took long walks when the weather was clement. It was as though the war didn't exist. Then Dad was recalled to London and it seemed to be a reminder of how brief our time together would be. We all found it hard to say

97

goodbye to him. London was now almost as dangerous as the front line. When the time came for me to return to Falmouth mum and Mary were on the edge of tears. It had been like a countdown. As children, we had had a countdown to Christmas: '*how many sleeps?*' Now we had that for the end of my leave. I remembered Dad's words and I tried to be as jolly as possible, even though I didn't feel like it.

The war re-entered our lives when we heard on the radio that Pearl Harbour in Hawaii had been bombed and the Americans were in the war. If Dad had been there I could have discussed its implications. He had told me what a difference that had made in the Great War. Mum and Mary just saw it as another example of man being cruel to man. This was now, truly a world war, Japan and Hawaii were on the other side of the world. I had thought North Africa was a long way away. This was something different altogether.

Mum drove me back to the station. The length of the journey meant I had to be at the station by seven. It seemed an ungodly hour to be saying goodbye.

Mary hugged me and burst into tears, "Take care big brother!"

As mum embraced me she whispered in my ear, "I love you, my big brave boy, but please don't be the hero all the time. I want to be a grandmother and see your children grow up. One medal is enough. Don't try for more."

I felt her tears running down my cheek, "I don't try, mum. I just do my duty."

She shook her head as the train hissed in. "A typical Harsker! Always doing your duty. Just like your father. Well keep your head down at least."

"I will mum, I promise."

As I waved goodbye from the train I realised that was a promise I could not keep. I was a sergeant in the commandos. I could not take it easy. I settled down in the corner of the compartment and watched England roll by. Mum's words had set me to thinking. I was just twenty but I had not even thought about a family. I never even got to meet any girls. If I was to be honest with myself I was actually a little afraid of meeting girls. I had done it so rarely. Much as I wished to heed mum's words I knew that I would not be able to keep that promise. If there was danger then I would be in it. If you were hesitant, you might die. It was safer to be fearless; fear brought its own dangers.

After I had dropped my bags off at Mrs Bailey's I went to the local we used. I knew that I was the first one back for Mrs Bailey told me so. We were not due back until the following day anyway but I had been lucky with the trains and had no delays. I was delighted to see Troop Sergeant Major Dean and Sergeant Jack Johnson when I walked into the lounge bar. Both looked thin and pale but they grinned when they saw me. I bought three pints and joined them.

"Good to see you both up and about. How is the jaw, Jack?"

"Getting there."

"Don't listen to him, Tom. He is in agony and he drinks more than he eats."

"I deserve it. It is my penance for being such a soft bugger. You were all right about Waller but I had to be pig headed!"

Reg gave him a stern look, "Water under the bridge. The subject is closed! Understood!"

"Yes, Sarn't Major."

"Are you able to move well, Sergeant Major? After the knifing, I mean."

"Aye Tom. I am fine and that is definitely an end to it. And tell the others no questions!" I nodded, "Did you have a good leave?"

"Yes, I went hunting with my Dad and we talked. It was good."

"But hard to leave the bosom of your family and come back here eh?"

"You had better believe it. Is anyone else back?"

"Just the Major and then he went off again; a message from London."

"Seems a little harsh at Christmas; surely they can't have anything planned for us."

99

"The war won't stop for Christmas. Still it might just be for a briefing or to get a new officer. We are short of one." He looked at me. "The Major said he wanted you to go to Officer Training."

"He did but I think I am better employed here."

"You are a bit dim for someone so bright!" I did not point out the contradiction in his words. I knew what he meant. "Everyone in the Troop know you would make a superb officer. It would only be for three months."

I shook my head. "I want to be an officer but I don't want to waste my time at Officer Training Course. Remember I was there before I joined up. I have learned more about being an officer since I joined the commandos. They could teach me nothing."

Jack nodded, "You might have a point there. If Grenville is an example of an Officer Training Course then we are better off with blokes who haven't been through that."

Reg decided that was enough about the Troop and we chatted for the rest of the evening about the inconsequential stuff which filled most bars: football, the weather, radio... the usual.

I took the opportunity, the next day, of catching up with Daddy Grant. He too had been granted leave and had spent his with his wife and children. He had given up more than most. His wound had meant he could have been invalided out but he had loyalty to the Troop. He was cheerier than I had seen him for some time. "I had the best leave. We even managed to get a big chicken for our Christmas dinner. I didn't ask our lass where she got it. I didn't care. It was bloody lovely and the kids have grown up. They made a real fuss of me. We had the in laws round two nights ago and had a grand party. Yes, that was the best leave I have had in a long time."

"Aren't you sad to be back then?"

"No. They made a fuss because my time at home was so short. That was why we had no rows and everybody was happy. There's a war on and you never know what is around the corner. If I had been home longer it would not have been as good. We crammed in everything we could."

100

He was right and his words echoed my mum's comments. The war was just part of my life. It wasn't my whole life.

The Major returned two days later and his face told us that, despite what we had thought, we were going into action again. He had with him another officer; a lieutenant this time. All of the NCOs were gathered in the canteen. "This is Lieutenant Eliot. He is joining our compliment and I have recommended that Lieutenant Marsden be promoted to Captain. We are awaiting confirmation."

We all cheered. He was a popular officer.

"That is the good news. Now the slightly more unwelcome news. We have a job behind enemy lines. We are being dropped into the Low Countries on Christmas Day. Our job is to destroy two radar stations which have just been built north east of Dunkirk." I saw Horace begin to open his mouth. "Before you say anything Sergeant Maguire, bombers can't go in because they have built the two of them very close to civilians. One is next to a church and the other next to a village. We are the scalpel and not the sledgehammer. We leave on Christmas Eve and we will be picked up at dawn from the beach. The RAF and Coastal Command will cover our withdrawal. We have until then to practise. You all know what Freja looks like. The new lads won't. I am hoping our recent training at the mine will pay off. The Brass hope that the timing will catch Jerry unaware. If will be Christmas day and he won't expect us to attack."

We all looked at the maps. We had not been to that part of France and I knew there were issues with the aeroplane drops. Being picked up after the raid was a clever idea. There was little chance of the enemy being alerted before the raid. However, there were far more things which could go wrong.

"I will lead Sergeant Jackson's section. We will go in with Sergeant Barker and Lieutenant Eliot. Captain Marsden and Lieutenant Green will take in Sergeant Maguire and Sergeant Harsker's teams."

I was pleased; I knew Captain Marsden. He was a good leader. Lieutenant Green still looked young and nervous. He would be the unknown quantity on this mission. It was the young lieutenant who handed out the maps.

The Major continued, "De Panne is on the beach. It is low lying and there are no cliffs to assault. There is a pier and that is how we will escape. It is guarded; our aerial photographs indicate that they have a pair of heavy machine guns mounted there. That implies about eight men. As they are guarding the pier from the sea it should be possible to take them out from the land." He pointed to me, "That will be Sergeant Harsker's task. When his section has set their charges, they will go to the pier and secure our safe departure." He smiled, "I understand that some of his men are now learning German. That may well come in handy."

"Sir, what about the guards for the two Freja?"

"There is a small guard hut next to each one, Barker. At night, there should only be a couple of men."

"And why have they two so close together sir? They don't normally."

"I know, Corporal Price; Intelligence seems to think that they regard this as a key site for their defences. Our bombers are visiting Germany regularly and that is the main route they take. Now that our American friends are in the war it won't be too long until there are American bombers flying there too. The second one was only completed last week. We don't think they are both fully functioning. Certainly, the photographic aeroplanes have not seen any activity around them."

"Do we want to bring any bits back, sir?"

Sometimes Intelligence and the boffins wanted to know if there were any changes in the way the enemy machines worked but, in answer to Gordy's question the Major just shook his head. "They asked us to but I said it was too risky. The priority is the destruction of these things." He smiled, "I offered to take one of their scientists with us so that he could examine one in situ.... They said we could just destroy them." We all laughed. No one but a commando would do what we did.

We dispersed to brief our sections. I sketched what Freja looked like and showed it to the new men. "They want these destroying

102

completely. Here is how we do it. We have one charge here under the wire array and a series of charges under the bottom of the whole unit. We will be with Sergeant Maguire's team. Technically it only needs one team to set the charges but we are going in by parachute and it may be that only a couple of people actually get to the Freja." I pointed to the new men. "If that is you then you will have to use what we have learned up at the mine and destroy it yourself." They nodded, seriously.

We did not have long to prepare. As we were going in by air we all had to have explosives and times with us. With the Bola and Thompsons, we would be landing heavy. The one advantage we had was that it was the Low Countries. The landing would be relatively flat. However, we were going in lower than we normally did. The Major was trying to minimise the risk of us being spread out over a large area. The Low Countries also meant that while it would be cold it would be unlikely to be a snowy landing.

It was early on the morning of Christmas Eve that we headed for the airfield where our Whitleys awaited us. The two Freja were just half a mile apart and so we would fly together. Once on the ground we would operate independently. The rest of the troop would be relying on the skills of my section to overcome the guards at the pier. If anything, untoward occurred in the landing then the rest would have to improvise. We waited until late afternoon. The airfield was full of preparations for Christmas. Homemade decorations were in abundance and we could smell the spiced puddings that were being steamed by the cooks. When they were waking up to Christmas and good will to all men we would be trying to kill Germans a few hundred miles to the east. It was bizarre.

We boarded the aeroplanes in daylight. We had to be in the air before it was dark. We needed all the dark we could get to do the job. I hated the flying coffins. They still smelled of leaking petrol and I knew that the noise during take-off would be unbearable. Dad had been surprised that they still used the antiquated bomber. In his position, he knew the vast array of aeroplanes we now had. My own theory was that the bombers, like us, were expendable. The old hands showed the new ones the procedure. I had alternated my section so that one of the

103

original crew was next to a new boy. Fletcher stood behind me. Lieutenant Green was bang in the middle between Harry and George. They would look after the young officer. Ken Curtis would be the last out. When the hatch was slammed shut it reminded me of the submarine. This too felt like a tomb- this time an aerial one.

As soon as the huge engines started the aeroplane began to vibrate and shake. The noise was horrific. It continued as we hurtled down the runway and only abated slightly when we were in the air. We would have a relatively short flight time but we were to rendezvous with some ancient Wellingtons which would act as a diversion. They would bomb the railway line which went through Diksmuide a few miles to the east. It was a good plan. I just hoped that all of the Wimpey bomber crews would survive. I did not want anyone dying for us. I preferred going in my small boat. Of course, the German guards at the pier would make that impossible.

It was a relatively short flight and the co-pilot popped his head out of the cockpit and shouted. "Fifteen minutes to the drop zone."

The Flight Sergeant went to the hatch in the floor and removed it. There was a rush of icy air and it became impossible to talk. We would use hand signals from now on. We all hooked on. Our Bergens and our Thompsons were in front of us. I felt Fletcher pressing as close to me as he could. That would be Ken pushing up from the back. It was important that we all exited quickly. Horace's team would be right behind us. The pilot came out and gave the thumbs up. Even before the flight sergeant had turned I was stepping into the black void. With my arms on my Bergen I hit the night. All was dark below us. There were no landmarks. I orientated myself to look west by using the departing Whitleys as a point of reference. I caught sight of white caps. It was the sea. I reached up to adjust my parachute. To the east I could hear the sound of flak as the Wimpeys began bombing the railway line. I wanted to be as close to the coast as I could get. The lower altitude meant that the ground came at me very quickly. As I descended I saw an empty field and I tugged one of the cords. I flexed my knees before I struck. The ground was rock hard but I managed to keep my feet. I began gathering in the parachute as soon as my feet touched the ground.

I heard the rest of the section as they thumped to the ground. Scouse Fletcher had a hard landing and I heard him grunt. With my parachute bundled up I took off my Bergen and my harness. Looking around I saw a ditch running along the field. I put the chute in the ditch. It would be found but, hopefully, not until we were long gone. I slung my Thompson and took out my Colt. As I had been descending I had fixed a couple of points in my head. The house to my left was in the direction of the beach. When we reached the road, which ran along the coast we should be able to see our Freja.

Lieutenant Green ran up to me. He was grinning. A successful landing did that. I pointed to the house. He nodded. Ken brought up the rest. I saw that Fletcher was limping. We had our first casualty. He would have to keep up with us. The Lieutenant signalled for me to lead. I trotted off towards the house. It was in darkness. I could not smell smoke and I guessed that it was unoccupied. I went down the track which led from the house to the road. As soon as I reached the road I held up my hand and dropped to one knee. We had landed about half a mile further west than we should have. We had two ways to go. We could risk the road and get to Duinhoek and turn left or we could risk the dunes. Both involved risks. The dunes could be mined.

In the distance, I heard a vehicle and that decided me. The dunes were less risky. I waved the section across the road. I followed Ken. There was no sign of Horace and his men nor Captain Marsden. They might have landed even further west. When I reached the Lieutenant I said, quietly, "There are vehicles on the road. I will lead, sir. There may be mines."

"Right, Harsker, you have done this before. Lead on Macduff!"

I went directly north and east. It would bring me, I hoped, to our Freja. I kept glancing to the ground but, as we had not seen signs and the sand, although frozen, looked to have been well used.

I saw the distinctive wire array of the Freja one hundred yards from us. A glowing pinprick showed me where the sentry was having a smoke. I waved the Lieutenant and Ken forward. I pointed. They both nodded. We had already planned this part. Ken took Polly, Harry and George. They would disable the sentries. The Lieutenant followed with the others. I took Scouse and we headed for the beach. We were far enough away from Freja to have our words masked by the sound of the surf. "How is the foot, Scouse?"

"I twisted my ankle, Sarge. Sorry."

"Never mind. I have something for you to do." We reached the beach and I saw, forty yards away, the pier which led into the sea. It was used by fishermen although in 1940 the BEF had used it as a mole to board the little ships. I took Scouse along the dunes keeping below the top. When we reached the end of the pier I said, "You stay here and keep watch. I want to know how many guards you see."

That done I ran back to the Freja. The two guards were trussed up like chickens. Their eyes were closed and I guessed that they had been laid unconscious. Before we left we would move them away from the blast although our charges would be precisely placed to do the maximum damage but make the least noise. The Lieutenant stood to one side. "I wonder where Captain Marsden and Sergeant Maguire are."

"They may have drifted too far to the west. I will take the lads and secure the pier."

The Lieutenant nodded, "Should I blow up the Freja?"

"Wait until I send a messenger back, sir. We have to contact the launches yet."

I tapped Polly and the new lads. They would be my team. The launches were waiting off shore in the dark. When Polly flashed his light then they would come to the end of the pier. I led the men to Scouse. "Fletcher, you are tail end Charlie. How many are there?"

"I counted four of them Sarge. There may be more but just four are moving about."

"Right. Drop your Bergens at the end of the pier. Polly, you are with me at the front. Crowe, Hewitt and Grimsdale you are with us as well. We can't afford any firing." I took out my sap and smacked it into my hand. "I will use this. If you haven't got one use your toggle ropes.

106

No guns! Scouse stay here with the bags. Use your charges to rig the end of the pier. Don't attach the timer yet."

"Right Sarge!"

Once the bags were dropped I stepped onto the pier. The sound of the water swirling beneath would cover most noises. We moved, crouching down the one-hundred-yard pier. I could see the shadows at the end. The guns, which pointed to the sky looked like heavy calibre machine guns. Scouse had been right, I could see the glowing ends of cigarettes and smell the smoke. I could even hear their voices. They were in a good mood and anticipating being relieved in a few hours. That was all we needed. More soldiers for us to fight.

When we were twenty yards from them I held up my hand. I dropped to all fours and crawled. I could see that they were not wearing helmets. They had field caps. That would make the problem of taking them easier. One of them was telling a ribald joke. Their attention was on the teller. We drew closer. My two new men were on the extremes. Polly and I would be the ones who would strike first. I glanced at Polly and nodded. I jumped up and, grabbing the nearest German around the neck with my left arm I smacked the sap against the back of his head. He went limp. Poulson's German was also taken but Grimsdale had not managed to overcome his German and the two of them fell into the sea with a loud splash. Hewitt was quick and he jumped in after them. Private Crowe held his man in a Japanese stranglehold until Polly smacked him with his sap.

"Crowe get back to the Lieutenant, tell him we have the pier and he can blow the Freja. Tell Scouse to bring the bags up. Groves go and help Scouse." Poulson had not needed orders and he had his torch and was flashing out his message. I went to the side and threw the lifebelt which was there. Hewitt and Grimsdale were hauled up. Grimsdale shook his head, "Sorry Sarge."

"Don't worry about it. Where is he?"

"He smacked his head off a strut. He is dead."

"Get these three tied up and then shove the guns into the sea." I went to Polly at the end. "Any sign of the ML?"

Not yet, Sarge."

"Keep trying." Just then I heard the chatter of machine guns. Someone had been spotted. Fletcher and Groves arrived with the bags. "Use these sandbags and pile them up across the pier. It sounds like we have been spotted." At that precise moment, I saw a flash of light. There were four explosions and then another two. The whole night was illuminated and the fire fight intensified.

I glanced at Polly who was still signalling. Unless he contacted them quickly we would all be in the bag! I saw figures approaching and I cocked my Thompson. Behind me I heard a splash as the German gun was dropped into the sea. To my relief the men who ran up were the Lieutenant and the rest of my section.

"The Freja gone, sir?"

"It is Sergeant."

"What was that firing?"

"I think it was Captain Marsden. It came from the west so it can't have been the Major." As if to prove it I heard feet racing down the pier and recognised Major Foster and the other two sections.

"Sarge, I have them!" Poulson pointed out to see where I saw a pinprick of light flashing.

"Tell them we are under attack." There was little point in a silent approach now.

"Well done chaps. The firing?"

Lieutenant Green said, "Sergeant Maguire's section and Captain Marsden."

"Harsker, you and Barker take six men and go to the dunes. They made need help."

"Right sir. Ken, George and Harry, with me." I cocked my Thompson as we ran down the pier. I could see the flash of muzzles in the dark. When we reached the dunes, we threw ourselves down and I took a grenade out."

Gordy said, "I thought it was too good to be true. It went like a dream."

"Horace is a canny old bird. He will make it."

The firing drew closer and we could hear shouts in German. Gordy gave a whistle and repeated it. Behind me I heard the sound of the MGB and Motor Launches as they drew close. George said, "I can see them." He pointed in the dark and I saw at least three Commandos.

"When I give the order spray just above their heads." I counted on the fact that these were our men and would obey orders instantly. When they were forty yards from us I shouted, "Horace! Down!" A heartbeat later I shouted, "Fire!"

We all gave a short burst. One of us was lucky for we were rewarded with a cry as a German was hit. "Come in now lads. The boats are here." One of them must have thrown a grenade for there was a sudden flash and an explosion and then four of them hurried towards us. I could see that two of Horace's section were carrying him and the Captain was covering them with his machine gun. Horace looked to be in a bad way as they almost collapsed behind us.

"Gordy take Horace back. I had Fletcher put charges at the end of the pier. It needs a timer. Ten minutes should do it."

"Ten minutes? That is cutting it fine."

"Just do it eh?"

As they hurried off we gave another burst of our Thompsons. Captain Marsden threw himself over the top of the dune. Now that he was safe we needed to buy some time. "Right lads, on three, grenades." I took out a Mills bomb and pulled the pin. "One, two, three!" We all hurled our bombs and then dived down. We heard shouts and screams as the shrapnel tore through the advancing Germans.

"Right sir, let's get the lead out eh? The end of the pier is rigged to blow in five minutes!"

We ran. It was just fifty years to the pier but it felt longer. Gordy was half way down the pier, "Come on lads!"

I heard the crack of rifles behind us. We just ran. Ken fell as we reached the pier. I reached down and picked him up. I could see that he had been hit. I reached under his arm and pulled him along. Harry saw us and came back. We were in a race. Would we reach the boats before we were either shot or blown up by our own charges?

109

I saw that the launches had all been loaded save one. The gunners were throwing lead and bullets at the pursuing Germans. I could hear shouts of encouragement from our comrades. All of a sudden there was a flash behind me and the concussion of the explosion threw the three of us to the floor. I lost my hearing. I groggily rose to my feet. Harry had also been hit by something. There was a gash in the back of his head. I helped Ken to his feet. "Can you make it on your own?"

"Yes Sarge!" Using the safety rail on the pier he hobbled towards the launch. I picked up Harry. He was a big lad and I put him over my shoulders. Polly and George ran to help me onto the launch. I collapsed in a heap. I knew they were talking to me, I could see their mouths moving, but we had been so close to the blast that I could hear nothing.

The launch spun around and we headed west. Scouse took off my Bergen. He held it for me to see. The back had been shredded. Shrapnel and pieces of wood had torn through it. Luckily for me the steel frame and the equipment inside had taken the impact. I was lucky again.

The leading hand came around, as dawn broke, with stoker's cocoa. He had a piece of holly in his cap. "Merry Christmas Sergeant!"

It was Christmas day. We had had our present. None of our section had died and the injuries were superficial; twisted ankles and cuts to the head. Sergeant Maguire's section, in contrast, had lost six men. We were not certain if they were dead or captured. I also had no idea what injuries Horace had suffered; he was in another launch.

When my hearing returned Lieutenant Green filled me in. He had managed to get some of the story from Captain Marsden. "They lost two men who drifted a long way to the west and they went to look for them. they were so late when they found them all that they decided to use the road." He shook his head, "You were right Sergeant, it was the wrong decision. A German lorry and Kubelwagen came down the road. They hid but one of the Jerries must have had sharp eyes. They opened fire and our lads had to leg it towards the beach. Then the two Freja went up."

"Just bad luck then. How is Horace sir?"

"No idea. He took a bullet. They put him on the MGB they have an SBA."

"Horace is a tough old bugger, sir. He will survive. He is too awkward to die peacefully!"

The wind was so cold that Christmas day that we all went below decks. Normally we liked to watch the horizon and see Blighty appear but it was too unpleasant for that and we huddled below decks.

As Lieutenant Green and I entered the mess Ken said, "Thanks for coming back for me Sarge."

"We never leave anyone behind Ken, you know that."

"And me too Sarge. Sorry I am so heavy." Harry looked to be embarrassed that I had had to carry him.

I laughed, "I didn't realise until I tried to pick you up! I bet you were a rugby player."

"I was sir, Rugby League, second row."

"What happened to the prisoners?"

"Major Foster took them on the MGB. He was pleased he said it was an unexpected bonus."

I almost felt sorry for the Germans. They had been expecting to be celebrating Christmas one minute and the next they were POWs. At least our lads knew what Christmas Day might bring. Rather than going all the way to Falmouth we headed for Newhaven. We needed the medical facilities there. It meant we were back on British soil within a couple of hours. While the wounded and injured were being whisked away I joined Major Foster and the other officers and sergeants.

"A shame about this one hiccup chaps. We would have had a perfect mission but for that."

"Parachutes, sir, they are unpredictable. Perhaps they should have dropped us sooner. We had a fair walk to get to the beach."

"I think they were worried about our chutes being seen."

"How is Horace?"

"The SBA did a good job and stopped the bleeding. There was an exit wound so that is one good thing." He smiled, "I had hoped to get to

111

camp before night but I think we will be lucky to get there by tomorrow. We will be using lorries."

Gordy said, "Well, sir, the sooner we start, the sooner we get home. Are those our lorries over there?"

There were two lorries with their drivers having a smoke. "I believe so."

Gordy turned, "Right lads get your gear aboard the lorries while I have a word with these drivers. Let's see if we can get back sooner than the Major says eh?"

The Major shook his head as Gordy raced off, "He will be lucky! It is two hundred and eighty miles to Falmouth. That is eight hours at least."

I shook my head, "Gordy might be right, sir. There will be no traffic on the roads. We don't need to stop and we can relieve the drivers if we have to. It is nine o'clock now. We could be home for six or even earlier."

"I admire your optimism. Let's try it then."

I think after the raid the race to camp seemed a bit of madcap fun. Gordy and Captain Marsden offered to relieve the drivers after an hour. They made those lorries achieve speeds I doubt even the designer had envisaged. We rocked and we rolled down country lanes. I was just glad that most people were at home enjoying Christmas. It reminded me of the story Dad told of Lord Burscough driving him from London to Burscough in a sports car. And we made it before night had fallen. Even the drivers were impressed. Of course, we had not thought this through. There was no meal prepared and everyone had already eaten their Christmas dinner. We were commandos and we improvised. Every section scavenged and returned an hour later with a variety of food. It was an eclectic mix. Major Foster managed to find beer and whisky so that we celebrated Christmas all together.

Before we all became completely inebriated Troop Sergeant Major Dean insisted we toasted and remembered those who had not returned. We all prayed that they were just prisoners and not lying in some Belgian

112

field but we all remembered them. And then forgot everything as the alcohol kicked in.

Poor Mrs Bailey did not know what hit her as the drunken, though quite pleasant, commandos arrived back late. Her face although stern had the hint of a smile at the corners of her mouth. "Get your men to bed, Sergeant Harsker, and I hope no one is ill tonight!"

I picked her up and hugged her. I kissed her on the cheek. "Don't worry Mrs Bailey, if anyone is ill I will clean it up for you!"

I saw the smile in her eyes as she said, "Ah go on with you!"

Of course, no one was ill but we all slept late, even me. The Major had said, while we were all still semi sober, that we had Boxing Day off. We took advantage of that. I walked down to the beach and just watched the waves. It seemed reassuring somehow. This was the same sea I had seen in France. We were all part of the same world. We had been lucky. The ones who were still in France would not begrudge us our freedom. It was all in the luck of the draw but I thought of those who would be prisoners of the Germans until this war was over.

Surprisingly enough when we all reported on the twenty seventh everyone was in good spirits. The news from Newhaven was that all those who had been wounded were doing well. Horace had pulled through. The Major had a meeting with us all in his office. "We will have to wait a few weeks for the replacements. Troop Sergeant Major Dean will take over Sergeant Maguire's section until he returns. We have lessons to learn but not as many as I might have expected. I want us to use the mine to continue the training."

Captain Marsden said, "But sir, there is nothing left there to blow up!"

"True but I want us to play ducks and drakes. Half the Troop will be guards and the other half will try to take the mine. I want every section to be as good as Sergeant Harsker's."

I did not like the attention we were being given. My section was well trained but we were no better than the rest. I hung back after the others had gone. "Sir, don't make us out to be special; we aren't."

"Wrong, Tom, you are. Lieutenant Green's report makes it quite clear that you led the section and you were responsible for the success during the attack on the Freja. Your decision to cross the dunes and not take the road was the right one. Had you gone down the road then the mission might have been a disaster. Instead of being back here celebrating we might all now be either dead or in the bag. I have recommended you for a field promotion." My mouth opened and close. He smiled. "Now these things take time; paperwork and bumf. However long it takes, you will be a Lieutenant soon."

The confidence which I gained from that knowledge was immense. I told no one. Why should I? It was a recommendation and that was all but I threw myself into being the best sergeant that I could be. And to be honest the games we played, one half of the Troop against the other, were fun. We all improved. As the wounded and injured men returned it seemed to make us stronger. The cold weather, the snow, the frosts, did not make us dispirited; they made us stronger. We revelled in the hardship. By the end of January, it was hard to tell who were the new men and who had served with us for years. We were a well-honed and trained team. We were ready for something major.

At the end of the first week in February Major Foster was summoned to London. That usually prefaced a major operation. What we could not know was how major it would be. Even when he came back he remained close mouthed but when other Troops began to arrive at the camp we knew that this was not just a raid across to France or the Channel Islands. We were suddenly the centre of the commando world. Was this the invasion of Europe?

Part 2

St. Nazaire

Chapter 10

Falmouth became a sea of brown as commandos found every spare bed and billet that they could. The camp numbers were expanded so that we no longer had as much as we had previously. Inevitably there were conflicts. Man is, by definition, territorial. We had become accustomed to little corners of the camp that we regarded as ours. Major Foster saw the problem early on and he arranged for engineers to come and erect more huts to minimise the conflict. He also acquired a marquee for us so that we had somewhere to brief larger numbers.

At our level, the level of sergeants and their sections, the new buildings and activity merely served to increase the pace at which we trained. Horace was still recovering and Troop Sergeant Major Dean had taken over his section temporarily. Something was coming and we had to be ready. Our Troop found the mine to be a haven. Other sections did not know of its existence and we were able to play guards and attackers to our heart's content. We practised with our bola; some men became incredibly adept at using them. We began to improvise even more elaborate booby traps. We even took to using the long nights to create even more effective scenarios. It was one thing attacking during the day but our natural environment was the cloak of night.

As February drew to its close the Major was increasingly missing. Then, one day as my section was attacking Jack Johnson and his men one of the new American jeeps we had recently acquired drove up. The Major was driving and he had with him a Lieutenant Colonel and a Royal Naval Commander.

"Sergeants, could we have a word please?"

The four of us ran over and snapped to attention. "Sir."

"At ease. This is our new commanding officer, Lieutenant Colonel Newman. He is in command of our latest operation; Operation Chariot. This is Commander Ryder who will command the naval element."

We saluted. I was desperate to know more but knew better than to ask. The Colonel smiled and leaned on his stick. I learned that he carried it everywhere- even into action! "All very secretive eh? Don't worry we will let all you chaps know the details when it is the right time. I am here because the Major here sets special store by you. I must confess having read the reports of some of your missions I am impressed myself."

The Major pointed to me, "This is Sergeant Harsker. You asked about him, sir."

"Ah yes. You are Bill Harsker's boy, aren't you?"

"Yes sir."

"I know your father. You and your men did a good job when you rescued him last year. Could your corporal take over, we need to chat with you."

"Yes sir. Corporal Curtis take over."

The Colonel saluted, "Carry on and keep the name of the operation hush hush for the time being eh?"

The other three saluted and said, "Yes sir!" The grins on their faces made it quite clear that they were delighted to have another operation.

I sat in the back next to the Colonel. "The Major and I need your special skill set for a key element to this mission. It is why we have taken you away." I was intrigued but I had to be patient. I would be told what I needed to know and no more. I knew that already.

They said little on the way back to the camp other than chatting about my father. Both officers seemed to know him. I knew a little of what he did but my Dad had always kept the details of what he did a secret. I suppose that rubbed off on me.

Once back in the office the Major put a sentry on the door to give us privacy. "Operation Chariot," the Colonel began without preamble, "has been designed to go to St. Nazaire and to blow up the only dock

116

outside of Germany capable of repairing the Tirpitz." He saw my reaction. "Yes, Sergeant Harsker, you are in a unique position. You have already been there and escaped. Your information about the submarine pens was invaluable. It is one of the many reasons you have been chosen to take a vital part in this operation." He nodded to Commander Ryder and began to fill his pipe.

Commander Ryder went to the easel and revealed a map of the coast of France. He took a pointer and tapped the Loire estuary. "Now their Lordships are still approving the plan but we believe they will give it the go ahead. The details of the ramming of the dock gates and the destruction of St. Nazaire are not of direct concern to you. We are going to use a submarine to act as a sort of beacon. She will lie off the estuary and guide in our flotilla. You, Sergeant Harsker, are the back up." He tapped the coast line on the map, "This is La Pointe de Chémoulin. There is a heavy artillery battery here and anti-aircraft batteries too. You will be landed by our submarine and make your way here. You will use this elevated position to signal the flotilla should anything happen to the submarine. Of course, if the submarine is on station then you will not be needed and you can make your way into St. Nazaire and join the other commandos to destroy the facilities in the port."

He sat down and they all watched me. "I take it that we would be going in the night before the raid and we would have to hide up during the day."

Lieutenant Colonel Newman nodded, "Quite right. Is that a problem?"

"It could be sir. We don't need a whole section. The more men there are then the harder it is to keep them hidden. I would prefer just to take three other men. It will be easier to remain hidden. We don't need any more. It is not as if we are going to attack anything is it sir?"

Commander Ryder smiled, "You are right Major, this man is a thinker."

The Colonel tapped out his pipe. "I think that is a good idea too. Right so you will take three other men and you will land the night before the submarine has to be on station."

117

"Now what you will have to do is to identify yourself to the MGB which will lead the ships in." He smiled, "I shall be on that one myself. If we know where you are then we can work out our course. The normal shipping channel passes almost next to the battery at La Pointe de Chémoulin. We shall be risking the shallower Les Jardinets channel."

I nodded.

"Any questions Harsker?"

"No, Major. I am guessing that we will be training with the other sections and our particular part of the operation will be kept secret?"

"I told you he could join the dots. Yes Harsker, you need not tell those you are taking until two days before we go. The whole troop will be part of this operation and they will all have a target within St. Nazaire."

"Right sir."

"You don't have a problem with keeping this from your men?"

"No sir, it is necessary, I can see that. Besides they don't need the distraction."

The Lieutenant Colonel stood and came over to me. He shook my hand, "I am pleased to have met you. For what it is worth I have told the Major he has my support to get you a commission. We need officers like you, Harsker. Too many who come from Officer Training know just the theory. You have the experience and that cannot be bought."

I left the office and my mind was a maelstrom of thoughts, worries and ideas. I guessed that, as the powers that be had yet to authorise the operation I had at least a week. I headed for the Quarter Master's stores where Daddy Grant worked. There were some things he needed to acquire for me.

"Now then Tom, a rare visit. I haven't see you since you came for the new Bergen. I thought you and your lads were up at the mine."

"I was. The Major needed to have a word with me."

Daddy was shrewd, "And the two senior officers as well." He nodded and went back behind his counter. "What do you need then?"

"I don't need it yet but we will want some camouflage netting."

He nodded, "Woodland or urban?" I looked surprised, "Aye, we have both now."

"Three of each. Two good torches too." He began writing down what we needed. Now that I had started the list flowed. I made it excessively long. I wanted to have everything to hand so that we could pare it down closer to the time.

Daddy nodded when I had finished, "I will keep it all for you until you are ready."

"This is just between the two of us, Daddy."

"You'll be trying to teach me to suck eggs next!"

When the Troop returned from the mine I saw the questions on their faces but I saw them all glance nervously at Reg Dean. I had no doubt that they had been told not to ask me anything.

In the event they did not have to wait too long. Lieutenant Colonel Newman returned in the first week of March and spoke to the sergeants and officers who would be taking part in Operation Chariot. This time he brought his own team with him. We soon learned that his own men called him Colonel Charles. The majority of the Commandos were from his own brigade, Number 2 Commando. He seemed to like the informality of that and so we all adopted the title. He had an easy manner with the men. He told them largely what he had told me except that he left out the actual target. We were told that we would be attacking a port in occupied Europe and that it would be at the end of the month. That, in itself, caused a ripple of conversation. He smiled and allowed it. From the numbers of officers and sergeants in the marquee I estimated that there could be more than five hundred commandos on this attack.

His sergeant came around with specific tasks for each section. Captain Marsden and our Troop were given the task of capturing the lifting bridge and lock gate across the entrance to the old port and holding it. Others were given quite specific demolition tasks. I guessed that they would have to be told more details than the rest of us.

As we left, to brief our men, the others were all buzzing. Troop Sergeant Major Dean gave me a shrewd look, "Something tells me you

119

weren't surprised by that eh, Tom?" I shook my head. "And unless I miss my guess you have something else you will be doing."

I smiled, enigmatically, "I couldn't possibly say, Troop Sergeant Major!"

Falmouth was a hive of activity. Motor Launches arrived daily and an accommodation ship, 'HMS Princess Josephine Charlotte' arrived. Most of the other commandos used her as a floating hotel and she would take in a large number. We had the luxury of staying at Mrs Bailey's.

We were in the pub one night when some sailors came in. I recognised Bill Leslie and waved him over. I saw that he had gained one stripe; he was now an Able Seaman. "I see you have been promoted."

"Aye. Is that bastard Grenville still with your lot?"

"No, he couldn't cut it."

I told him the story of Waller and Grenville. He burst out laughing, "I would have paid money to see him wetting himself. I'll buy you a pint my friend!"

When he returned I discovered that he would be part of the operation. His ship was ML 160. We chatted about the operation. Like us the sailors only knew the vague target. As he was leaving he said, "You ought to come down to our end of the harbour. We have an E-Boat which was recently captured. They are going to take her off at the end of the week but she is moored next to us for the moment. Enough of them have chased us from one end of the Channel; I reckon it would be good to have a shufti eh?"

"Will they let us?"

"I know the CPO in charge of it."

"Right, I 'll bring a couple of lads tomorrow after training."

I knew that Harry was interested in engines and so I took him and Ken with me. I had almost decided already whom I would take but until the Major confirmed our mission I would not get anyone's hopes up. Ken was rapidly improving his German and I thought there might be information on the E-Boat which we would find handy.

Bill was waiting for us. The CPO was quite happy for us to go aboard. The captured boat was covered in a huge tarpaulin. "I don't know why they are being so secretive about this. I think the Germans know what an E-Boat is like."

Bill and I were interested in the armament. Ken and Harry went with the CPO to look at the engines. The E-Boat, surprisingly, only had three gun emplacements. When they had chased us they seemed capable of firing more guns than the three we saw. When Bill examined them, he whistled. "These are big machine guns, Tom, they are massive. They look to be twice the calibre of our Vickers and Lewis guns."

When we visited the bridge, I saw that it was very streamlined. Bill was even more impressed than I was. "This is good. Look at this; steel plate! We have bits of wood!"

When we caught up with the others they were in as much awe of the boat as we were. "These are serious boats. They have three huge diesel engines." Harry looked as though he was in love. "How I would like to get my hands on one of them."

Ken asked, "You understood them?"

"Oh aye, they are simple enough. Diesel engines are better than petrol and Jerry makes good engines. There was nowt wrong with the engines. If they had fuel we could have started them easy enough."

It was good to understand your enemy. The fact that we had seen how the E-Boats worked meant we had a greater respect for them. Bill had seen that there was little point in firing at the bridge of such a vessel you had to go for the gunners who had far less protection. It was a tiny chink in the enemy armour but you used what you could.

I was summoned to MGB 314 to meet with Colonel Charles and Major Foster. The MGB would be the Headquarters during the raid. It was a cosy place to hold a meeting. "We have the green light for the attack, Harsker. You should choose your men and brief them. You will leave for Southampton on the twenty third. The raid is scheduled for the night of the twenty eighth. You will land on the twenty seventh."

Major Foster handed me a sheet of paper. "Here are the call signs. You and your team will need to memorise them. But you don't need telling that. If you are not needed then you will have to make your way to the lock gate and bridge in the old port. It may well be that you beat

121

Captain Marsden to that vital crossing. If you do then you will need to hold until relieved."

"Yes sir."

Colonel Charles began to fill his pipe, "You are a cool customer, Harsker. I can't think of many men who would be so stoical about hiding for twenty-four hours behind enemy lines."

I smiled, "It won't be my first time, sir. And, as you say, I know the area. That helps."

Major Foster said, "We are going to have a practice attack on the Devonport docks. You and your team will be part of the defenders. You are there to observe. As soon as it is finished then we will have an ML take you to Southampton where the 'Sturgeon' is waiting."

"Is that an S-Class submarine sir?"

"It is. Why?"

"We have used one before. They are er...cosy."

Colonel Charles laughed, "Thank God you are human! I was beginning to wonder. Well off you go and pick your team."

"I'll come with you, Harsker." Major Foster followed me out. Once outside on the harbour wall he said, "I take it you know who you will be taking."

"Yes sir, Ken Curtis; if anything happens to me he is a good leader. Harry Gowland. He is a whizz with anything mechanical. You never know when you need a mechanic and Polly Poulson. He is clever, good with explosives and a sound signaller. He is Ken's back up."

"You have thought it all out then?"

I laughed, "As much as you can when you are here where it is safe. Over there? We'll see. I just hope we don't let you down. There is a lot resting on this."

"You are just the back up. The 'Sturgeon' should be able to do the job. You might have an easy time of it."

"And one day they will teach pigs to fly, sir. I always think it is best to expect the worst and then you are never disappointed."

"Well Captain Marsden knows you are to be detached. He is not planning on using you. if you do help him at the bridge then it will be a bonus."

The section was with the Captain and they were practising attacking the harbour master's office in the centre of the complex. The Harbour Master and his men were watching with amusement as the Troop collected rocks to represent hand grenades. When the Captain saw the Major and me approaching he said, "Troop, take five!" The Harbour Master and his men all clapped ironically.

Captain Marsden came over to us, "I hate an audience."

"They are a better one than the one we will face at the end of the month."

His face brightened, "We have a date then?"

"A rough one. Harsker is going to take three of your men."

"I haven't given them specific roles yet. Who are you taking, Harsker?"

"Curtis, Poulson and Gowland."

"All old hands. Good choice."

He gestured with his arm and I shouted, "Curtis, Poulson, Gowland; get your gear. You are coming with me."

We jogged up to the camp which was now largely deserted. I said nothing all the way up. I forced the pace so that we arrived out of breath.

"Bloody hell Sarge! Are you trying to kill us?"

"Not yet, Gowland! But that day is coming. We will get some gear from Daddy and then I will outline what we have to do."

Daddy had a kitbag with all my requirements and we took it to the empty marquee. I handed them the pieces of paper with the call signs. "First learn them. We burn the paper in an hour." While they did so I divided the equipment into four piles.

When that was done and they all looked at me I explained our mission. Ken said. "A submarine again?"

"I am afraid so. I have camouflage nets which I asked Daddy to get. I am not certain yet where we will be laying up so we take both types. From the aerial photographs, I think there is some scrub ground

123

just a mile from the coast. We will use that. There are just four of us and we may not be needed but whatever happens we stay there until the attack starts. If they find us we have to hold out and stay put. There are over six hundred men and eighteen ships depending on us and the 'Sturgeon'. We do not run. We stay and we die if we have to. If I fall then Ken takes over. This is the most dangerous mission we have ever been given. We have two days to prepare and then we go to Plymouth. We get to watch the lads go into action."

We spent the rest of the day poring over the maps and the aerial photographs. We came to the conclusion that the beach to the west of the German gun emplacement would be the best place to land. The Pointe de la Lande hid it from the gunners and we would be just five hundred yards from the wood where we hoped to lie up and wait out the long day. We packed all the equipment we would need into the Bergens and returned the kitbag with the unwanted elements to Daddy.

As we headed down the hill to our digs I warned the three of them, "Don't let anything slip out. It is as much for our mates' safety as ours. The only chance the flotilla has lies in the hands of the captain of the 'Sturgeon' and us."

"Right Sarge."

Harry said, "We'd like to thank you for picking us."

"Thank me if we get back. I could be signing your death warrants; you know that."

Ken laughed, "We have more chance with you than without you."

Troop Sergeant Dean must have had a word with the other lads for there were no questions. He had not spoken, however, with Mrs Bailey and she showed that she knew something was up. "Mrs Ferry was telling me today that there are hundreds more like you all over the town. Is something going on? Are the Germans going to invade?"

The others looked at me, "No, Mrs Bailey. We are just training. We are all Commandos and they want us to get used to working together. That is all. You won't find Germans landing here. You have my word."

She looked relieved, "I thought she was wrong but you boys be careful!

"We will."

Horace Maguire was returned to us the next day. He was determined not to miss this raid. There was an air of excitement from everyone. We had missed the other big raid, the Lofoten Islands. We would be part of this one.

My section packed our bags and headed for Plymouth, just along the coast, on the twenty first. The Major wanted us to try to hide in the port and evade capture. We were given blue armbands to mark us as Germans. We joined the local Home Guard and a company of regulars to act as Germans. The Captain in command was bemused when I said our job was to hide. "Sort of like a fifth column eh?"

"Something like that sir."

"Well we will give your chaps a stern test when they come."

They were as good as their word. When Lieutenant Colonel Newman and the commandos attacked on the night of the twenty second they were easily repelled. It was a shambles. Nor did they discover us. We took great amusement from watching Captain Roy and his men of Number 2 Commando walk right past us. When the whistle went to announce the end of the exercise we stood up behind them. Our camouflage nets had worked well.

Captain Roy enjoyed the fact that we had beaten them. He came over to us and spoke quietly. He was third in command. "You are the chaps who are going in early eh? Good. It bodes well. Colonel Charles speaks highly of you. I can see why."

I heard a voice I recognised, "Hi there, Tom. It's me Fred Harris, from the demolition course."

I shook his hand, "Good to see you. Well you will get some action now eh?"

"Aye, me and the lads are fed up of hearing about Number 4 Commando. Folk will be talking about us soon!"

"Well good luck!"

The ML was waiting for us in Plymouth harbour. It was Bill's boat ML 160. We had a daylight run to Portsmouth. There the 'Sturgeon' was waiting for us.

125

Bill came aft for a smoke as we raced along the coast. "A submarine eh?" I nodded, "You wouldn't get me in one of them."

"I know. They are horrible."

"They should let us take you over." There was no secret where we were going.

"I think they are using the sub so they don't alert the defences. An ML would be a dead giveaway."

"We have never let you down before." I could not tell him the real reason, that the submarine was the beacon for the boats.

The submarine was waiting in a quiet corner of the busy harbour. The ML's captain, Lieutenant Boyd, nodded as we clambered over the side to the metal hull of the sub. "Good luck you chaps!"

"Thank you, sir."

The Petty Officer on the sub grinned as he opened the hatch and we descended into the bowels of the sub. It felt like descending into hell. All my memories of 'Sunfish' resurfaced. I could still feel the concussion from the depth charges. Just before we entered the dark nether reaches of the sub I saw an ancient American destroyer leaving the harbour. I did not know it but it was the 'H.M.S. Campelltown'; it was the floating bomb which would destroy the harbour. The next time we saw her we would be behind enemy lines and the attack would have started.

Chapter 11

We would be aboard the floating coffin for a couple of days and we were assigned bunks. We stored our gear in the forward torpedo room. That was where we would leave when we disembarked. The captain was another young lieutenant, Lieutenant Wingfield. He seemed a little put out that we were being landed, "No offence Sergeant, but I don't like this implication that we might not be able to do our job."

"I think it is just belt and braces, sir. Lieutenant Colonel Newman seems like the sort who wants to cover every eventuality. Besides this just helps our lads when they attack the lock gates."

Mollified he said, "Well we shall try to make you comfortable eh?"

"We have been in a submarine before, sir, the 'Sunfish'."

"Then you know what to expect."

"Yes sir but I hope we won't be depth charged this time. Commandos are used to fighting back and not just taking punishment."

"If we are depth charged then it means the operation has been compromised so let's hope we have a safe journey. We will travel at night to charge up the batteries and then submerge during the day. We will surface again at night to land you chaps and then return to the Loire and our station."

The crew were friendly enough and made us feel welcome but the food still tasted of oil and battery acid. The walls were still damp and the whole vessel felt like it was closing in on me. I found the only solution was to keep my mind occupied. One of the officers had a chess set and so the four of us played non-stop. As Gowland could not play when we first started we did remarkably well to teach him to a standard where he could give us a game. We became so engrossed that we barely noticed when we set sail and headed out in the dark night. The conning tower hatch was still open and the air was fresher than it would be when we submerged.

We changed our body clocks. Instead of sleeping at night, when we would have fresher air we waited until the time we would hide on the bottom waiting for nightfall once more. This would help us when we landed and had to lie up during the day. The Germans had anti-submarine patrols in the Channel and they stood more chance of finding us if we were moving. Submariners were the most patient men I ever knew.

Ken and Harry were playing chess. I sat on one of the bunks with Poulson. He seemed in the mood to chat. "What will you do after the war, Sarge?"

"I have not thought that far ahead. I suppose I will go back to University. I had a place at Manchester to study Engineering."

He nodded, "There will be plenty which needs fixing that is for sure."

"What about you?"

"I don't know Sarge. I just had labouring jobs and such before the war. I couldn't go back to that." He tapped his head, "I have started to use this a bit more. Besides I like the action. Perhaps I will stay in."

"After the war I am not certain it will be as exciting. Dad stayed in and it was not the same."

"He's still in now though isn't he Sarge? So, it can't have been that bad."

He was right. Would I want to stay in? I shook my head. First, I had to survive the war.

The klaxon sent shivers down my spine as did the tannoy. "Diving stations! Close all watertight doors!"

As the doors slammed shut I consoled myself with the thought that at least we were not in the torpedo room. Even so as the ship went silent and we descended into the depths I found myself curling up in a foetal ball. This was the most unnatural thing I had ever done. I had thought that jumping out of an aeroplane was weird but this was worse. The heavy air made me sleep but it was not a pleasant sleep it was a nightmare filled horror which had me waking up bathed in sweat.

Ken had the bunk above me. He leaned down as I put my feet over the side. "You were shouting in your sleep Sarge. Are you all right?"

128

"Just nightmares, Ken. I thought I had grown out of them. I had them as a kid. I suppose your fears never really leave you."

"You are afraid of nothing, Sarge."

"Everyone is afraid of something Ken. I just hide mine better than most."

One of the ratings came along with a Dixie of tea and biscuits. "Not long now lads. Jimmy the One reckons we surface in an hour and then we take you lads in." We felt the movement as the electric motors were started and we began our slow rise from the bottom of the Channel.

We made the most of the tea and the sugarless biscuits. We would be on just the dry rations and water once we went ashore. The fresh air which raced through the submarine told us that we had surfaced. It would be dark and the submarine would be running with just the conning tower showing. We would not come up any higher until we were within sight of the beach and then we would have to move very quickly. The submarine did not want to hang around.

We made our way forward to the torpedo room. The torpedo men had semi inflated the dingy. They would be able to man handle it through the hatch and then fully inflate it on the surface. It was what Gordy called 'war paint time'. We darkened our faces and hands. We did not apply it evenly we found that if you used stripes it helped to break up the contours and was like dazzle camouflage on a warship. We examined each other's faces to make sure we had left no white bits.

The Chief Petty Officer arrived, "Captain says we will be on station in five minutes."

"Thanks Chief."

He pointed to the torpedo men, "I want you up and out faster than a stoker can hide his wallet when it is his round!"

"Aye, aye Chief."

Perhaps the Chief had senses that we did not for he said, "Get the hatch open!" When the water flooded in I thought he had given the order too early but he knew what he was about and the crewmen had the dingy out and on to the bow in a flash. We held our guns and Bergens. I clambered out into the chilly night air. It felt refreshing. By the time Ken had joined us the dingy had been fully inflated and the two men had it in the water. We slithered down the side and climbed aboard. I looked east. The coast was hidden in darkness but a hint of white flecked water showed the shore. I had no doubt that the Captain had found the right place. I slipped my Bergen on my back and held my Thompson across my knees. The two sailors were powerful men and they powered us through the water. I suspected that the tide was on the way in for we were leaping off the dingy in no time at all.

Goodbyes were superfluous and we waded ashore and ran to the rocky point to our right. I glanced back and I could barely see the dingy which was hurrying back to the submarine. They would be able to deflate it this time and then return to the depths to wait for the flotilla of small boats and the floating bomb. Once we reached the rocks we threw ourselves to the ground to take stock of our position. As we did so I heard voices. They sounded German and were coming from the rocks above us. I signalled for the others to remain still and I climbed up a little closer. They were German voices and the soldiers were complaining about the duty they had drawn. They thought they were being picked on. There were two of them. I risked going closer for if they were not looking out to sea then they might spot us when we moved behind their post. My hand felt concrete. It was a pill box and the men were inside. We could avoid that. We had been lucky. Had they looked out to sea they would have seen the submarine. I made my way back to the base of the point and waved the men to follow me.

We scrambled across the rocks which led to the coast road. We had to be beyond the road well before dawn. The coordinates of the position the 'Sturgeon' would take the following night were locked in my head. We would need daylight to accurately identify the place where we had to signal from but I knew we needed height first. Our rubber soled shoes made no noise as we ran along the road. There was a curfew in operation and I hoped we would see no one. To our left the ground rose and I spied a track. I led my men up it and we disappeared into the scrubby bushes and trees. I kept us heading east towards the gun emplacement which we knew lay close to our position. That would be our rough guide to the position of the submarine.

After a hundred and fifty yards, I held up my hand. I dropped my Bergen and slipped through the undergrowth back to the road. I saw, just twenty yards to my right, the entrance to the gun emplacement. There was a barbed wire barrier. I could just make out, eighty or so yards closer to the sea, the concrete and sandbags which marked the position of the four huge 155mm guns. This would do. I returned to my men. Slinging my Bergen on to one shoulder I looked around for somewhere to hide.

We moved deeper and higher across the scrubby ground. We left the trail. We did not want to risk someone stumbling upon us. I spied a bush which was thicker than the others. Kneeling down I found that I could raise the lower limbs of the bush. There was no growth lower down towards the bole and it looked big enough for the four of us. I waved them underneath. Ken and Polly held up the branches so that I could follow them. There were no leaves close to the base of this hedgerow and we could sit up if we wanted. I risked snapping off a couple of the thinner, dead twigs. They made less noise than I had feared and they gave us more room.

We had seen no one and I risked speaking quietly to them. "The gun emplacement is just over the road. Tomorrow morning, I will go and find the exact spot we have to watch. We use the camouflage nets to mask us even more. I don't think anyone will give this bush a second glance. I will get my head down first. I want waking at dawn."

"Right Sarge."

It did not take long to rig two of the nets to cover the inside of the front of the hide. It was cosy beneath the huge bush which had not been cut since it had grown, goodness knows how many years earlier. We used our Bergens as pillows and kept our Thompsons close to hand. I left Ken to organise the rota and I slept. The traumatic journey on the submarine had not resulted in a decent sleep. Here on terra firma, beneath the scrubby bush I slept the sleep of the dead.

131

When Polly shook me awake I was alert in an instant. I nodded to him and, after swallowing a mouthful of water I placed my Thompson next to my Bergen and rolled out from beneath the net. It was dawn but only just. It was that thin grey light between dark and light. The light was perfect for skulking around. I drew my Luger and headed down the slight slope towards the road. I knew that the 'Sturgeon' would be a couple of miles offshore. It would be hard to see in the dark which was why we had brought binoculars. I needed to find a vantage point close to the flak guns. The submarine would be south west of that position. All I would need to do was find the shape of the submarine and wait for the flotilla to hove into view.

I stopped and hid in the ditch when I heard the German voices. I looked up and saw thirty yards from my position, the entrance to the gun emplacement. This morning, however, there were two sentries there. The barrier I had seen last night had been removed. I also saw a sign. It identified this as the Headquarters of the coastal artillery. We had not known that. A car approached from the west and the two sentries held their hand up to stop it. I took the opportunity to roll out of the ditch and disappear behind the hedge again. I continued east to find the flak.

The flak battery was easy to spot. They had cleared the ground around it. The emplacement lay just forty yards from the road. There were tents, for the gun crews I imagined, and a Kubelwagen. I could smell the coffee as they prepared for another day. I checked my map again and used my compass to establish the correct bearing. It was the right place. When it was time we could wait here to see if the submarine had reached the rendezvous successfully. Taking out my dagger I put a Free French Cross on the tree which was in direct line with the spot the submarine would surface. It would identify the place for me and yet would appear to be the work of locals. The spot the submarine would surface seemed a long way away. I slipped back up the hill and reached the bush. I knew that my comrades were hidden there but I could see nothing. I felt satisfied. We would be safe hidden there but it would be a long day to wait.

I raised the lower branches and slipped under. I found myself facing two Thompsons. I held my hands in mock surrender. It was still early and I risked speaking again. "I have marked a tree with a Free French Cross. We have to be careful. The German Artillery headquarters is close to the big battery and is not far away. You lads can sleep if you like. I am staying awake."

Polly and Harry took the chance of more sleep but Ken stayed awake. We ate some rations and drank water. Dehydration could be a problem. We needed to drink regularly. I watched the day as it became lighter through the netting. We watched animals as they either returned to their burrows or rose to feed. We were so still that birds ate the insects which were on the bush while others gathered twigs to build nests. Even in a war life went on.

I used the time to go through our plans in my head. The flotilla was out at sea now. The submarine would surface at 22.00 hours. Once we saw it then our work was done but I had decided to wait until we actually saw the ships. The ships should be in position and ready to enter the Loire by 22.15. They were the plans but as we all knew they could go wrong. It was a long way from Falmouth to St. Nazaire and the flotilla would be sailing during daylight. Anything could happen: aeroplanes, ships, submarines. I knew that there were plans to deceive the German gunners. I hoped they would work but if they did not then the flotilla of launches would be sitting ducks. The flak guns could depress and add their firepower. I knew that I was deviating from the plan when I began to work out how to disrupt the gunners should they fire. I had seen the wreck of the 'Lancastria' sunk in 1940 and I did not want the 'Campelltown' to suffer the same fate. The attack on the bridge could wait; the flotilla had to get beyond these guardians of the estuary.

We heard people in the woods at about noon but saw nothing. I deduced they were foragers picking mushrooms, wild greens and herbs from the scrubland. The other two awoke and we ate. I was luckier than they were. I had taken the opportunity to relieve myself on the way back from my dawn walk. They would be desperate. As soon as it was dark

133

we slipped out from under our den. We had four hours to get in position and await the submarine. They would be four long hours.

Although I had made the journey earlier that morning it was more difficult in the dark. There were also more people around. The road which passed the headquarters and the flak emplacement were busier. There were vehicles and people moving along. Before the war they might have used a bus to get to St. Nazaire and back to their homes. Now they walked. Every time we heard something we dropped to all fours and hid. It made the journey much longer. Finally, I saw the mark I had made on the tree. I took off my Bergen and removed the binoculars. I hung them around my neck. I scanned the sea from beneath the green canopy. I saw the navigation lights of trawlers as they returned to port. Of the submarine, there was no sign.

We checked our guns once more. We drank more water and we ate more rations. We waited. We watched the fingers of the clock as they moved slowly around. The traffic below us became a trickle. Ken checked on the guards at the headquarters. He discovered that they came on duty at eight. I presumed that was when the night crew took over. As the hour of ten drew close we peered anxiously out to sea. At nine forty I saw something rise from the water. Had I not been looking for it I would not have seen it. They were good binoculars; Quarter Master Grant had kept them especially for me. Apparently Captain Grenville had ordered them. Had I not been looking on the correct bearing I might have missed the periscope as it rose from the sea. I saw the ripples first and then the stick like black shape. It was the flurry of foam at the base which confirmed it was the submarine. Having been on a submarine I knew the procedure. Lieutenant Wingfield would ensure the sea was clear before he came up. Sure enough I saw the tell-tale bubbles as the tanks were partly emptied and the conning tower appeared. Again, its size was so small as to be almost indistinguishable from the sea. We could have gone then but I waited.

"Sub is here. We will wait for the flotilla. I want to make sure everything is going to plan." It should not be a long wait and I thought the risk worth taking.

Time seemed to drag. I had to keep removing the glasses to keep my eyes from watering. I had just peered through them when I saw a flash from the submarine. I barely caught it. I traversed the binoculars to sea but saw nothing. I checked my watch and saw that it was 22.15. The flotilla should be close. I wanted to cheer when I saw the dark shape of the old American destroyer. It was barely visible but the dark shape was there.

"They are here."

"What do we do now, Sarge? Head to the bridge?"

"It is less than a mile. We have no need to go yet. Let's wait until they pass the guns here. We might be able to help the lads out."

"But Sarge, our orders are to go to the bridge."

"We are commandos, Ken. We improvise. It is my decision."

I looked again and saw that Lieutenant Wingfield was bravely keeping station at Point Z. His position would confirm the channel and make it easier for the ships to strike their target. As soon as he began to submerge I knew that the flotilla was on course. I put the binoculars inside my battle dress. I might need them again. "Right lads. Let's get to the artillery headquarters. Gowland and Poulson, when we get there take out the sentries."

"Right Sarge."

We moved back through the bushes to the road. It was pitch black but we knew where the sentries were. While my two men slipped across the road Curtis and I moved to a position to cover the entrance. It was 22.45. The attack was timed to begin after 01.00 hours. The boats and ship had a gauntlet of guns to run. I had my Thompson slung and my Luger in my hand. Ken had his bola ready. We did not need either. Our two men used the Japanese stranglehold and the sentries were incapacitated. While they were trussed like chickens Ken and I took their potato mashers and rigged a booby trap across the entrance.

We moved down the track which led to the emplacement. The ground had been cleared and we could see out to sea. I took out the binoculars. The flotilla was approaching the entrance to the Loire. I waved my hand to the left and the right. The other three scurried off in the dark. I could hear, below us, in the concrete emplacement, the sound of music. The gun crews had a radio playing. Further down, close to the edge of the rock face I saw the sentries. They had their backs to me and were staring out to sea. Without binoculars and being lower down they would not see the ships. Soon, however they would for the flotilla would have to come towards this shore. The twin lines of boats would have to sail between two sets of sand banks, Les Jardinets and Le Vert. it would bring them within seven hundred yards of the shore and the deadly batteries.

My three men came back. Through hand signals I discovered that the two guards I had seen were the only ones. Ken pointed to the east and we followed. He led us to the ammunition store. It was well away from the guns, for obvious reasons. It was unlocked. I signalled for Poulson and Gowland to rig a booby trap in the door. When the Germans opened it, they would set off the bombs. It was a risk but I reasoned that they would only need to open the store if they were firing. If they were firing it would be because they had seen the flotilla.

As midnight approached we headed back towards the emplacement and then we heard them. It was the drone of bombers approaching from the west. The sirens went off and we ducked down to hide behind the bins which were there. An officer came out, with binoculars, if he looked to sea I would have to kill him but he did not. He stared up at the sky. A sergeant came out.

"It looks like St. Nazaire is going to get it tonight. Telephone the Twenty Second Naval Flak Battery. Those dozy bastards will probably be asleep."

"Should I have the gun crews stand to and load the guns, sir?"

"Have them stand to but this is an air raid. I will go to the communication centre and tell Kapitan Diekmann. He is probably awake now anyway."

The two of them disappeared. To our left the flak guns opened up and the sky was lit up with tracer and exploding shells. The bombers were too high for me to identify them save that they were twin engined. I looked out to sea. The flotilla was now almost at the sand banks. I turned

136

around and saw that the bombers were just flying over St. Nazaire. It was proving effective. Every eye and pair of glasses would be drawn to the skies and away from the sea.

There was a flash of light as the door of the gun emplacement opened. We ducked down again. Two Germans came out to relieve themselves. "Kapitan Diekmann is not in a good mood is he, Hans?"

"I don't think he likes being woken up. Still he is right it is a strange air raid. They are just flying around and not dropping any bombs."

"Lieutenant Kobbel thinks the Tommies might be invading and the air raid is a ruse."

The other one laughed, "The Tommies are finished. We are chasing them out of Africa and they are only waiting for the Americans to join them. They have not enough ships to invade us."

The door opened again and the sergeant's voice bellowed out. "When you two have quite finished the Kapitan has ordered everyone to scan the horizon!"

A few minutes after the door had shut we heard the guns stop. They were no longer firing at the aeroplanes. That was ominous. I looked at my watch. It was one o'clock. I could not see the boats because of the buildings between us but I guessed that the flotilla would almost be at the sandbanks; perhaps even past them. They would be less than thirty minutes from the dock gates. I pointed east. The ships had not been spotted. We would go and help to capture the bridge. We made our way back to the road. I reckoned we had between one and two miles to go to get to the bridge. We avoided our booby traps and began to double down the road. There were no civilians about. I daresay they were sheltering from the bombs which had not been dropped.

We passed the flak guns and could smell the cordite in the air. Turning left along the coast road I saw the flotilla. They looked close enough to touch. The old American destroyer led two columns of launches towards the dock gates. It looked as though they had done it. Then suddenly searchlights played across the water and illuminated the boats. Guns opened fire at the flotilla. I saw the German flag flying

137

from the destroyer. A signal lamp flashed from the bridge and was answered from the guns below us. I held up my hand and we stopped. I waved my men down towards the searchlight and flak emplacements which were just yards from the river.

The guns, miraculously, stopped firing and then a moment later all hell broke loose. Even the large guns at La Chémoulin opened fire too. I cursed. Had we waited just a little while longer then we could have attacked the guns and disrupted their fire. Battle flags mushroomed on the flotilla as they returned their fire. I took out a grenade, "Right lads let's knock out this searchlight and upset these Jerries."

The Germans were less than thirty yards from us. Although protected by sandbags they were below us and had no idea we were there. We hurled the four grenades high in the air. They exploded in the air and we were up, on our feet as soon as the wave of concussion had passed over us. I fired a short burst from my Thompson into the carnage of the emplacement. To my right I heard a dull double thump. The booby trap on the ammunition had exploded at the German battery. Suddenly a sheet of flame leapt into the air as the magazine exploded. That would disrupt their firing. Ken Curtis sprayed the searchlight and it went out instantly. In the dark, we could hear the moaning of the wounded and the dying. The crew of the searchlight had all been incapacitated or killed.

We had done all that we could and we ran back up the slope towards the road and St. Nazaire. We ran with guns cradled in our arms. If we saw any Germans we would fire instantly. I saw that the flotilla was pouring their fire into a small guard ship which was being riddled with fire. The 'Campbelltown' however was also being targeted by every gun the Germans had. The gun on the foredeck disappeared as a shell hit it. The bridge was being targeted by every gun the Germans possessed and yet the ship still headed towards the gates. And then the flotilla was through the narrow entrance to the river proper. St. Nazaire's Normandie dock was less than a mile away. I saw one of the MLs hit and as it burned I saw sailors and commandos leaping into the water. A second

ML stopped to pick them up and it was struck by tracer. We were too far away to help.

Poulson suddenly called out a warning, "Sir lorry!"

I turned in time to see a German truck barrelling down the road towards St. Nazaire. I dropped to one knee and began firing my Thompson in short bursts. The other three joined in. Although the truck was hurtling towards us none of us faltered. As I emptied my magazine the truck lurched to its right as the driver was hit and it plunged off the road to plough into the gun and searchlight emplacements below us. I turned and led the men towards St. Nazaire. I changed magazines as I did so. To my right I heard an enormous crash which accompanied grinding metal. I didn't know it at the time but the 'Campbelltown' had struck the dock gates. The Navy had done its job and now it was the turn of the commandos to do theirs. I looked at my watch, it was thirty-four minutes past one. The attack and the raid had begun.

Chapter 12

There were more guns below us but I was acutely aware of our mission. The rest of our Troop would be racing from their launches towards the bridge at the western end of the old port. I estimated that it would be less than two hundred yards away. This part of the town was familiar to me. I saw grey uniforms as they emerged from a building to the right of us and ran towards what I assumed was the bridge. Their attention was on the port and not the road. We were unseen.

"Spread out!"

There was too much noise for our words to be heard by Germans. Shell and shot were firing and there was the sound of battle all around. Within a few seconds there were ten yards between each of us and we were almost at the bridge.

"Halt and fire!"

We dropped to our knees and gave short bursts. The German soldiers were scythed down as bullets poured into their backs and sides. Having emptied my second magazine I slung my Thompson and ran towards the building from which they had emerged. I threw in two grenades in quick succession and then flattened myself against the wall. A wall of flame leapt out and I heard shouts from those that I had hit within.

I drew my Colt and, pausing only to pick up a fallen potato masher grenade led my men to the far end of the bridge. There were six Germans there and they were manning the machine guns they had set up to cover the bridge. Their backs were to us. They saw us and tried to turn the gun. The Colt bucked in my hand as I fired at the right hand crew. The others let rip with their Tommy guns. I threw the German grenade. "Grenade!" My men and I dropped to the ground. The grenade went off and the last of the crews fell dead.

"Quick, Harry and Ken, set one machine gun up to cover the west. Polly with me."

In the distance, I could hear grenades going off, the chatter of Thompsons mixed with the sound of German weapons. But around us was a little haven of calm. The Germans here were dead. "You be the gunner and I will lay for you." I reloaded my Colt and my Thompson; we watched the empty road.

The brief peace did not last.

"Sarge, Germans!"

Polly added, "And there are some coming from the port too Sarge."

That meant they were coming at us from both sides. "Hold them as long as you can. Our lads will be here shortly."

I heard Ken and Harry's heavy machine chatter. Polly's joined it. I saw a German take a potato masher and smash the porcelain top. I fired three bullets as he arced his back ready to throw. He fell back and then the grenade went off. His squad all fell to the ground.

Ken's voice from behind us was urgent. "Sarge! There are too many of them!"

I gambled. We had stopped the attack from the port side, "Poulson bring the machine gun to the other side of the bridge." I ran the few yards to my men. The Germans were setting up their own machine gun. I fired from the hip as I ran. One lucky shot hit the man carrying the barrel of the heavy calibre gun in the knee and he tumbled to the ground, taking his companion with him. I kept firing until my Colt clicked empty. I holstered it and drew my Luger. I emptied that too. I was firing blindly for there was so much smoke it was hard to see men; just the flashes of their guns. I took a Mills bomb from my webbing, pulled the pin and then threw it as high in the air as I could manage. "Grenade!" I dropped to the ground and the grenade went off above the Germans showering the air with shrapnel.

Poulson dropped next to me as I took my Thompson and took aim. I heard Colts behind me. They struck the lifting bridge wall. It was our men. I yelled, "Commando! Sergeant Harsker!" I glanced towards the Germans and saw that there was no movement. The threat was gone; at least for the moment.

I heard Captain Marsden as he shouted, "Cease fire!"

141

We had relief. There was a flurry of muzzle flashes from the dark. Poulson's German gun began to fire and the flashes from the dark diminished. I turned and saw Captain Marsden and Reg Dean. "Well done, Harsker. You have save us a job. Sergeant Barker, get those charges set. Sarn't Major Dean, bring up Harsker's section and cover this end of the bridge."

"Sir. Come on lads!" I saw that the Sergeant Major was limping. He had been injured.

I saw that the whole of the section appeared to have made it. As Reg knelt down next to me I said, "Where is the Major and the rest of the troop?"

"One of the MLs got hit on the way in and he has gone to the Old Entrance Bridge." He tapped the smoking German gun. "These would have made mincemeat of us."

"Just doing our job. Are you hurt?"

"Just landed badly and twisted my knee. Don't worry son, I can still fire my gun!" As if to prove it he suddenly whirled and fired a dozen shots at four Germans who appeared around the corner of a building to our right. One fell and the rest scurried back.

The smoke had cleared and I saw German trucks appearing from the dark. Sergeant Major Dean shouted, "Get a move on, sir. Reinforcements!"

The two heavy machine guns sent their bullets into the engine block of the leading truck. It swerved to the left and took its occupants to a watery grave in the submarine basin. We had, however used the last of the German ammunition. The other two trucks stopped and Germans flooded out.

"Let's close with them!"

It was the right decision for Reg to make. It allowed those laying charges to put them at both ends but it took my tiny section towards forty German soldiers.

"Charge!"

The twelve of us ran at them spraying them with .45 slugs. It was a withering wall of fire. The Germans fired back but they were using just

142

rifles. Even so I saw Reg Smyth pitch forwards, his chest a bloody mess and another bullet took Bert Grimsdale in the head. We made the German lorries and the men within flee to the safety of nearby buildings.

"Right lads, we can get back now!"

The words were hardly out of his mouth when there was an enormous explosion behind us as the lifting bridge gates were exploded prematurely. We were showered with wood and debris. We were trapped on the wrong side with no way of getting back. Already the water was rushing through the gap we had made. It was unintentional but it had given us a problem. The plan had been to embark the launches from the other side of the bridge we had just destroyed.

I turned to Reg, "Where are the launches?"

He pointed to the other side of the bridge. "Over there."

"Then we have to go down to the river. They will have to pass us to get back to sea and we might be able to signal them. Curtis still has his lamp."

"It is worth a try. You now the way, you lead."

I didn't but I followed the channel. As we ran down I saw the bridge at the seaward end of the lock. It was destroyed by Lieutenant Swayne and his men. If they had been less efficient then we might have got across there. We stopped at the wrecked bridge. There was nothing left for us to cross. That had been our last chance to use the planned escape. I waved my arm and led the section down to the small beach.

"Polly, Harry, keep watch."

I could see to our left the fire fight still going on. Motor Launches were burning and I could see bodies in the water. I looked at Reg he looked like he had been through the mill. "Did the ship hit the dock gates Sergeant Major?"

"Oh aye. That part went well but the rest of it?" He shrugged, "The Germans still have the mole and three launches went down there. I think the pumping house went up but…." Just then we saw MTB 74 stop just fifty yards away to pick up two men who had drifted down on a Carley float.

143

"Over here!" We all began to wave. I saw a sailor raise his hand in acknowledgment and then the big guns to our right began to pound the MTB to matchwood. The flak guns close to us had been depressed and their rapid fire began to punch holes in the boat. I watched as the officer ordered his men to jump into the river. Our chance had gone. The two commandos on the Carley float began to kick their way to shore. Sergeant Major Dean shouted, "Fletcher, Crowe, pull those men to shore." We had a little haven and we appeared to be safe from German fire on this little beach. The two destroyed bridges afforded us protection from the Germans on that side of the port.

I looked up at the gun emplacements. They were less than fifty yards away.

"Sarn't Major I will take my lads and try to stop those firing. We have no chance of being picked up while they are still firing." He nodded. "Gowland and Hewitt drop your bags, grab some grenades and come with me!"

Without waiting for them I ran up to the road. I paused at Ken and the other two. "I am going to try to do something about these flak guns. Give us some cover."

"Right Sarge. Things have quietened down here but there is all hell on close to the submarine basin."

"I know. We are going to try to get a launch out. If we can't then we will break out and go back the way we came."

I saw that Gowland and Hewitt were with me. "Come on."

We ran along the road. I had seen the other flak positions and knew that there was no protection from the land. It was our one chance to hit them.

"When I give the command then throw two grenades in quick succession. Throw them high. We want the shrapnel to do the damage. Then go in with your Tommy guns. In and out; no messing about."

"Right Sarge."

I saw, as we descended, the cannons hammering shells into the MLs trying to head out to sea. I pulled the two pins and shouted, "Now!" I hurled them both high and then dropped to the ground. I landed

144

between two concrete walls and the shrapnel from the grenades flew over our heads. I jumped to my feet and swung my Tommy gun around. I ran towards the carnage that was the gun position and I sprayed the twitching bodies.

Gowland shouted, "Duck Sarge!"

I ducked and a wall of .45 bullets tore into the German who had risen like Lazarus from the pile of bodies. He was almost torn in half. The guns had stopped firing. "Back to the beach!"

We ran down the road. As we did so I glanced to the left and saw more vehicles coming down the road. We would not be quiet for much longer. When we reached the beach I shouted, "Incoming! Gowland, Hewitt, Lowe stay with the Corporal and Poulson."

I ran to the Sergeant Major, "We will have company soon."

He pointed to the two commandos we had rescued. They had both been wounded. "These lads are in trouble too."

Just then I saw an ML begin to head towards us. It was ML 160. I saw Bill Leslie waving from the bow.

"We have a chance. I'll get the other lads." I turned to fetch the men from the road.

Sergeant Major Dean began to lift one of the two wounded commandos to his feet. "Right come on you pair, get these lads out into the sea."

As I headed towards the road I heard a rattle of bullets. To my horror I saw Ken Curtis pitch backwards. Blood poured from his shoulder. "Hewitt, Lowe, get the Corporal to the beach. There is a launch coming in. We will follow!"

I threw myself to the edge of the road and levelled my Thompson at the Germans who had taken advantage of our inattention and were racing towards us. I had a full magazine and I let rip. They were just twenty yards from me when I fired and I scythed through them all.

Polly said, "There are more of them Sarge. If we leave they will get the lads on the beach."

I turned and saw that the section and the two rescued commandos were wading through the water to the ML. Polly was right. I shouted to them, "We will find another way! Go!" I turned back to my men, "We have to lead them away. Fire and head right. I'll bring Ken's Bergen! Run back to the bridge."

"But it is blown up!"

"Just do it Poulson. Let me do the thinking!" They both fired and then ran. Picking up Ken's Bergen and Thompson I turned and shouted, "Sergeant Major! Leave while you can!" He shouted something back but I just waved him away. I turned and ran back to the road. As I reached the road I saw four Germans. They were less than ten feet from me. They were aiming their rifles at Poulson and Lowe. I fired Ken's Thompson left handed and kept pulling the trigger until it was empty. Their heads looked like ripe tomatoes when I had finished. I ran after my two men. Bullets filled the space I had just occupied.

We had to watch our footing as we ran. There were bodies and debris all over the road. Behind us I heard the fire from the pursuing Germans. We would be hard targets in the dark. Even as we ran I began to formulate a plan. The best and fastest way out of the town was the one we had taken last time, north. We could not take the first road north for we would be too close to the Germans who were chasing us. "Run to the place we first attacked the Germans, the far bridge."

I was counting on the fact that we were fitter than those behind. To our right we could hear the battle still raging. The ship had yet to explode. I vaguely remembered that they had put timers on board. I knew how notoriously inaccurate they were. The ship could go up at any time or even the next day. When they reached the bridge my two men stopped and dropped behind the bodies of the dead Germans. I joined them and we levelled our Thompsons at the line of men who ran towards us. There were just six. I guessed that the rest were busy trying to hit the ML which had more targets for them.

I whispered, "Wait!" When they were twenty yards away we fired. We used very short three bullet bursts. They tore into the Germans who had taken us for dead Commandos.

"Quick grab any grenades you can while I transfer stuff from Ken's Bergen."

146

I took the magazines, rations, water bottle, signalling lamp and camouflage nets. I jammed them into my bag. I had used some of my magazines and everything fitted; just. Poulson and Gowland reappeared. "Right we head up there. Polly, tail end Charlie. Keep low and don't fire unless you have to. We are going to find somewhere to hide."

The fighting was on the seaward side of the submarine basin. On the landward side, it appeared quiet. None of our men had penetrated that far. It was the last place they would look for us. I had a bold plan. We would wait out the initial search and then leave when they were looking further afield for the commandos who had attacked their dock.

As we made our way along the side of the submarine basin I glanced to my left. We had sheltered there last year in a building. We had blown up the building. I wondered if they had cleared it. When we reached the railway lines and crossed them I saw that they had not. They were a jumble of broken bricks and debris. I ran towards them. This part of the port was quieter for no Commandos had reached this section. The rest were contained on the far side of the port. We needed somewhere to lie up. It would be dawn in a few hours and the Germans would sweep the countryside looking for those commandos who had escaped. It was obvious to me that many commandos would be stranded. I had seen too many MLs destroyed. I knew my fellow commandos. Surrender would be the last thing on their mind and they would try to get somewhere; perhaps even Spain! We were tough, resilient and resourceful.

I led them over the pile of bricks and debris from the demolished buildings. It was a mighty pile of uneven rubble. I wanted a nest similar to the one we had used the night before. The bricks shifted beneath our feet as we moved. That was good. We would be warned of any search. When we reached what would have been the back of the house there were fewer bricks and we found a depression. I guessed this had been where the yards of the three-story buildings had been.

"Clear a space and rig the nets. Use the brick coloured ones. We are going to hide out here for the day." Despite the strange order they complied. I went back across the bricks and lay on the highest part of the bricks keeping watch. I saw squads of Germans as they hurried along the

147

roads but they all headed for the Normandie dock. The flashes and bangs showed that Colonel Charles and his men were still fighting. Part of me told me that I should go and help but another part convinced me that our escape was of more importance. I was not certain if the raid had been a success or not. Until the dock gates were blown then it was a failure but even if the gates were blown I had seen enough dead commandos to wonder if the price we had paid was too high.

Polly's voice came from behind me. "Done, Sarge."

"Better pee now while we have the chance! Do it away from the camp in case they use dogs." If they used dogs to search they would home in on the smell of human urine and excreta.

Once relieved the two of them hunkered down and I viewed our den. We were hidden unless someone came right up to the edge and even then they would struggle to see us. I slid down next to them. We used our Bergens as sandbags in case we were attacked although, in that case, they would merely delay the inevitable. "Eat now. Check your magazines. There are spares in my Bergen."

"Right Sarge." I ate some of the composite rations, husbanding them as I did not know how long they would have to last. I refilled my magazines, using the half empty ones to give me three full magazines. I had four clips for my Colt and four for my Luger. I had not managed to acquire any more German ammunition yet. Poulson and Gowland kept the potato mashers.

"Do we stand any chance of getting out, Sarge?"

Harry Gowland was worried. "I have been here before, Harry, and we got out. Until they stick us behind barbed wire just believe that we will get out. So long as we are alive we have a chance."

"What is the plan, Sarge?"

"Lay low tomorrow. There will be a hue and cry. It is like a game of hide and seek. If you hide close to the den then there is a risk that you will be found but if you hide well enough then the searchers move away. That is what I am counting on. This is a good place to hide. The bricks are treacherous and we will hear anyone coming close. As soon as it is getting on to dark we leave here and make our way north and east

148

towards the coast." In my head, I had the map. We either needed an airfield or a small port; both would afford us the chance to escape. "We will avoid the coast around here. They will be searching every inlet and beach for miles, if only to find the dead bodies of our mates. The further north we go the less chance we have of detection."

There was silence save for the sporadic gunfire from the other side of the submarine basin. Harry said, quietly, "But how do we get across the Channel!"

Polly laughed, "Once the Sarge stole a German aeroplane and back in the day he stole a French fishing boat. He will get us out alright. I just don't know how."

Polly had more confidence in me than I did, "You lads sleep. I will wake you in two hours Polly."

"Right Sarge."

They were good commandos and they were asleep in next to no time. I crept up the bricks to peer over the top. If we were attacked we would have some protection from our brick parapet. In the port, the fire fights had ended. There were now just single shots which we heard occasionally. I shuddered. Was that the sound of commandos being executed? I looked at my watch. It was four o'clock in the morning. When I woke Polly, it would be light. I began to second guess myself. Perhaps I should have taken the first watch in daylight. No, I should trust my men; I had trained them well.

At five thirty I heard the tramp of feet. As it was still largely dark I risked a glance over the top. I saw Germans marching prisoners along the road which flanked the submarine basin. Many of the commandos appeared wounded. I recognised Jack Johnson who was supporting a commando I did not recognise. Jack was a prisoner of war. Part of me wanted to leap out and rescue them. I knew that would be doomed to failure. At least, if I got home, I would be able to tell Jack's family that he had survived. Poor Jack had had no luck since Waller. First a broken jaw and now he suffered imprisonment.

149

They had not been gone very long when a patrol of Germans arrived at the gates opposite us. The Sergeant pointed over to our side of the road and I heard him shout, "You two search the derelict buildings."

The others began to search along the road where there were places a man might hide. The two Germans headed towards us. For some reason, they appeared to be heading directly for me. I knew that I could not be seen. I was just another lump. Perhaps it was an illusion but I took out my Luger and cocked it. Suddenly one of the Germans slipped as his foot found a hole in the bricks.

"Shit!" His friend laughed. The German was stuck in the bricks. "Stop laughing and get me out of here! There might be rats!" They managed to get him to his feet. "There is no one here!" He turned and shouted. "There is no one Sergeant."

"Get over here then. There are some commandos in the cellar of a house at the other end of the town. Come on!"

I breathed a sigh of relief as they ran off. That had been close but I saw how lucky we had been the previous night. That could have happened to any of us. We were camped in an unstable pile of rubble. It would make our departure doubly hazardous. Polly opened his eyes and I put my finger to my lips. A short while later a second column of commandos was marched past heading for a future ringed by barbed wire and watch towers. We had paid a high price.

At eight I shook Polly awake and curled up in a foetal ball. I fell asleep. In many ways, it was miraculous but a commando learned to be stoical; so long as we were alive there was hope. When Polly woke Harry I also woke up. The two hours' sleep had been more than enough. I rinsed my mouth out with water and rubbed my teeth with my finger. I resisted eating more rations. We had a limited quantity of those. Polly rolled over for his sleep.

I let Harry watch while I took out my map to study it. There were many small ports to the north and west of us but we had to get further away before we risked stealing a ship. Lorient was a large German base and we would have to avoid that. It left us with a short area from

Damgan to Plouharnel. If that failed we would have to skirt the German Naval base and head for the Channel ports.

I glanced at my watch. It was ten thirty. Dusk would come after five. The sun was so bright that I suspected it might be late. It would be a fine day. I had just put my map away when there was an enormous explosion from the other side of the submarine pens. I had never experienced such a loud bang in all my life. The concussion washed over us and made my ears ring. We were showered with bricks and pieces of metal. Luckily none actually hit us but I heard a thump as a solitary brick slammed into the net just a foot away from my head.

Polly woke up, startled, "What is that?"

Harry grinned and slapped him on the back, "The ship has blown up! The raid was a success."

I nodded, "Right and that means the Germans will be doubly desperate to get to round up every commando who was on the raid. It has not made things easier for us. It will be harder."

Chapter 13

We heard the sound of German soldiers and vehicles all morning. There had been casualties as we heard ambulances. That would not endear us to them. The afternoon dragged on and still we waited in our bunker. I was right about dusk and it was later than we had expected. It also promised to be a chilly night. We sipped our water and husbanded our rations and we hid. As soon as it was beginning to darken we removed the nets and packed them away. Who knew when we would next need them. In our secure hollow, we slung our Bergens. I rose, gingerly from the depression in the bricks. We would not be heading towards the submarine pens, rather we would be heading to what had been the back alley. There were boarded and shored up buildings along that side of the rubble. When we had first come they had been occupied. Now they had been abandoned and gave us hope that we could use them to leave unseen.

I scanned all around three hundred and sixty degrees and saw no one. We were below the highest level of the demolition. I crawled north, towards the alley. Here the bricks were fewer but I was acutely aware of the danger of air pockets which would not support our weight. Just as bad was the prospect that an avalanche of bricks would alert the German patrols to our presence. With no one in sight I stepped towards the cobbles just thirty feet away. The hardest part was the first few steps where we had to climb. Once on the solid cobbles I took out my Luger. It was a handier weapon than the Thompson.

I signalled for Polly to bring up the rear and we headed along what had been the alley. At the end, I stopped. Glancing around the corner I saw a German armoured car heading in our direction. It was going towards the submarine pens. I flattened myself against the wall. The other two did the same. I did not move my head as the vehicle passed. If anything, my face was even better camouflaged. The brick dust had joined the black make up. I looked like a sooty wall. So long as I didn't move I would remain invisible. At the end of the road the armoured car turned left and headed along the road adjacent to the submarine pens.

Once I could no longer hear its engines I peered around the corner. It was empty. I used the doorways of the derelict shops as cover and we made our way north. I remembered from my last visit that St. Nazaire was smaller than one might have expected. However, that meant they would put road blocks and checkpoints at the main points of egress. I kept taking left turns and then a right turn to keep us heading north and west. As I turned one corner I almost tripped over the body of a commando. I turned him over. It was Fred Harris from Wolverhampton. His war had last one raid and no more. I felt for Fred Harris who had been so keen to see action and continued to negotiate the treacherous streets.

It was more commandos who saved us. We were silently creeping along the dark, rubble filled streets when we heard a commotion ahead. Peering around a corner I saw six commandos being dragged from a cellar. There was a road block at the end of the street and the six stood no chance. Now that we knew were the road block was we backtracked to the last right turn and headed up that street. When I looked down the intersection I saw that the German's attention was on the six commandos. I waved the other two across the road and I followed. We ran down the next road and then turned left. To my horror a German sentry stepped out from a doorway. He saw me and tried to bring up his rifle. I reacted instinctively, I fired one shot into his face. He died instantly. The only saving grace was that it was the sound of a Luger that the road block would have heard.

"Run!" We raced like gazelles. Crossing the road, we darted into an alleyway behind terraced houses. Half way down I led us left and it brought us out at another road which led north. I saw trees. We were almost out of the town. However, behind us I heard the whistles and shouts of alarm. They had discovered the body of the sentry.

"Run straight and get to the woods."

This was where all the training paid off. We made it to the woods and collapsed in a heap. We had run the last mile in a speed which might

153

have won us a gold medal at the Berlin Olympics. We stopped in the eaves. "Drink! And get me out a couple of potato mashers." It was important that we remained hydrated. You thought better. I took out some cord and, when Harry had given me the two grenades I made a trip wire across the path. It would alert us to pursuit and slow down the Germans. I took my own advice and drank from my canteen. We had a spare now, thanks to Ken. I heard shouts and the clatter of boots in the cobbles. They were following. We were now hidden in the woods and they would have to close with us to see us. We ran through the woods.

The day had been bright sunny and warm. The night was clear and cold. Thankfully our exertions warmed us up. I remembered this area. We had booby trapped a German truck here but, as I recalled, the wood soon petered out and we would be on a road again. There was little else to do but keep going and pray that we would lose them. We had left the woods and were making our way through the tiny huddle of houses that was Brais when we heard the distant crump of the booby trap going off. That gave us an idea of where they were. It would slow them down and we had a chance to extend our lead. I know we could have asked the French there for help and shelter but I was loath to involve innocent civilians. I would get us out of this. I saw a curtain flicker as we passed one of the houses. If it was a collaborator then we were done for.

At the next junction, I turned left. I saw fields and I took us across them. The pursuing Germans were too far away to see us and we risked the open. The cold night and the dry day had hardened the ground so that we made no prints as we ran across to the next field. We made a mile by taking this cross-country route. We crossed another road and I saw, to the left, a German airfield. Hope sprang in my breast. Perhaps we could steal an aeroplane. I had done it once before. I led my two weary men to the barbed wire fence. It was a small field with one wooden building and tents. To my disappointment I saw that they were Focke Wolf 190s. I could escape in one but I would have to leave my two men behind. That was not an option.

Just then I heard a German lorry coming from the direction of St. Nazaire. There was a drainage ditch at our feet and we dived into the

154

foetid water. I heard the brakes on the truck as it stopped just twenty yards from where we lay hidden.

I heard voices. "Are you certain you saw them crossing the field, private?"

"Yes Lieutenant. I thought we would see them on this road."

Just then I heard a voice which seemed to be coming from above us. It was a sentry in the airfield. "Who are you looking for?"

"Tommies. British Commandos. They raided the port and destroyed the gates of the dock. Have you seen anyone?"

"No one came this way."

"Well you keep watch for them. Come. They must have headed up the road." I heard the truck start and drive off. Then there was the sound of a match being struck and the smell of smoke. The discarded match fell and hissed into the water close to Poulson's foot. When the cigarette butt followed I willed the sentry to continue his patrol. I heard him move off his feet on the gravel path which ran along the fence. After five minutes, I rose and peered left. He was not in sight. I tapped the other two on the shoulder and back to the other side of the road. We slipped over into the field.

We had a dilemma. There was a lorry between us and the coast. However, if we retraced our steps we might run into others. "We stay in the field next to the road. When the German lorry comes back we hide."

"Right Sarge."

We moved ever north and west. We moved slower than before because we had to use the fields. We dared not risk the road or the open. We had been careless crossing the field and it had nearly cost us. An hour later I saw dim lights along the road. We dived to the ground as the German truck came back down the road. We continued along the fields for another mile or so. We were so close to the sea that I could smell it. I took a decision. "We risk the road. We can move faster. Be ready to dive into the hedge if we hear anything." I hoped the lights of a lorry or the sound of the engine would carry to us before we could be seen.

I checked my watch as we set off. It was midnight. We would need to lie up in four hours at the most. Depending upon the sun it might be earlier. I wanted as much distance between us and the port as possible. We used the darkness and the roads to make good time. We ran, our rubber soled shoes silent on the tarmac. We would hear any vehicles and I gambled that we were far enough away from any German soldiers to avoid the patrols.

We were eventually stopped by nature; the Marais. It was an area riddled with tidal creeks and marshes. We would need some time to cross it but it was too good an opportunity to miss. We could lie up here and no one would ever find us. The map in my head told me that the village of Le Poulprio lay to the north of the swampy area. We crossed a footbridge and found ourselves in treacherous country. We moved through stunted trees and bushes. Beneath our feet the ground went from a relatively solid footing to leg sucking mud. Gowland went into one such hole and disappeared up to his waist. We pulled him out.

We were deep enough now and I did not want to risk a major accident. "I reckon we will be safe here. Set up the nets, Harry. I'll scout around and make sure we are safe."

I dropped my Bergen and Tommy gun. I would not need them. I back tracked to the village. It seemed quiet. To the east I saw the faintest of glimmers. I returned to the place we had entered the Marais. Dawn was not far away. I walked fifty yards in each direction and saw that there was no buildings close by. I returned to the path we had taken. I saw that it was not a path as such but one of a number of routes across the soft ground. It was tidal and I suspected that different areas flooded at different times. I was just forty yards from our camp when I had a shock. A flurry of ducks took flight as I almost stepped into their nests. I knelt down and pocketed the four eggs I found in the two nests. I could not see the camp but I knew that come daylight it might be a different story.

Like a magician with a special trick I flourished my find before my two men, "Duck eggs!"

Polly rubbed his hands, "Now if you had some bacon and bread this would be perfect."

"I'm afraid it is raw eggs tonight lads but the protein will help us. We are running short of rations."

"I've put some lines in the water. You never know we might get lucky. Fresh fish is good too."

We ate the eggs and had some of the rations. We were running dangerously short of water but I did not want to risk the water here. It might be salty. "Poulson take the first shift. Wake me at dawn. I want to make sure that the hide is well camouflaged."

"Right Sarge."

I knew that it would only be an hour at most but I had to be sure that we were safe. It felt like I had just touched my head to the ground when I was shaken awake. "You told me dawn, Sarge."

"I know. Get your head down."

I crept from under the hide. The nets had more than done their job. I took the opportunity to explore. There were reeds and spindly trees all around. We had managed to find the part with slightly bigger trees. I saw that we were surrounded on three sides by water. I headed north and after forty yards saw that the stream was big enough to jump. I cut down a bundle of reeds with my knife. I used three of them to bind it into a faggot. After I had made three or four I laid them across the stream and stepped on them. They sank alarmingly but did not disappear below the water. They supported my weight. I crossed to the other side. It was firmer ground for almost five hundred yards but there was less cover. Luckily the land was the same colour as my battle dress and I risked it.

Once on the other side I saw there was a wide channel. I crouched down and tasted it. It was not tidal. I peered to the west and saw that it was a mixture of mud flats and water. That was no good. I followed the channel north; it narrowed rapidly. I found a place where it was just twenty yards wide and looked shallow enough to ford. I heard a vehicle and I dropped behind some scrubby bushes. It was a German convoy and the road was just a hundred yards north of where I nervously waited. When the convoy had gone I headed back to the hide. We now had two options. We could risk the channel or risk the road. Both were not without danger and I would decide which was the bigger one when night fell and we reached the point of no return.

157

By the time I got back the day had warmed up considerably. I went to check Harry's fish lines. We had two small fish. I took them off the hooks and laid them on the bank. I dug up a couple of worms and put the lines back in the stream. Taking out my dagger I gutted the fish. It was a pity we could not cook them but they were fresh and I had heard that the Japanese ate raw fish regularly.

I woke Harry at ten. He was delighted with his catch. I told him about the surrounding area and I curled up to sleep. I was happier now for I had a choice of escape routes.

We left before dark. Harry managed to catch an eel too. I ate the fish but drew the line at the eel. Harry and Polly seemed happy enough to risk it. We packed up and I explained my plan. "We head for the road. If it is too busy then we cross the channel and work our way around to Vannes." I took out the map and showed them. "It looks to be smaller than St. Nazaire but it will still have a garrison and I would prefer to avoid it. If we can pass through the suburbs at night then I think that we stand a chance."

Then both nodded. They seemed to have complete faith in me and my ability to get us home safely. I wished I was as confident. When we reached the channel, I saw that the tide was out and the water looked shallow. I saw that the road was still busy and there was plenty of traffic. I had no doubt they were still searching for commandos and the port would need repairs.

"We will risk the channel. Take off your shoes and socks. I don't want to lose them in the mud." We took off our shoes and socks and rolled up our trousers. It proved to be a wise move. The water only came up to our shins but our feet sank into the grey slimy mud of the channel. We might have had our shoes sucked from our feet. Once dressed we headed across the scrubland towards the distant town of Vannes. Some of the fields had sheep grazing on the salt grass but we saw neither people nor dogs. Sheep do not give the alarm.

We reached the River Marle. There was a military bridge across the river. That was when my cleverly constructed plan came unstuck. There were two guards at the Vannes end of the bridge. They would see

158

us as we crossed. I had to come up with another plan. We clambered up the bank and I saw that the bridge was made of girders. There were struts and crosspieces. A mad idea came to me. We could use them to cross under the bridge. No ships would be passing below at night and even if there were they would be unlikely to look up. Once over the other side we would need to escape into the town without the guards seeing us.

I pointed to the bridge and mimed climbing it. At first, they looked confused and so I mimed it again. Then they nodded. We would be safe from observation as there was no one on the river. However, it would not be an easy climb. The first part was not difficult. I found myself under the wooden boards which made up the surface of the bridge. Once there I discovered that I would not need to hang from the bridge as I had feared; the struts and braces were close enough for me to crawl. I moved like a huge four-legged spider. The problem was the Bergen which scraped along the wood but I managed. The water was not that far below but if we fell into it then the splash would easily be heard and I doubted that we would escape. I kept my attention on the other side. Once I reached the other side of the bridge then I turned and saw the other two making their way along the girders after me.

I took out my Luger and made my way down to the base of the bridge. There was no path close to the river. We would have to climb up and risk the road. I waited until the other two joined me and I pointed up. They nodded. We crawled slowly towards the checkpoint. With luck, the guard's attention would be on the other side of the bridge. As we neared the top I heard them talking. I rose slowly so that I was hidden by the huge metal post which supported the cable supporting the bridge. I saw that the road was clear and I waved Polly down it. He scurried away and disappeared across the other side. He had not been seen. I waved for Harry to follow him. He was half way across when I heard a German shout, "Halt!" And then, in English, "Hands up Tommy!"

Harry briefly glanced in my direction and I nodded. I was still hidden. Unless they turned around they would not see me. The two sentries made the mistake of walking together towards Harry. He raised his hands. I saw that he still held his Tommy gun in his right hand. Their

159

rifles were pointed directly at him. I knew that Polly would have them covered but it would be a disaster if he were to use his gun. I silently stepped out behind them and had my gun pressed into the back of one of them before they knew.

"One false move and I blow a hole in your back! Drop your guns!" I poked my gun hard and one dropped his rifle, followed by the other one. "Poulson get out here!"

As soon as Polly appeared with his Thompson they raised their hands. Harry immediately took out his cord. I said, "Put your hands behind your backs." While my two men trussed them up and took their grenades I looked around for somewhere to hide them. There was a sentry box to one side and a motor bike and sidecar combination. "Stick them in the sentry box. Gag them with something." The motor cycle had given me an idea. "Fetch their helmets!"

When they returned I said, "Harry, can you get the motor bike going?"

"I think so Sarge. Why?"

"We are going to drive through Vannes. Two of us can wear the helmets. In the dark, we might be mistaken for Jerries. Polly, you are lighter than me. You get on the back of the bike." I took one helmet and I gave the other to Harry. I jammed Harry's Bergen into the sidecar. It was a tight fit but I managed it. "Harry, just keep going straight. Don't turn right! That will take us into Vannes. Once we get into the country we will stop and study the map."

The German motorcycle seemed inordinately loud as he started it. He looked at me and I nodded. We headed west. The Germans had made the headlights a bare slit. It made visibility poor and our speed was reduced. It was only later I realised that this meant we did not attract attention. I kept my Luger in my hand for the only people on the streets were the Germans. The curfew kept the French indoors. I relaxed a little and ran the map through my head. To the south of us, our left, there were no ports and no boats. We had another twenty miles to go until we reached Plouharnel or Carnac; both were close to each other. I guessed, at this speed, we would reach one of them in under an hour.

160

It was not to be for we were spotted at Ploeren; it was a few miles short of Carnac. It was a small village and perhaps the two sentries were bored. They heard us coming and stepped into the road. One held a lantern and the other had his rifle in his hands. "You had better slow down, Lowe, but be ready to go as soon as I give the word. Polly keep your head tucked in."

We slowed and I saw that the rifle was not levelled at us but hung loosely in the sentry's right hand.

"Halt!"

I kept the Luger hidden but pointed at them. I said, "What is the problem? We have a message to take to Lorient."

We were just six feet from them and the man with the light approached. I saw suspicion on his face. He saw Polly. "Why are there three of you on this..." He did not finish the sentence for his light showed Harry's brown tunic. "Fritz, they are Tommies!"

The man with the rifle was the danger and I fired two shots at him as he raised his weapon. He was less than ten feet away and I could not miss. The man with the light had a dilemma. He had no weapon and rather than using his light as one which we would have done he panicked. I swung the Luger around and said, "Do not throw your life away my friend. Raise your hands. Give me the light." He did so. "Polly tie him up." I had no idea what sort of garrison the town contained but the two shots would have woken them. "Take his boots." I threw the light to the ground and it shattered covering the road in broken glass.

As Poulson remounted I said, "Have your Colt ready."

I holstered my Luger and drew my Thompson. Harry roared off down the road. We had to be ready for anything. I saw, in the dark ahead, the shadows of another small village. A light appeared. "Lowe turn off your headlight."

"I might as well. It is bloody useless." As soon as he did the road ahead became just a black mass. Luckily the road was relatively straight. I peered into the darkness and saw, by the light ahead, that there were Germans and they were attempting to put a barrier across the road.

161

There were just six of them. "Straight through. Poulson, you take the Germans on the left."

Perhaps they recognised the motorcycle and the German helmet in the dark but they hesitated. I gave a short burst when we were twenty yards away and they dived for cover. I heard the bark of Polly's Colt. As we passed them I reached for a grenade, pulled the pin and threw it high over my shoulder. "Grenade!" Gowland accelerated and I felt the force as we leapt down the road. The explosion behind was accompanied by the shouts of injured men. We passed a crossroads and kept heading west. I suddenly realised that the road was now heading south and I could smell the sea. There were many inlets hereabout. "Lowe, Stop! Turn around and go back to the crossroads. We need to head north." The road south would trap us on the wrong side of the inlet.

"But you said...!"

"Just do it." I had to think quickly for seconds would now be vital if we were to escape this trap.

I readied another grenade in case we needed it. When he struck the crossroads, we headed north. The road twisted and turned but after a mile we, thankfully, struck a main road heading east to west.

"Turn left!" The alarm would have been given. I had no doubt that the telephone lines were humming. There would be roadblocks ahead. We needed to make some miles and then get off the road. The question was, would we be allowed the time? I looked behind and I could neither see nor hear any sign of pursuit. They had radios and telephones. They did not need to pursue. They could just tighten the net around us.

162

Chapter 14

A mile and a half after we had joined the larger road I saw a wood to one side of the road. "Lowe, find a track into the wood. We need to hide up."

This time he obeyed instantly and we turned down a forester's track. Just inside I said, "Stop here and turn the motorcycle around." I needed time to find our bearings.

I took the torch from the Bergen and shone it inside the sidecar so that no light spilled. I wanted to be able to read the map and find out exactly where we were. We were beyond the map in my head. The other two manhandled the bike so that it was facing the way he had come into the wood. I wanted a speedy exit. "Come here, you two, in case anything happens to me." They peered at the map. "That last village was called Plougemelen. A mile or so up the road is Auray. Once we have passed Auray then we can choose our route to get to the coast. We have to get to Auray now as fast as we can. When we hit the town take the first major road to the left that you can." I jabbed a finger at the map. "That should be here."

"Righto, Sarge."

"Fresh magazine Polly, and keep a grenade handy. Lowe give me a couple of yours. I am almost out." He handed me two Mills bombs.

Just then we heard a Kubelwagen as it headed along the road in the direction of Auray.

"Quick, follow that German. We might be able to sneak through behind them."

As we set off I knew it was a gamble but a calculated one. The Kubelwagen would be ahead of us. Their attention would be on the road in front of them. I hoped that if they did see us they would assume we were men sent to help them. I had Gowland use the headlights; it would make them less suspicious of us. We caught up with it and when we were about two hundred yards behind I told Gowland to maintain that distance. A Kubelwagen is noisy and I doubted that they would look behind. I saw the houses and buildings of Auray in the distance. I could see lights and saw that we had another bridge to cross and another roadblock to pass. "They will open the road block for them. When you see it open then give it all the power you have Lowe!"

"Sarge!"

We were at one end of the bridge when the Kubelwagen slowed and they opened the barrier to let it through. When they heard the sound of the motorcycle they turned. Without lights to see us clearly, we would appear as two Germans in a motorcycle combination. However, I saw one suspicious sergeant holding his rifle at high port. He was ready.

"Go!"

I had a grenade in my lap but I first fired a long burst at the sergeant. He fell to the side and the others dived for cover. It was a tight fit. Polly hit a soldier who fell across the road. I threw my grenade into the Kubelwagen as the motorcycle ran over the stricken soldier. I turned and emptied my magazine. I saw the Kubelwagen lit up by the exploding grenade. They would be going nowhere in a hurry. It took a few moments for the stunned Germans to react and by then we had disappeared into the dark. The shots they fired were blind.

We passed one left turn almost immediately but that was no good. They would know we had taken it because of the change in engine noise. We kept going and were rewarded, a half mile later by a second smaller one. It was narrow and even the motorcycle appeared too large for it. I hoped that it would be devoid of Germans. For the first time that long night our luck held. We saw no one and we heard no sounds of pursuit. Dawn was less than a couple of hours away. The Luftwaffe would have spotter aeroplanes up and then our goose would be cooked. I planned on being at our destination by then and lay up until we could reconnoitre the area.

As we raced along I began to feel more confident. Suddenly Harry jammed the brakes on and we squealed to a halt. There was a river ahead. I jumped out and said, "Harry turn it around." I stepped into the narrow channel. I could ford it but not the motor cycle. I took a decision. "We have had it with the bike. Hide it, grab your bags and follow me."

I slung my Bergen and headed across the river. It was not wide but it came almost to my thighs at one point. I waded ashore on the other side and made my way through the trees. It was another wood. I heard nothing and, while I waited for the others I risked the map and the torch. I used the inside of the bag to hide the light. I worked out that we had just crossed the Ruisseau de Gouyanzeur. We had been lucky. Had we hit it another fifty yards downstream we would not have been able to cross. Harry and Polly joined me, "A shame about the bike, Sarge."

"Don't worry about it." I pointed into the Bergen where the map was illuminated by the torch. "I think we are here about a mile and half from the first little port. We can be there before dawn and see what there is there. Polly, you take the lead. Head south and west."

"Sarge."

I brought up the rear. In the distance, I could hear the sound of trucks and other vehicles. Occasionally, as I turned, I saw flashes of light. They were using lights to search for us. They were not close and appeared more like the lights of fireflies. We were not out of the woods yet, literally.

After half an hour of tramping through, first woods and then fields, we saw houses. This had to be Carnac. Poulson stopped and I ran forward. It was still dark but we needed to find somewhere close to the harbour. This was the smallest of the ports I had seen. I hoped for a fishing boat to take us home. Once again, I gambled. We ran along the lanes towards the sea which I could now smell. It would be light in an hour and false dawn was behind us. The road began to descend towards the beach and the harbour. I saw figures in the distance heading up towards us. I led my men to the left and we ducked into a track between two houses. They looked like fishermen's cottages and, as we hid against the wall I felt the chimney. It was warm. The people were up and about.

I waved my arm and we moved along the back of the houses. There was no fence but they used the backs for vegetable gardens. We ran along them. We emerged on a road above the harbour. I could see

165

the fishing boats. There were eight of them and they were heading out to sea. The tide was coming in. We had missed them by minutes. I did not want to risk moving back through the houses and so I looked for somewhere for us to hide close to the harbour. It was not a crazy idea for I saw the last of those who had helped to launch the boats, heading up to the village. There would soon be no one left in the harbour. We could hide there until the fishing boats returned. When the road was empty I led them down to the circular harbour. It was small. I reckoned it could hold no more than twelve fishing boats at most. There were tables covered with a roof. That would be where they would land and sell their fish or perhaps sort it. The only other buildings were what looked like somewhere they sold things in the summer months, a vending hut, and the other was a large hut which had a flagpole. Possibly something to do with a harbour master.

I whispered, "Lowe, keep watch!" I led Polly down to the two buildings. The hut was open and there was a smell of tobacco and smoke. I saw that there were crumbs on the floor and an empty pot with used cups. This was where the fisherman had eaten before they left. We went to the second one and it was bolted. The lock was flimsy and rusty: it had not been opened for some time. I suspected since before the war. I took out my bolt cutters and had it off in a moment. Inside there was a musty smell and it was filled with cobwebs. No one had been inside for years. It was perfect. I doubted anyone would give it a second look and we could wait there until the fishing boats returned. It would be simplicity itself to steal one at night and sail home.

"Get Harry. We will hole up here."

While he went for Gowland I examined the interior. There were two rooms. One was obviously where they sold things. I saw ancient postcards and metal pails with children's shovels. There had obviously been other items but the rats and mice had had them. The only things that remained were non-edible. The other two came in. "Shut the door."

The back room showed more promise. There was a tap and a sink. I turned the tap and it squeaked before turning and a trickle of rusty water came out. I left it running and examined the rest of the room. It was where the owner had had their lunch or waited for customers. The water ran clear and I tasted it. It was fine. We could refill our canteens.

"Fill your canteens now and then find somewhere to lie. We are going to sit it out until dark."

The other two lay with their eyes closed but I could not sleep. Had I made a mistake? If anyone came then we were trapped. There was only one way in and one way out. I was counting on the fact that the lock was rusty and no one had been here for some time. Perhaps the owner was dead. I could second guess myself all day. It had not been planned that we were stuck in France. I was just lucky that I had had maps. The commandos who had landed with the destroyer were not as lucky. If they had escaped they would be wandering around France just using their compass. As we had discovered that could be disastrous.

I drank some more water and looked at my watch. It was almost twelve o'clock and the fingers wound around exceedingly slowly. I had just put my canteen away when the door opened with an ominous creak. An old French woman stood there with her hands on her hips and a face as black as thunder. I was so stunned I didn't even reach for my gun. Instead I stood and said, "Good morning Madame!"

Her face changed in an instant. She pointed to my shoulder flashes, "English?"

"Yes, Madame."

She closed the door. "You are the ones who blew up the dock?"

"Yes, Madame. We were stranded here."

She reached up and brought my face down to hers so that she could kiss me on both cheeks. "Good."

"Madame, you must go. If you are found here with us then you might suffer for it."

Poulson and Gowland were staring open mouthed. The woman was speaking too quickly for them to pick up anything. I saw Polly reach for his gun. I gave the slightest of shakes with my head.

"Pah!" She said, "I am eighty years old and buried my husband in the Great War. The Boche do not frighten me! Let them come!"

167

I was curious. "Why did you come in here?"

She gave a sad smile and swept her hand around the room. "This was my shop. I sold things to those who came here before the war. It was little enough I earned but I enjoyed the smiling faces of the children. I come here each day to make sure that no one has damaged it." She wagged a finger at me. "And you have!"

"I am sorry Madame. We are hiding here until it is safe to move tonight. We hope to get aboard a fishing boat."

"Do not worry about the lock. I will get a new one. I know the fishermen. I will get you on board. They will be back by six or seven." She suddenly disappeared out of the door. For an octogenarian she moved really quickly! She reappeared with a basket covered in a cloth. She shut the door and, like a magician theatrically removed the cloth to reveal a baguette, wine, cheese, ham and an apple. "You will have to share it between you, I am afraid."

I shook my head, "We could not deprive you of your lunch."

"I have more at home and it is a small price to pay to those who still fight against our enemies. Now eat. No one comes here during the day. We are safe until night time. I am the only one who comes here each day to eat my lunch and to watch the sea." She broke the bread into three and tore it open. I had not noticed the butter but she spread it liberally and then placed ham and cheese in each sandwich. She handed them out and then poured wine into a glass for me. Handing the bottle to Harry she went to a cupboard and brought out three more odd sized glasses. She rinsed them under the tap and then poured the rest of the wine into them. Raising her glass, she said, "Death to the Germans!"

Bemused we joined in the toast and then devoured the food. After composite rations it was like a banquet. I was pleased it was just one glass of wine for it was rough and strong. It went straight to my head. She collected her things and put them in the basket. "I will put the lock so that it looks as though it is still attached and I will return when the fishermen do." She pointed behind her. "There is a German hut in the village and they have a radio. Do not leave until I return. Come and kiss an old woman!"

We all kissed her on each cheek and she nodded approvingly. "Your French is good Sergeant."

"My father was a flier in the Great War and we had a cottage to the north."

"Good, then you now our country. We stand together. I am glad that you broke into my shop. Do not leave!"

After she had gone Poulson said. "Will she not betray us, Sarge?"

"I think I can say categorically that she will not. We have dropped lucky and no mistake."

The wine made me drowsy. If it had not I might have heard the approaching engine noises sooner. First there was the sound of German trucks pulling up on the road above us. Gowland shook me and made the sign for danger. I pressed my eye against the crack in the door and I saw two ambulances on the road above and white coated medics rushing to the beach with stretchers. Then I heard the unmistakeable throb of an E-Boat's diesel engines. I ran to the front of the hut and peered through the crack under the counter flap. There was an E-Boat coming in and it had been shot up. I saw blood running from the scuppers and bandaged seamen. It tied up just forty yards from us. I could hear some of what they were saying. They shouted to the medical staff who were on the other side of the hut. Men were lowered on to stretchers. They had been badly hit in some sea battle. I counted twenty men being taken away by the ambulances.

By my reckoning that left just ten men on board; an E-Boat had a crew of thirty. The Captain obligingly sat with his back to the hut while he smoked a cigarette. Two of his officers were with him.

"We were lucky then and no mistake, Heine. Those damned MTBs suckered us into that trap as efficiently and effectively as we might have done."

"If it were not for the Hurricanes, Captain, we would have destroyed those two boats."

"You fool, Heine, that was the trap. We were just lucky that their engines were damaged or we would be prisoners already."

169

"We were unlucky Captain not lucky. Those exploding shells incapacitated the gun crews."

"No Heine, luck was with us. If those shells had penetrated the engine room that would have been unlucky. We only lost four men. The engines work and we can replace the ammunition. We were lucky and I intend to celebrate our luck. Leave Gerhardt and Klaus to watch the boat. I will send a relief at nine. We will go and enjoy a night in Carnac. Tell them."

I saw the older officer, he had white hair, stand and shout, "Everyone ashore. Gerhardt and Klaus, you have the first watch. You will be relieved at nine."

I glanced at my watch. It was three o'clock. If the two men on watch went below deck then we stood a chance. It was a wild one and filled with risks but we could sail back to England in a German E-Boat. I stared at the two crew men. They went around the E-boat to make sure that the ropes were all secure and, when they were certain that the officers had gone, they went below decks.

I turned to the other two. "We are going to capture the E-boat that is in the harbour. In a moment, we will go outside and drop our Bergens on the harbour wall. There are just two sentries and they are below decks. We find them and incapacitate them. Then you get the bags Polly, and untie us. Harry, you have seen these engines before. You reckon you can start them?"

"Yes, boss. So long as you can drive the bloody thing!"

"Then we are on!"

We opened the door and, after making sure that the coast was clear scurried around to the harbour wall. I dropped my Bergen and Thomson. I took out my sap and kept my Luger handy. When the other two were ready we boarded the boat. Our rubber soled shoes meant we made no noise and the two Germans obliged us by talking. They appeared to be in the cabin behind the bridge. There had to be two entrances and so I sent Polly aft to find the other one. I watched and he waved. This was it. I descended the steps.

A voice said, "Who is it?"

170

"The Captain sent me with some Schnapps!"

I was just buying time but it appeared to work   The dim light below decks meant they did not seem to notice my battle dress as I descended the stairs.

"Well he has changed then. He is normally as tight as..."

He got no further for I had reached the bottom of the steps and turned. He saw my battledress. He leapt at me and I swiped him, blindly, across the head with my Luger. His momentum and my blow smashed his head off the edge of the cupboard. Unfortunately, he took me with him and I lost my footing. His companion whipped out a wicked looking knife. As he stabbed at me Polly brought his own sap across the back of his head. They were both out for the count.

"Quick get to the engines. Polly tie this one's hands." I took out some cord and tied the hands of the man who had tried to knife me behind his back. I hauled him up the steps by his feet. His head clattered off every one. I dragged him to the harbour wall and dumped him. I ran to the forward rope and untied it. Poulson already had the second one on the harbour wall. As he went for the Bergens and guns I went to the aft line which held us to the harbour wall. I heard the engines start. I was just about to jump on board when one of the Germans swung his feet and took my legs from under me. I jumped up, pulled out my sap and smacked him again. Just to be sure I hit the other one too. There was no time to waste and I jumped aboard and ran to the bridge. Poulson untied the bow line and leapt on board. He waved at me.

Bill Leslie had explained how these boats were steered and moved. I prayed he was right. There was a voice pipe next to the wheel. "Harry, I am about to move us away from the harbour. Everything all right down there?"

"Aye, aye skipper."

Polly joined me. I nodded towards the two throttles. "Just push these levers."

As he did so we leapt forwards and I turned the wheel hard to port. We surged towards the entrance which looked remarkably narrow.

171

Poulson glanced over his shoulder. "Sarge, there are Germans running towards the harbour."

"Get on the rear guns but don't fire unless you have to. Jerry said they were short of ammunition. We may need it before we get home."

There was a compass. I headed west once we had cleared the harbour mouth. I should have used a proper course but I had not had time to plot one I just improvised and sailed west north west. I knew that the coast line jutted out here. It would take us closer to home and away from France. That was my sole intention. The old lady had said they had a radio transmitter in Carnac. It would not take them long to summon air support. I had to get us as far away as possible before they came. "Harry, is this the maximum speed?"

"I think so. Have you pushed the throttles as far forwards as you can, Sarge? We are nowhere near the red here yet."

I pushed hard. There appeared to be a notch and we clicked through it. Suddenly we took off. This was full speed. Poulson came to join me. He pointed aft with his thumb. "Those Germans had no weapons but they looked fairly unhappy Sarge."

"You had better find a gun you can fire. Try them all out. From what they said they had a problem with ammunition. I daresay Jerry will send someone after us."

"I don't fancy swimming for it, Sarge."

"Neither do I and remember that our lads won't know this is captured. When you have checked the guns get the swastika down and see if you can find a White Ensign or Union flag."

"I doubt it."

"So, do I but look eh? You never know they might have tried to fool us by flying a false flag too. There will be a flag locker near to the mast."

There was a whistle. I leaned over the voice pipe. "Yes Harry?"

"Do you want the bad news, Sarge?"

"Go ahead."

"We only have a quarter of a tank of diesel. I have no idea how far that will get us."

172

"I will slow down after dark. Until then we go as fast as we can. If we end up drifting then so be it."

I heard the different calibre guns as Poulson tried them all. Then there was silence as he searched for a flag. I saw the coastline to the north of us. It was German territory now and I imagined the messages being relayed down the coast, *'Watch for a captured Schnellboote!'*

He came back with a Royal Navy flag, the White Ensign. "You were right Sarge. I wonder why they had one."

"Probably the same reason the 'Campbelltown' did, to deceive the enemy. Get it run up and then we can't be accused of fighting under false colours. Which is the best gun?"

"There is more ammunition for the 20mm so the single one would be best. We would use less of it that way."

"Good thinking." I looked up as the flag snapped at the mast. "That feels better. See if you can find a chart eh?" I knew the course I had been following but I had little idea of the speed. It would have to be an estimate. I glanced at my watch it was not even four o'clock yet and we were hours from both darkness and safety.

Polly came racing up the steps and handed me a map. He pointed aft. "Trouble, Sarge, a Focke Wolf 190 approaching rapidly."

"Get on your gun then. I intend to make us a hard target so give him short bursts and fire just ahead of him." The appearance of the German made my estimation of our position academic. I glanced over my shoulder and saw that he was racing along at just above sea level. He intended to destroy the rudder. I gambled and swung the wheel to starboard and after the count of three returned to our original course. The bullets whipped across the sea and I heard Poulson firing back. I needed the German to waste his bullets on us. He would have to return to base to rearm and by then it might be dark. Instead of coming around and attacking the bow he flew around to come after our stern again. That was a mistake. I could predict what he did and I suspected that he would try to predict my movements. I would have to throw him.

"Poulson this time I intend to make a full swing all the way around, full circle. I will cover three sixty degrees."

173

"Right Sarge!"

I shouted down the voice pipe, "How is the fuel, Harry?"

"Going down steadily."

I pulled the throttle back a little. That too might throw the pilot's aim off. I was just grateful there was only one of them and he had no bombs.

"Here he comes, Sarge."

I heard the Focke Wolf's guns and I swung to port. The boat heeled alarmingly. I hoped that Poulson was strapped in. I heard a couple of bullets hit the stern guard rail and then Poulson's gun fired. As it came over I saw a tendril of smoke from the engine. We had a hit. I brought her back on to our original course and kept the same speed. We might as well save fuel.

"Here he comes again and I only have one more drum after this one, Sarge."

"Then make them count. The last ones worked."

This time I tried something totally different. As he zoomed in low I pulled the throttles right back. Poulson had a long clear shot at him and his bullets hit the mast and then ploughed into the sea. As he zoomed overhead I heard the change in the sound of his engine. The smoke was thicker and he was in trouble. As he turned to starboard I knew that he was heading back to base. I pushed the throttles forward. One danger was behind us. How many more lay ahead? I resumed the same speed we had been doing before we were attacked.

Chapter 15

"Poulson, see if you can make a brew or something. We might have a long voyage ahead of us."

Harry came up to see what the damage was like, "It sounded horrific, Sarge, from below decks but there appears to be little damage."

"They are a tough boat. What about the engines?"

"Sweet as a nut but we are using the fuel at a prodigious rate. I reckon we have three hours more cruising at this speed."

"Well you are the boss when it comes to the engines. I will slow down." I brought the throttles back so that we were doing what must have been twelve knots. It made sense but it went against every fibre of my being.

Poulson brought up three mugs of something hot. Harry took a sip and wrinkled his brow. "What the hell is this?"

Poulson grinned cheerfully. "No idea but it was in a pot in the galley. I tasted it; it seemed all right to me and I heated it up."

I recognised the tastes. "I think it is a malted drink. Think of it as German cocoa."

Poulson shook his head sadly, "No rum though Sarge, never mind."

I raised my mug to them, "Here's to you two. You have done really well. I couldn't have asked for more. I shall mention you in my report. You deserve some recognition for this. There might be a stripe or two." Promotion meant more pay.

"We are just like you, Sarge, we just did our job."

We were heading into the setting sun. The clement weather of the last few days had continued. Behind us the sky was rapidly darkening. Black clouds appeared in the eastern sky. The only difference to the previous day was a stiffer breeze from the east but as that was pushing us closer to home and saving fuel I did not object. While drinking our German malted drink we pored over the map and came up with a rough position. When I decided we had headed far enough west we turned and sail due north. We had allowed a margin of error but I calculated that we would miss Ushant by at least fifty miles. Once we turned to steer north by north west we saw how quickly day was turning into night. A commando liked the night, it was his friend. We could hide. The E-Boat was a big target and the huge Focke Wolf Condors which patrolled this part of the sea and the Atlantic would soon spot us. I glanced behind, at the mast. The last attack by the 190 had damaged it and it hung at an alarming angle. The White Ensign, however, still flew.

I almost jumped when Harry's voice came up the pipe, "Almost out of fuel, Sarge. We will be on fumes soon."

"Do your best. Poulson, see if you can get the radio to work. We may have to send out a signal for help."

"But Sarge that will pin point our position for Jerry."

"I know, old son, but with this breeze from the east we could end up in the middle of the Atlantic. The swells are bad enough here but out at sea they would turn us like a pancake." I pulled the throttles back even more. The darkness would soon hide us and we would get a few miles closer to home before the fuel ran out.

He returned half an hour later at about the same time the engine gave its first cough which warned that it was almost running dry. "I have found the radio and turned it on. I heard German chatter but no English. I didn't use the microphone, Sarge," he shrugged, "I left that for you."

"You did right, Poulson. Were there any coats down there? It is going to get nippy soon."

Happy to have something to do he disappeared, like the white rabbit below decks. He had hardly been gone a minute when the engine stuttered and coughed and then died. Harry's disembodied voice drifted up. I could hear the despondency. "That is it Sarge. We are out of fuel."

"You did your best. Best come on up and we will decide what to do next." I turned and went down to the charthouse. The batteries were well charged and would give us lights for a while but we also needed batteries for the radio. My decision had been made for me. We needed to radio and send for help.

176

Poulson had found some warm coats and we donned them. I roughly estimated our position and then wrote it down on a piece of paper. "Right Poulson, radio room."

I heard the crackling as we entered the tiny space. I saw down and looked at the dials. There looked to be one for frequency. We did not use radios and I had no idea which frequency our ships and aeroplanes would use. I guessed they were nowhere near the German ones. I turned the dial and the crackling gradually became a German voice. I listened briefly in case we were mentioned but it turned out to be a German convoy approaching Brest. I turned the dial. There was more crackling. I heard something faint but I could not make it out. I wrote down the frequency and then continued to scan.

I stopped when I heard an English voice. From the words, it sounded like an anti-submarine patrol I knew it would not be a convoy. They maintained radio silence. I had no idea of a call sign. I would just have to send the message in open language. I saw the switch for transmit. Picking up the microphone I flicked the switch. "Mayday! Mayday! We are three commandos from Number 4 commando. We are adrift in a captured E-Boat. We are drifting west. We have run out of fuel. Our position is 48 degrees and 52 minutes north; 6 degrees and 11 minutes west. Mayday! Mayday! We are three commandos from Number 4 commando. We are adrift in a captured E-Boat. We are drifting west. We have run out of fuel. Our position is 48 degrees and 52 minutes north; 6 degrees and 11 minutes west. Mayday! Mayday! We are three commandos from Number 4 commando. I repeat, we are three commandos from Number 4 commando. We are adrift in a captured E-Boat. We are drifting west. We have run out of fuel. Our position is 48 degrees and 52 minutes north; 6 degrees and 11 minutes west."

I flicked the switch to an ominous silence. I looked at the other two and saw that their faces reflected their despondency. They hated being helpless. On the land, they knew what to do and they could fight back. Here there was nothing to rail against.

I flicked the switch. " Mayday! Mayday! We are three commandos from Number 4 commando. We are adrift in a captured E-Boat. We are

177

drifting west. We have run out of fuel. Our position is 48 degrees and 52 minutes north; 6 degrees and 11 minutes west."

I flicked the switch. Then I heard a crackly voice. "This is HMS Atherstone. What is your unit, repeat, what is your unit? Over."

"Number 4 Commando. We were at St. Nazaire. Over."

"Stand by. Repeat, stand by. Over."

"What does that mean, Sarge?"

"That means that they are checking we are who we say we are." Just then the boat heeled alarmingly to port. The wind was getting up. "Lowe, go to the wheelhouse and keep us bow on to the waves."

"Aye, Aye captain!" He was cheerful once more. He had something to do.

"Polly get some hot food on the go. I don't think this is going to end soon." With both of them occupied I waited. Atherstone could be anywhere. All I knew was that she was close enough to hear our message; however, as we were less than fifty miles from Ushant and Brest, so could the Germans. They had radio direction finders. Each time I flicked the switch they were closer to finding us.

An hour passed. Polly brought some fried German sausage and eggs for us with a rye bread. Harry joined us while we ate. Neither of my commandos was happy with either the bread or the sausage but it was hot and it filled a hole. I quite enjoyed its spicy taste. Hot food always makes a soldier more hopeful.

The radio crackled into life, "Atherstone to commandos; Atherstone to commandos. Over."

"Commandos to Atherstone go ahead, over."

"What is the name of your Commanding officer, over? Repeat, what is the name of your Commanding officer?"

"Major Foster, over."

A brief silence and then, "What is the name of your Quarter Master over? Repeat, what is the name of your Quarter Master, over?"

"That is a daft question, Sarge!"

I smiled, "No it isn't. It is a perfect check to identify us." I flicked the switch, "Quarter Master Daddy Grant, over."

178

There was hardly a break and then the voice came back. "We are on our way, over. We are on our way, over."

"Thank you, over."

"Have a white sheet rigged over the deck in front of the bridge for identification, over. Repeat. Have a white sheet rigged over the deck in front of the bridge for identification, over."

"Understood, over and out." I flicked the switch and turned off the radio. We needed to save the batteries. "Go and find a sheet Poulson. Harry turn off every light you can. We need to save power."

I went on deck. The swells were building up. I went to the wheelhouse. Gowland had lashed the wheel but the wind had turned a little. I untied it and manually brought us around to face east. The motion became easier. I would have to stay on the wheel. My two men emerged with a large sheet. "Spread it out and lash it down. I guess they will use an aeroplane as soon as it is light to find us. The white sheet will be easy to spot from the air." Having understood its purpose, the two of them made a much better job than they might have otherwise done.

They joined me. "Poulson, sit by the radio. Switch it on every ten minutes. Listen for one minute and then turn it off again."

He disappeared. Gowland said, "Will they be here soon, Sarge?"

He wanted an answer I could not give. "I doubt it. They will wait until daylight. The ship might be on its way but we are a small target in a large ocean. If they have radar then we have a better chance but we just sit tight." I pointed to the east. "At least the wind is taking us further away from Jerry."

The night dragged on. It was the longest night I could remember. The destroyer was coming to our aid but if she was in the west then she would be fighting the wind. This close to the French coast she would have to zig zag for fear of submarines. Lowe brought up more of the German cocoa. He was just keeping himself busy. At other times, he waited with Polly in the radio room. I was facing east and I saw more false dawns that morning than I could ever remember. When it did break I almost cheered. "Lowe keep your eyes peeled eh? Look to the north. Go and get the binoculars; they are in my Bergen."

179

I was keen to keep both of my men busy. Poulson came to the bridge. "Sarge, the navy says they have sent a Sunderland up to find us."

"Good lad. Back on the radio eh. With any luck, we will be back in Blighty before you know it." I had to sound confident but it was a big ocean and I had no doubt that the Germans would be looking for us. While Gowland scanned the skies to the north I stared east. The wind had abated somewhat but the rollers were still rougher than I would have liked. I had to keep adjusting the steering wheel to keep us bow in to the wind. As the sky lightened I saw a shape high in the sky. "Lowe, swing your glasses around to due east. Eleven o'clock. What do you see?"

It took him a moment or two locate it. "A four engined job, Sarge."

"Condor?"

"Looks like it."

"Then we can expect company soon. Come here and take the wheel."

When he reached me, I went around to examine the guns myself. Poulson had been correct we had little 20mm ammunition. There were about thirty rounds of 37mm ammunition but that would take two men to operate. I made sure that both guns were loaded and ready to fire. If push came to shove we would use the last of the Thompson's magazines. We would go down fighting. It was now a race against time. The Germans had the advantage; they had seen us. We had even made it easy for them by putting the white sheet for them to see.

I returned to the bridge and took over the wheel again. The Condor was clearly visible now. I had no doubt that it would have signalled other aeroplanes and ships to come and get us. He would, no doubt, continue west to patrol for convoys. "If we are attacked I want you and Poulson on the flak cannon. There are thirty rounds left. I will stay here and try to keep us from spilling into the sea."

The Condor kept flying overhead, almost mocking us. There was no point in firing at him, he was too far away. We could have done with a second pair of binoculars but we had to make do with the one. Gowland and Poulson both shouted at the same time; one from the radio room and one from next to me.

180

"Sarge, I can see the Sunderland!"

"Sarge, the Sunderland has radioed it can see us!"

I felt relief wash over us before Poulson continued. "He says a fast German patrol boat is heading for us. It will be here before the Sunderland."

The flak gun was aft. It was our only defence. "Lowe and Poulson get on the flak gun. I am going to bring us about. We need the stern facing the enemy and that way you can fire the guns. It will be rough for a minute or two." It was yet another risk to add to the many I had already taken. As I turned the rudder the wind and the waves began to make us roll. I saw Harry Gowland cling on to a stanchion for dear life as we came beam on to the waves and then it eased. One advantage of having our stern to the east was that we were being pushed away from danger by the offshore wind. It was little enough but you clung on to things like that.

"Give me a shout when you are ready and when you can see the Germans."

To the north I could see the huge flying boat. I wondered if he would be able to land and pick us up before the Germans attacked. Then I realised that was impossible. The sea was too rough. As if to rub salt in the wound Poulson shouted, "Patrol boat astern!"

"Use the glasses. Is it an E-boat?"

There was a pause and then Harry said, "No Sarge. It looks like a smaller version of the motor launch. It has a pair of machine guns at the bow."

"Use your gun when you have the range but ration the ammo!" The Sunderland had guns and bombs. Perhaps the crew could come to our aid.

I lashed the wheel and hoped that the wind would not change too much over the next hour or so. Sixty minutes would determine if we were rescued or captured. I had no doubt that the Sunderland would be sending more radio messages but I had no men to spare for that. I ran to get the Thompsons. As I passed the radio room I switched on the radio

181

and said simply, "We have only three men. We cannot man the radio. Over!" I switched it off.

Once on deck I saw how close the launch now was. My two gunners were waiting for the right moment to fire. There was armour plating around the bottom of the gun. They could shelter there if things became too hot. I, in contrast, was totally exposed.

The flak gun sounded much louder than I was expecting. They were firing over open sights. The motor launch aided them by coming in a straight line. And, we were helped by the waves which made aiming harder for them than for us. We were just moving with the waves. They were bouncing across the whitecaps. The fifth shot from the flak gun hit the forward machine guns on the launch and the captain swung sideways to allow his other guns to fire. Polly and Harry took advantage of the beam on target and pumped three shots at the launch. One of their shells hit. Nature and the sea took over as a large roller hit the launch. It began to fill up with water and within a short space of time had capsized. I could not believe how easy it had been.

I saw that the Sunderland was much closer to us and was now flying obliquely across our bows. I saw why. A flight of three Messerschmitt 110s were coming towards us. These had no bombs but they each had four machine guns in the nose and they could tear us apart. The Sunderland was coming to our rescue. Known as the flying porcupine to the Germans it bristled with machine guns. It wisely flew higher than the three fighters.

I saw Poulson as he cranked up the flak gun. This target was aerial. The 110 was a very stable gun platform and the first one's guns tore into the stern. I was impressed that my two gunners held their ground. It would have been tempting to flee. I levelled my Thompson. They managed two shots at the approaching fighter but both missed. As it flew over me I managed to stitch a line of bullets into his belly. I doubted that I had hurt it but it gave me satisfaction. I watched it climb away as the second one attacked. The Sunderland's guns chattered and I saw them hit the port engine of the fighter which had just peeled off.

182

There was a crack and I looked to see the second 110 with smoke coming from its starboard engine. They had managed one hit. It had a brave pilot and he continued his attack. I finished off my magazine at the cockpit. It shattered and the 110 did not pull up but cracked the top of the mast, taking the ensign with it before plunging into the crest of a wave. The Sunderland came lower to attack the last fighter. It came in hard and low. Gowland and Poulson fired shell after shell. One hit the wing but it continued to come. Then I heard Harry shout and fall to the side. Poulson kept on firing and he hit the nose with a shell. The front exploded with such force that both Poulson and I were thrown to the deck. I stood quickly and ran to the injured Lowe. The surviving fighter headed east, smoking. Harry had been hit in the left arm. He was bleeding heavily and he was unconscious. I took a length of cord from my pocket and tied a tourniquet high up on his arm.

"Polly, fetch a first aid kit and some water. See if you can find some Schnapps or something." He hurtled below decks to the Bergens. I turned Lowe's mouth to the side. Mum had told me that it was called the recovery position and stopped someone swallowing their tongue when they were unconscious.

Poulson returned and threw himself next to me. He handed me a half bottle of Schnapps while he tore open a gauze dressing. I poured the fiery liquid on the wound. There would be no infection. I used the first dressing to clean away the blood and then to press hard and stop the bleeding. Polly had a second one ready. The wound was now just seeping blood; the tourniquet was working. He sprinkled the antiseptic powder on the wound and then he applied the gauze dressing. He started to fasten a bandage around it. We then bent his arm and I loosened the tourniquet briefly before tightening it again.

I was aware of a light flashing. I looked up and saw that the Sunderland was signalling. I waved as I read the message. "The Atherstone is on the way. I hope she hurries. I am no doctor."

"You did all right, Sarge. You can tend to me anytime."

"Give him some water. Hold his nose to make him swallow if you have to."

183

I was reluctant to move. I was afraid that if I did the wound would bleed again. Every five minutes I released and then tightened the tourniquet. Polly was putting the top back on the canteen and he pointed, "Eh up, Navy's here." I glanced to the north and saw the destroyer ploughing through the sea.

We did not have long to wait. The Sunderland continued to be our guardian angel while the destroyer slowed down. As the captain stopped his ship he reversed his engines to bring his vessel alongside ours. Four of the crew leapt down to the deck and fastened us to the destroyer with two ropes. Once secure they were thrown a stretcher. The Petty Officer hurried over with an SBA. He smiled at me. "It's all right now Sergeant. We have a professional." They gently lifted the wounded Gowland on to the stretcher and secured him. With four sailors lifting and the four on our deck helping they soon hauled him up.

"Poulson, go and get our gear."

While he went the Petty Officer offered me a cigarette. I shook my head. "You lads are a sight for sore eyes."

"Aye and you are lucky too. We had just spent two days down at St. Nazaire covering the launches and looking for survivors like you. We were almost at Falmouth when we got your radio message." I saw a scrambling net thrown over the side of the destroyer as Poulson reappeared. "Right lads you get aboard our ship. We will look after yours. There is a dixie of stoker's cocoa waiting for you. I reckon you deserve it."

It was a struggle to get up the net. I suddenly felt exhausted. My arms and legs felt like rubber. The lack of sleep over the last three days had finally caught up with me. You can only survive for so long on adrenalin. Willing hands hauled us over the side. We were patted on the back. An officer's voice snapped, "Give them some room you chaps." They all disappeared and a young sub-lieutenant stood there. "Sub Lieutenant Garvey, welcome aboard. The Captain told me to take you to the Petty's Officer's mess. He will join you there when the tow is attached. Follow me."

As we went down I said, "Were there many other survivors?"

184

He shook his head. "No, I am afraid not. Only a couple of hundred made it from the town. The captain reckons that over three hundred and seventy were either killed, captured, or are on the run in France but the gates were destroyed. It was a great success."

As we followed him into the bowels of the ship I thought that would be cold comfort to the men who would be prisoners until the end of the war. Number 2 Commando had largely ceased to exist in a single night. We could build more tanks and aeroplanes but commandos were harder to train.

We were left alone with the rum infused cocoa. It tasted good but what I really needed was sleep. Polly's eyes were red rimmed and his face covered in salt. I daresay mine looked the same. He smiled weakly. "Well, Sarge, it is never dull."

"No, that it isn't."

"Do you reckon Harry will be alright? I mean Daddy was invalided out but he was old. Harry would be mortified if he couldn't carry on."

"They have doctors aboard these ships. He has a better chance here. But I don't think he will be ready for active service any time soon."

"Surely we will have to have some leave and a bit of a rest."

"From what the subbie said most of Number 2 Commando has gone west. We are the ones left to go behind enemy lines. But we will probably get a few days leave." I drank some of my cocoa. I could feel my eyes closing, "I wonder how many of the lads got out."

"Well we know Jack Johnson didn't."

I felt us moving and the door to the mess opened. "Lieutenant Commander Cartwright." I began to rise, "No, sergeant, sit down. Let me shake your hand. What you have done is quite remarkable. You escaped from occupied France, captured an E-Boat and fought off attacks from the air and sea with three men. What do they feed you Commandos on? Steel?"

I smiled, "They train us hard sir. Do you know if any of the other lads from our Troop escaped?"

185

"Well I know that your commanding officer did because it was he who came up with that question. I thought it was a rum one myself but it worked. We worried it might be a German trap to sink us. We had been stooging around for a few days. Brass thought they might have captured you and made you talk. Your Major took umbrage at that and said you were the last person who would give that kind of Intel away. Anyway, you gave the right answer and here we are. "You lads get your heads down. Your Oppo is doing well and we should be in Falmouth in six or seven hours." He pointed to the hammocks. "Use any of the hammocks. The petty officers won't mind."

"Thank you, sir. I reckon we will."

I had used a hammock before. Once you were in one it was almost impossible not to sleep and we were exhausted. We slept.

Part 3

Behind Enemy Lines

Chapter 16

The sub lieutenant who had greeted us when we boarded us woke us. "Sergeant, we are approaching Falmouth. The Captain thought you might want to freshen up."

I frowned, "Freshen up?"

"There are newspaper journalists there. Apparently, the Ministry thought this was good publicity. You know; brave commandos escape Germans, steal a boat and all that."

I sighed, "Right, sir. How is Private Lowe?"

"Awake and the doc has given him the all clear to go ashore. There is an ambulance waiting."

We dutifully washed up. There was no way I was going to shave but I was filthy. I confess I felt better when I was cleaner. We made our way onto the deck. I saw, from the darkening sky, that it was getting on for dusk. I could see a crowd gathered. There were some uniforms but they looked to be mainly civilians.

I sighed and Poulson said, "What's up Sarge? It will be great to have my picture in the paper. Me mam will be dead proud."

"I know but I could do without the fuss. I just want to get back to Mrs Bailey's and have a nice hot bath and some of her corned beef hash."

"But we are heroes!"

Shaking my head, I said, "Don't go down that road. We are not heroes. We just do our job and we do it well but we are not glory hunters. It was luck that led us to the boat. That and a brave old lady. She is more heroic than either of us."

A barrage of flashlights went off as the captain edged us closer to the wall. Poulson had Lowe's Bergen over his back. We looked after our equipment. I carried Lowe's Thompson. We did not look like soldiers, we looked like pirates. Two orderlies came up on deck and stood next to us carrying Harry.

"How is it going Harry?"

"Not so bad. I can't feel the arm yet but the doc says I will. He reckons I won't lose it." He looked at me nervously, "I will still be a commando won't I, Sarge?"

"If I have anything to do with it you will."

The Bosun came to stand next to us as the gangplank was lowered. He winked, "Give you pongos a good send-off eh? We reckon you deserve it!" He piped us from the ship and his assistants saluted. It was a nice touch.

The Sick Bay Attendant said, "After you two, Sarge. It is easier that way."

We walked down the gangplank to cheers. I could barely see anything because of the flashes and I understood why the SBA had let us go first. Our bodies deflected the lights and they had an easier job getting the stretcher down the gangplank. There was an Intelligence officer waiting for us standing next to Sergeant Major Dean. The officer saluted, "Well done Sergeant Harsker!" he leaned in and said quietly, "Don't say anything to the press that is why I am here. You just smile and look tough."

Sergeant Major Dean said quietly, "He is tough and that is why he is here!"

Only the officer heard and he flashed an irritated look at Reg who just smiled back at him. There was a barrage of questions which the officer deftly handled. He made it sound as though we had planned it all. He kept patting me on the back as though I was a collie dog! When they were satisfied he turned to me. They headed back to their cars. No doubt the photographs would be in newspapers over the next few days and the newsreel would be in the cinema. "We will need you for a debrief tomorrow at nine a.m."

188

"Yes sir." There would be no leave then. We waved goodbye to Harry Gowland as he was whisked away in the ambulance.

Reg Dean said, "Well done, son. We are all as proud as punch of you. We lost a few good lads over there but your survival has cheered us all up."

Just then an umbrella appeared between us, "When are you going to let these two lads get home! Haven't they been through enough?"

It was Mrs Bailey. Reg Dean looked bemused. As Sergeant Major he was not used to being spoken to like that. "Sergeant Major Dean this is our landlady, Mrs Bailey." I smiled at her. "Quite right too, Mrs Bailey. Is that all, Sergeant Major?"

I winked and he grinned. "Off you go lads and my apologies, dear lady!"

"Don't you dear lady me!" Reg beat a hasty retreat. She threw her arms around the two of us. "My poor boys and poor Harry too! How is he?"

Polly grinned, still happy about the way she had dealt with Reg Dean. "He's tough is Harry. He'll survive."

"When the other boys came back and told me how you had been left behind I was proper upset and poor Corporal Curtis is still in the hospital." She stepped back, "And look at you! You need a good bath and a good meal." She linked us and marched us towards her house. The onlookers parted like the Red Sea in the face of such a formidable lady.

As soon as we entered the house the others descended upon us. We were bombarded with questions. Mrs Bailey shooed them away, "When they have had a bath and some food then you can question them. Be off with you!"

She was right. We did feel immeasurably better after the bath and complete after the meal. We sat in the residents' lounge and we told them all. It was good for us to discover what had happened after they had left the beach. Bill Leslie's launch had been one of the lucky ones. The other Hunt class destroyer, 'Tynedale', had escorted them all back to Falmouth. They had been like chicks with a mother hen. Captain Marsden and Major Foster had both survived but had been wounded. It

189

had been a costly raid. Horace Maguire was also wounded but Lucky Gordy Barker had emerged, like me, unscathed.

One thing was certain; there would be little chance of us engaging in any large-scale attack in the near future. We would need at least a month to bring the wounded back to good health and train new recruits. We seemed to take three steps forward and two back. My bed felt comfortable, warm and cosy but I spared a thought for Jack Johnson and the others who would now be prisoners in Germany. I was the really lucky one and I knew it.

Despite my exhaustion the previous day my body could not rest too long and I awoke early. Mrs Bailey had washed and pressed my spare uniform. It felt good to be in clean clothes once more. Mrs Bailey was making the pot of tea ready for the boys. She silently poured me a cup at the table. Breakfasts were not the cornucopia of plenty that they had been before the war. You ate what was available. On that first morning back it was toast and margarine. The only luxury was the small jar of pre-war bramble jam which Mrs Bailey brought out for me. She shook her head sadly, "There won't be enough for the other lads, Sergeant but you deserve a treat. Private Poulson told me what you did. It is no wonder you get medals."

I did not like attention and I deflected it, "I'll tell you what, Mrs Bailey when the berries are on the bushes in September me and the lads will pick some. You can make a whole batch of it."

She shook her head, "A kind thought but we can't get the sugar."

As I ate the thin smear of jam on the bread I was suddenly aware of the shortages. The war was hitting not just us but all of the civilians. That Focke Wolf we had seen had been looking for more than us. It was spotting the convoys for the wolf packs to sink. We were three years into the war and there was little sign that we were either hitting or hurting Herr Hitler. St. Nazaire had made his eyes water, no more. She waved me off at the door. "I will make a special tea for you and the lads. I have enough meat rations for a nice piece of shin. I shall stew it all day with the carrots and the onions left from the winter store. I have some early tatties I can pick."

"I am looking forward to it." My sentiments were genuine; I was already salivating at the thought of a home-made stew.

I headed up the hill as soon as I had finished. I had two Bergens and two Thompsons to carry. I had to fight the urge to dive into the bushes each time I heard a vehicle. Here I was safe. This was England. When I passed the boarded-up beach huts I thought of the old French lady. Would she be having a picnic by the hut again? I suspected she would have raised a glass to us when we stole the E-Boat. It would give hope to those in France that Jerry was not getting it all his own way.

Sergeant Major Dean gave me a strange look as I entered the Headquarters building. He was alone. The clerks had not yet arrived. "Morning, Tom. Have a seat. I have just brewed up a pot of tea. It should have stood long enough by now."

I knew what that meant; the spoon would stand up by itself. He brought me a mug. It was heavily laden with sugar. He had a sweet tooth and, unlike Mrs Bailey, appeared to have no problems acquiring the white gold.

"Your landlady is a feisty lady."

"Mrs Bailey? She has a heart of gold. She lost her husband as a result of the Great War and they had no kids. I think she sees me and the lads as her surrogate children. I don't know what she will do when the war is over. I think she will find it hard to go back to being just a landlady."

"How old will she be? She looks young enough to still have children."

I shook my head, "I am not certain but she said she was in her teens when her husband died and he died in the last year of the war. Probably early forties."

"She is still young enough then. In our town, there were women in their fifties still popping sprogs." I sipped my tea. It was as strong as I had expected. He nodded towards the clerk's desk next to him. "Intelligence will be here to debrief you and Poulson later on this morning. You had best start your report off. I think that the brass are keen to use these sorts of experiences for training purposes. Up to now

191

you and the other two lads are the only ones who escaped the bag. The French Resistance has reported commandos being captured hundreds of miles away. Some almost made it to Spain."

I nodded and began to write. As I wrote I said, without lifting my head, "One thing is maps, Sergeant Major. Because we went in early and needed maps we were able to find our way out again. If we hadn't had them then we would still be wandering around the Marais."

"Right. Put that down then."

"And Gowland; I discovered he knew engines. If he hadn't been able to start that E-Boat we would be stuck there yet."

"Aye but we can't put a mechanic in every section."

"I suspect you don't have to. My Dad was good with engines. He liked to tinker. You can bet your bottom dollar there will be others like that. You need to get the sergeants talking to their men and find out what they are good at. Poor Reg Smyth was a poacher. That was a hell of a skill. If he had survived who knows when that might have come in handy. They should know their men."

"You know yours."

I nodded, "They are good lads and I am lucky but aye, I know my men. I know their strengths and their weaknesses; horses for courses."

I knew, as I scribbled away, that I had set a train of thought away in the Sergeant Major's head. Despite his gruff exterior he was a thoughtful man. It took a long time to write the report. The clerks appeared and set about their daily chores. I had almost finished when Gordy Barker came in. "The wanderer returns!"

I looked up and saw Gordy's grinning face; the inevitable cigarette hanging precariously from his bottom lip.

"Let Sergeant Harsker finish his report before you start bending his ear, Barker!"

"Sorry Sarn't Major. Is there a brew on?"

"Help yourself."

It did not take me long to finish and I handed the report to Reg. "You two cut along now. Don't go far Harsker, the Major will need you."

"Right, Sarn't Major."

Gordy lit another cigarette as we left the building and headed towards the training ground. "How are things here then, Gordy?"

"A bit of a mish mash Tom. We just have two officers left now and you and I are the only sergeants. We can't function as a Troop. The Captain said we would have two new lieutenants by the end of the week but that will just mean more work for us as we will have to show them the ropes."

"What about Sergeants? Have you any who could be promoted?"

"Norm Thomas is a good lad. He is lance corporal at the moment. He handled himself well in St. Nazaire; he didn't panic. The other good lads were in Jack Johnson's section and none of them made it back. What about your lads?"

"Ken is a definite. It just depends on his wounds. Paul Poulson is ready for promotion but I would prefer him to be a Corporal and learn the ropes that way. I think it helps you become a better sergeant. You are the grease which smooths out the bumps."

"You are right there." He gestured over his shoulder, towards the sea. "How the hell did you manage to sail that bloody big E-Boat back?"

"Harry Gowland is a damned good mechanic. If I were you I would find out what skills you men have got. His certainly came in handy."

We had reached the training ground and I saw his section, what remained of it, lined up and waiting for him to take them on a run.

My section had not wasted their time since their return and I found them at the shooting range firing their Colts. We were a smaller unit now. There were just six remaining. Poulson was the most experienced of those who remained and he had organised them. "I thought we could do with some practice Sarge. The Colt was the most useful weapon last time out."

"Good thinking, carry on."

Scouse Fletcher asked, "Any chance of some leave, Sarge?"

"I daresay there will but we will have to see the Major first. He will be along later."

193

In the event neither the Major nor the Captain returned from Intelligence and I was spared an interrogation by those who planned but never had to perform. At least when my Dad gave advice to pilots it was based upon his experiences. I called in to see Reg before I left. "In case you are asking for recommendations, Sergeant Major, I was going to suggest Ken Curtis for Sergeant and Poulson and Gowland for Corporal."

He nodded, "What about Poulson as Lance Sergeant? Do you think he is ready?"

"I like to give lads the chance to learn the ropes first but he could handle it. He organised my lads today."

"I'll tell the Major tomorrow. If he gets back tomorrow, that is."

When I returned to Mrs Bailey's I spent some time writing letters. I wrote a short one to mum. It was more to put her mind at rest and a longer one to Dad. I left out any direct references to the raid but he would be able to read between the lines. The I wrote a couple to the mothers of my dead commandos. They were harder and took much longer. I owed it to the dead men to tell their loved ones what they had done. After supper I wandered, alone, to the pub. There were none of the lads in there but I had a quiet pint. I like to think that the ones who didn't make it back were there in spirit. I could almost see their faces. I had a second pint for them and then headed back to the digs. I felt better; I don't know why but I did.

The next morning, we were playing our adult game of hide and seek when the Captain found us. "Good to see you Tom. We were worried that we had lost you."

"Thank you, sir, but I had a bit of luck and two good commandos with me."

He nodded, "Poulson, could you take charge here?"

"Yes sir, er, " he added cheekily, "any chance of some leave?"

Captain Marsden laughed and shook his head, "Where is the innocent, keen, young lad we first met eh Sergeant Harsker? He is an old hand now. Sergeant Harsker can ask the Major for you but I dare say a short furlough may be in order."

194

As we walked back to the office I said, "He didn't mean anything, sir. He is a good lad."

"I know he is. If it was up to me you would all have had leave as soon as you landed. That was a hell of an operation we pulled off." When we neared the office, I saw a staff car and a Naval rating. "Oh, by the way Tom, just a warning. There are senior brass about. Very senior brass."

He knocked on the Major's door. "Come."

When I entered I saw a flag lieutenant and an Admiral. The Major said, "This is Sergeant Tom Harsker, Admiral. The one you have been keen to meet."

Admiral Lord Louis Mountbatten had been a destroyer captain who had lost a ship at Crete. He was now in overall command of Combined Operations. I never expected to actually meet him. He was related to the King and Queen!

He stood and held out his hand, "I am damned proud to shake your hand young man. You have done great things. I was speaking to your father about you yesterday. He is damned proud too."

"Thank you, sir."

"Take a seat. Hugo, give the sergeant your chair. I want to pick your brains." He opened a gold cigarette case, "Smoke?"

"No thank you, sir."

He nodded, "I forgot, your father told me." He lit one and then said, "I shall come straight to the point. I like what you have been doing. More than that I want it to be a model we use elsewhere. You seem to handle yourself well behind enemy lines. In fact, my people tell me that you have survived longer behind enemy lines than anyone else." He pointed at a map of France which was on the wall with his cigarette. "And that began on the retreat to Dunkirk. Now I have my own ideas about that. I think your skill with languages added to your natural skills as a commando make you the perfect material for what we have in mind." He paused and stubbed out the cigarette. "Well?"

I was confused, "I am not certain what you are asking, sir. Do you want me to be an agent behind enemy lines?"

195

He laughed, "Good God no! We have SOE cloak and dagger merchants for that sort of thing. No, I want you to lead a small team to perform raids behind the enemy lines."

"But that is what we all do in the commandos."

"True but you will be operating directly under me. Major Foster here will pass my instructions on to you. This is not the large-scale raids like St. Nazaire or the Lofoten Islands. This is smaller, secret raids right under Jerry's nose." He stubbed a cigarette out and leaned forward. "The thing is this wouldn't have worked had you not captured that E-Boat. That was a brilliant move, by the way. We are having her repaired and crewed by handpicked men from the Royal Navy. The same sort of chaps you have been sailing with. She will be able to take you in easier and more safely and bring you out. We have a young Lieutenant for her and he speaks perfect German. We want you to be ghosts behind enemy lines. We want you to appear and disappear at will. What do you say?"

"I think it is a good idea, Admiral, but I think you overestimate the abilities of this humble sergeant."

He smiled and nodded to the Major, "And that is where you are wrong Second Lieutenant Harsker."

Major Foster came over, shook my hand and handed me my pips. "Well done, Tom. This was decided before you went to St. Nazaire. But the Admiral's new role is perfect."

The Admiral continued. "You will pick your own section. I think that eight would be the optimum number to operate behind the lines. You have shown us the benefit of using a small closely-knit unit." I nodded. I already knew who the men were. "Now choose your men and give them a seven-day furlough. You and Major Foster will come with me to London. I want you to see the set up there and it will be easier to get your uniform sorted out. Then back to Falmouth. You, I am afraid, will get no leave. You will meet Lieutenant Jorgenson there. He is the captain of the E-boat and when your men return we will have a working up exercise. I want you ready to go back to France as soon as possible. We have a mission for you already. The details are still being worked out but you have shown that you are what we need in the Commandos.

You think on your feet and that is what we need." He smiled, "I think your Sergeant Major has more details for you. We leave in an hour."

I discovered that Lord Louis was always this way. He spoke calmly and pleasantly but grass did not grow beneath his feet. Reg Dean had the biggest smile I have ever seen. "Well done, Lieutenant Harsker! Would you allow me to shake you by the hand?" His handshake showed that his sentiments were genuine. "It is good to see a good NCO get promoted. " He rubbed his hands. "Now then sir, I understand you will be picking your team?

"I believe so. I need eight men. I assume that means NCOs too."

He nodded. "The Major and I have already had a discussion. I know his thinking."

"You want some of my men for other sections."

"Bang on, sir. To be precise the major wants Ken Curtis. He is perfect sergeant material. We want him to take over Horace Maguire's section. His injury will keep him side-lined for a while."

I nodded, "Then I would want Paul Poulson as my Sergeant and Harry Gowland as either Corporal or Lance Sergeant." The Sergeant Major grinned. "Go ahead, Reg, tell me what you and the Major have come up with."

"Just as you said, sir, and George Lowe as your Corporal."

"That gives me three of my men. I have Hewitt, Groves, Fletcher, and Crowe. I am one short."

I think the Major said eight including you, sir. I might be wrong..."

"You are probably right. That makes sense. I confess it came as quite a shock to me. I had better go and tell them. I leave in an hour." I suddenly remembered Mrs Bailey. "I had better send a message to Mrs Bailey. She was making a nice stew for us."

"Don't worry sir. I will tell her. Are you still going to use the same billet?"

"The rank has changed, Sergeant Major, not the man."

He smiled, "Aye you are right there."

"I'll be off and thanks, Sergeant Major. I know that you put a good word in for me."

197

He shrugged, "I was just thinking of the Troop, sir and it is no more than you deserve."

The men were just heading for the canteen when I saw them. The nearby lecture hall was empty. "Poulson could you bring the men over here please I need to speak with them."

"Right Sarge."

I sat on the table at the front. "I have some little bits of news to give to you. Private Poulson, you are now Sergeant Poulson. Private Lowe you are now promoted to Corporal. When Harry is released from hospital he will be lance sergeant."

I was disappointed in their reaction. You would have thought they had been demoted.

"Did you not hear what I said? You are both promoted."

"Yes, Sarge but that means you must be moving off. We would rather be privates with you as the sergeant, Sarge."

Now I understood. "I am not leaving you. You do not get rid of me as easily as that. I have been promoted to Lieutenant."

Their reaction said it all. It was as though they had won the football pools. I held up my hands to quieten them. "I do not have a lot of time. I am going to London to be briefed but there is more. We are to be a special unit under the direct command of Major Foster. You cannot divulge to the other sections what we are about. We will be operating largely behind enemy lines. While I am away you need to improve your language skills, communication and demolition skills. However," I smiled, "Before then you all have a seven-day leave. Sergeant Major Dean has your travel warrants. I would make the most of it. I don't think we will get a second one any time soon."

"Thank you, Lieutenant Harsker!" They chorused it like children in a school. Then they saluted me. I had no hat and so I just stood to attention.

Paul Poulson hung back, "Thank you for this, sir. I hope I am ready for it. I will try not to let you down."

"After what we have been through that is impossible, Sergeant."

He grinned, "Me mam will be dead proud! I can't wait to tell her."

198

Chapter 17

The Sunderland was waiting for us in Falmouth. I wondered if it was the same one which had come to our aid. Probably. The Major and Lord Louis sat together and I sat next to Flag Lieutenant William Tree-Johnson. When we were airborne he asked, "What is it like? In action, I mean. I know you have the MM, I checked your records. What is it like knowing you could be shot at any time or captured?"

"I don't know." He gave me a queer look. "No, I am not being funny. You have no time to think and reflect you just react. Something happens and you try to do something so that the lads you lead don't die and the mission is successful. Then, when you are on your way home you wonder how in God's name you did what you did."

"I would love to take part in a raid."

"Show me your hands."

He held them out. "What have my hands got to do with it?"

"My hands were like that before I joined up in thirty-nine. Look at mine now. They are gnarly and tough as leather. They have sunk daggers into men's throats and they have clung from cliffs. I am afraid that you would need Commando training and that is rigorous. You would need so much time and then you would need the experience. It is not for everybody. I have seen men who I thought would be perfect material for commandos and they have not made it."

"I could do that."

"And then lead men who will have forgotten more than you know about fighting. The Germans we fight are not always noble and honourable. I have seen the results of the work of the Waffen SS. They are nasty bastards. Stay where you are; that is my advice."

"But I just help his lordship."

"And from what I have seen his lordship might just make the difference in this war. I like him."

"He is inspirational. He is related to the King don't you know?"

"I did."

We sat in silence and then he said, "Is it true your father won the VC and was a fighter ace in the Great War?"

"He is fairly inspirational himself, yes."

"God, what I would give to be a member of your family."

We did not land in London itself. There were too many barrage balloons but we landed instead, close to Essex where a car waited to whisk us into Central London. Lord Louis and Major Foster had spent a great deal of time talking close together. I wondered what this mission would entail. It seemed obvious to me that they were going over some of the details of the operation. As we headed into central London, a depressing sight these days as many beautiful buildings had been destroyed and everything appeared wrapped up like some sort of parcel, Lord Louis said, "Would you care to stay with me in my house, Lieutenant Harsker?"

"I believe you said my father was in town?"

"Yes, he is."

"Then I shall stay with him. I haven't seen him since Christmas."

"Of course, how remiss of me. I should have realised. Well if you give the driver the address he will take you there when he has dropped us off and pick you up tomorrow at nine. I fear it will be your busy day. I am afraid you won't have the time to have a uniform made tomorrow; still the day after should be fine."

I knew I should have telephoned my father but I could gain entry by using the spare key. Even without that I was certain that, as a commando, I would be able to break in. As it turned out I did not need to do either. I rang the doorbell and he answered. He did not seem surprised to see me. "Ah Tom. Good to see you. The Admiral said he was going to see you. I thought you might drop in."

I dropped my Bergen in the hall. "Did he give you the news then?"

"News? I am not certain. He said he had a role for you, sounded all very hush hush."

"I have been promoted. I am a second lieutenant and I have my own unit."

It was a lovely moment for he was genuinely pleased. He hugged me. "Then tonight we celebrate and tomorrow I shall take you to my tailors and have you a uniform made."

"Sorry, Dad. Tomorrow I have meetings all day with the Admiral. Perhaps the day after?"

He nodded, "Good. Then we shall dine at my club. It is the only place in London these days where you can get a decent meal and the cellar is still excellent."

He was right and both the meal and the wine were excellent. However, I still regretted not enjoying Mrs Bailey's stew. I hoped that Sergeant Major Dean had made my apologies. Once back in the flat Dad opened a good port and decanted it. "I had been saving this for a special occasion. This seems like one!"

Now that we were alone I told him of the St. Nazaire raid and the E-Boat. I saw him frown when I mentioned the 110s. "You were bloody lucky there, Tom. They are bloody useless against a Spit or a Hurricane but they are lethal against ground targets."

"There wasn't a great deal we could have done. You taught me never to give up but I thought we were dead in the water."

He nodded, "Never tell your mother I said that!"

I laughed, "Of course not! She is bad enough as it is."

"Be fair to her. It is harder sitting at home and worrying than being out there and enduring the danger."

"You are right."

"So, what does Lord Louis have in mind for you?"

"We are going to use the E-boat to land us behind lines and create mayhem although the first mission, next month, appears to be something bigger than that. I shall find out tomorrow."

He nodded, "Are you happy with your team?"

"The commandos I know. They are my section and I picked them all. Four of them are young and new but they are good lads. The navy boys are an unknown quantity but I have yet to be let down by the Jacks."

"We will be involved too."

201

"So, you knew about this?"

"No, Tom, Lord Louis wants more cooperation from the RAF and Coastal Command. I have been asked to expedite it. Some of the senior RAF officers are a bit too protective about their precious aeroplanes. They don't see we are all part of the same team. We have some good night fighters these days and we shall use those to provide air cover. I am pleased you told me what you did. I shall be able to give the pilots a clearer picture of what they have to do."

"Then you will be directly involved?"

"No, I shall just set it up and brief them. Then it is back to North Africa for me. We are planning a push across the desert. Now that the Yanks are joining us we can go on the offensive a little more."

We talked until half the decanter was gone and I must have fallen asleep. When I awoke, at four o'clock, I was undressed on the sofa with a blanket over me.

Before I left the next morning, Dad gave me a key. "I might not be in when you return but we shall have dinner and tomorrow I will find some time to take you to my tailors."

The room in the Ministry had high security. Apart from the Admiral, his aide and the Major, there were four senior army officers and Lord Lovat. He looked out of place. He was more like a country gentleman and the formal surroundings seemed not to fit him.

"Gentlemen this is Lieutenant Harsker. He is vital to the plan I am putting in place. I will not insult you by swearing you to secrecy. All of you have been appointed by me. If I can't trust you... well." He stood and went to a map. He took a pointer. "This is Europe. Now that our cousins are joining us we can think about invading. I want a plan from you gentleman. By autumn I want to have landed an invasion force in Europe. We will not stay but I want us to go in and capture a port. The operation will be a way for us to learn what we can and can't do." I think I was the only one who was surprised. He continued. "Lord Lovat and Major Foster have already given me their ideas. I want some from you." He pointed to me. This young man will land with his men at the site we

202

choose and reconnoitre the ground. This needs more than aerial photographs. This needs boots on the ground."

Lord Lovat's Scottish burr sounded as anachronistic as Lord Lovat himself as he said, "Rubber soled shoes, my lord."

"What?"

"My chaps don't wear boots. Too noisy. Rubber soled shoes!"

He laughed, "Well whatever the footwear Lieutenant Harsker will be our eyes on the target."

"How about Boulogne? It is a short hop over the Channel and our guns in Dover could support the attack."

"As Lieutenant Harsker can tell you that part of the coast bristles with heavy guns and the Germans are busy fortifying it. They see that as their most vulnerable coast."

Another general nodded. "Then we either think of north of Boulogne or south." The Admiral nodded. "North is not feasible. The ports are not on the coast. We need a port which sits right there on the coastline."

The first general said, "Then it has to be Dieppe."

I saw Major Foster and Lord Lovat exchange a smile and the Admiral said, "Exactly what the commandos said. Good. Then you gentlemen can come up with the plan. You, Lieutenant Harsker have your target. Major Foster will take you to operations so that you get a picture of what we do here at this end. The code name for this operation is Operation Rutter. We will work out more of the details."

Major Foster said, as he closed the door, "Sorry I couldn't give you a heads up on all this, Tom. I suggested you when Lord Louis was appointed but he is a careful man and he had you checked out thoroughly. Naturally you passed with flying colours."

He led me down to the basement. It was festooned with radios and maps. WAAFs and WRENs occupied the desks and soldiers manned the radios. On the wall were huge maps and there was a table which also had a map of the coast of France and the Low Countries. They largely ignored me. I was a lowly sergeant and I daresay much higher ranks normally visited.

"Here they monitor the radio traffic and pass messages sent by you or the radio operator in the E-Boat. For our purposes that is one and the same."

"But we don't use radios."

"You will now. You will have to have two of your lads trained as signallers and radio operators. As you have demonstrated, sometimes it is impossible to make a rendezvous. Now you can tell us. One of these radio operators and one of the female service personnel will be allocated to your team. One of them will always be available to speak with you. They will be on duty for as long as you are in France or the Low Countries or wherever. They will get to know you. This is important, Tom, we don't want you to be captured and used. They will get to know you. They will be as much part of the team as the crew of the E-Boat. I want nuances in your words to be picked up. That way, heaven forbid, if you are captured then you can let us know without telling us."

We spent an hour talking to them. We spent a great deal of time looking at the maps and discussing how we would operate and what we would need. It took a long time. Major Foster finally allowed me to return to my father's flat. I had two days before I had to return to meet with the Major, have my final briefing and then head back to Falmouth.

I had with me a notebook filled with everything I had learned. I decided to spend the afternoon coming up with a training regimen for my new section. I now had a better idea of what was needed. I felt like a schoolboy preparing for an exam as I surrounded myself with pencils and paper. With a small team, we would have to become specialists in certain areas.

I knew, from Major Foster, that I would need two signallers. Ken had been my signaller. We could all read Morse, of course, and use a map but the two men whom I elected to have trained would need more than that. Hewitt would be by medic. He was an easy choice. I allocated him his role. Scouse Fletcher suddenly came to mind as a signaller. His accent would make it difficult for a German to understand and to copy. The team in Whitehall would soon learn the inflections of his accent. He would be my first choice. As he got on well with the other northerner,

Alan Crowe from Manchester, he could be my second. George Lowe was a natural with explosives. He would be the demolition expert and Harry Gowland had already shown great skills with vehicles.

The team sorted I turned my attention to the training. We would not have long for this first mission; that much was obvious. I deduced that we would be around the Dieppe area, I made a note to get as many maps of the area as I could. The more I jotted down the more questions I had for the Admiral and his staff. Would we involve the resistance? Would we still be based in Falmouth? If we were using a German boat should we use German weapons?

I heard the key in the door as Dad returned. He looked drawn. He gave me a tired smile, "The sun is over the yard arm somewhere son! How about a couple of whiskies?"

I put my doodlings away and poured us a couple of glasses of the amber nectar. "Tough day Dad?"

"We had some heavy losses the other day. We lost some fine pilots. I thought the older I got the easier it would become but I was wrong."

I nodded, "I know. We lost some good lads on this last raid. When we all go out we assume that we will all come back. I know it is ridiculous but there it is."

He nodded, "You know what we forgot to do last night, old son? Telephone your mum. She will be miffed if she hears of your promotion from someone else. Let's telephone her now and then pop out for some dinner at my club again."

He was right of course. Mum was delighted with the news. She had always wanted me to be an officer. I don't think it was snobbery but she knew, from the Great War, that some of the officers had not been made of the right stuff. She was convinced that I was. When I had given her the news I handed the telephone to Dad and went to wash and shave. As I brushed down my battle dress I realised that there had been a time I had been proud of the sergeant's stripes now I was desperate for my new uniform. Would this be the last night that I wore my old one?

Dad had me up early. We were at the tailors in Saville Row by nine. He introduced me to Maurice, the tailor, and told him to put the uniforms on his bill. "I'll have to leave you now. See you for dinner eh?"

Maurice was a fussy little man but he knew his business. Everything was recorded and written on a fresh page in a well-worn ledger. I wondered how long I would be there. However, once he had measured me he became all efficiency. "I have no Commando flashes, Lieutenant Harsker. I am afraid I will have to take them from this battle dress. That means I can only do one uniform today."

"I have a spare. I will go and fetch it eh?"

"Oh no sir. There's no need." He took some scissors and deftly began to remove the flashes. "If you pop back later this afternoon I should have one uniform ready. You could bring the flashes with you then. When would you require the rest of your uniforms?"

I have to leave London, probably tomorrow."

He sighed, "Everything is in a rush these days. Still there is a war on. I am afraid that I can only get one more battle dress ready for tomorrow. The rest will take a week. I have to get the material."

"That is not a problem. The battle dresses will be fine. You can send the others to my father."

That was my one day of leave. I spent the morning visiting the sights of London. Before the war it would have been to wonder at them. Now it was to view them in case it was the last time. I wondered how many more fine buildings would be destroyed by German bombers. I had lunch in a small pub just down from Trafalgar Square and close to Horse Guards. The fresh marks where my flashes had been removed attracted some attention. However, the bar was filled with khaki and red collars. I was soon ignored. After lunch, I returned to the flat to pick up my second flashes; I removed these although it took me longer than Maurice.

Even though I arrived back early Maurice had finished. After I had changed I was more than happy to leave but the tailor tutted, "Not yet, sir. There may be a war on but you are still a gentleman and should dress appropriately." When he was satisfied he stood back. "There sir.

Perfect. Now if you require any more uniforms; tropical gear, mess uniforms and so on then just drop me a line. We have all your details now."

"Thank you, this will be fine."

As I donned my beret he frowned. "We have spare caps sir."

"This is what commandos wear, Maurice, thanks anyway."

The Major and I were not afforded the luxury of a flight back to Falmouth. We took a train. However, the Admiral wangled us First Class travel warrants and we had a compartment to ourselves. We caught the only train of the day. It was the 10.30. With just one change it would take just over seven and a quarter hours. There was a restaurant car on the train. As we pulled out of Paddington Major Foster said, "This is the Cornish Riviera Limited. I used it on a few holidays before the war. Happier times."

The compartment allowed us to talk freely. I had had all my questions answered and more. We had two weeks to get ready for a mission to Dieppe. By the time my men returned from leave that left us with just ten days or so. We had much to do. The tides and the phases of the moon meant that we would be landing in the last week of May. We would be dropped close to Dieppe and picked up two days later. Our task was to identify the defences around the port.

As we watched England race by I asked Major Foster about the rest of the Troop. "Will you be part of this raid in force, sir?"

"At the moment, no but because of my involvement in the planning we will be a strategic reserve. I am afraid the Troop's time in Falmouth is over. We will be moving back to Newhaven. Part of our job will be to help train the Canadians who will be going in. They are keen to do their bit, don't you know."

I had already learned that we would be staying at Falmouth. The narrow fiord like estuary was perfect for hiding the E-boat. The other one I had seen had been spirited away to the east coast where it, too, was engaged in clandestine activities. Faster than any of the British launches we could still be in France relatively quickly. I was sad that people like Daddy and Reg would be moved many miles east. Such was war. There

207

was a long stop at Plymouth where we had to change engines. The Major explained that the bridge at Saltash could not take the weight of the King class engine. We pulled in four minutes early at a quarter to six. It was a short walk to my digs.

When I entered the digs Mrs Bailey burst into tears, "A lieutenant! Oh, you do look smart. I am so proud!"

I smiled, "I am sorry that I had to leave so suddenly but..."

"I know, the Sergeant Major told me. Would you like a bit of supper?"

"No thank you Mrs Bailey, I ate on the train." As I headed to my room I wondered what the captain of the E-boat was like. His name sounded Norwegian. I knew that there were many pilots in the RAF from the conquered countries to the east but I had not found many Norwegians. Major Foster told me that there was a couple of sections of Norwegian commandos but they were based in Scotland.

Before I retired I cleaned all of my weapons. They would now be even more important. When I had been speaking with my father he had told me of something called a Maxim Silencer. It was a device to muffle the sound of a bullet. I had become quite animated when he had told me. Although neither of us had seen one he had described it in detail. I had decided to approach Daddy Grant and the armourer as soon as I could. Such a device might be invaluable. Especially if we were to spend long periods behind enemy lines.

I was the only one in the house and Mrs Bailey made me a delicious cooked breakfast. I had not used many of my ration coupons and I gave them to Mrs Bailey. One advantage of being away from England for long periods meant that we had more coupons left for the time we were at home. We ate better than most families.

I was so keen to get to the camp that I was there by seven. Reg Dean snapped to attention when I walked in.

"It is still just me, Sarn't Major."

"You are now an officer, sir!"

I shook my head, "Well this officer still likes your tea so, with your permission, I will have a mug."

"Help yourself sir. You look smart in that uniform. It looks tailored."

"It is."

He nodded approvingly, "Class always shows, sir."

I wondered if he knew of the move to Newhaven. It was still a month away but it would be a headache for Reg and his staff. He stood to reach for a file and I saw him wince. "Everything all right, Reg?"

"Just my leg, sir. The wound I received on one of the raids never quite healed." I looked at him and he nodded, "Yes sir, the doc reckons my days of derring do are over." He tapped the desk. Looks like I will be stuck behind one of these." He shook his head, "It isn't fair is it, sir?"

"You have done your bit Reg. Let us younger lads take the strain. You can impart your wisdom to them. That is worth more." He nodded. "I am going to see the Quarter Master but there are some things I need you to get hold of for me; if you can."

"Right sir."

"And this is on the QT."

"Of course, sir." He looked offended.

"Sorry, Reg, but at Whitehall they see spies and agents everywhere. I need maps, as many as you can get, of the coastline from Boulogne down to Bordeaux."

"What scale, sir?"

"As small as you can get."

"Right sir. Leave it with me." He rubbed his hands. "It will make a change from arranging cookhouse rotas!"

Daddy was also proud of my promotion. He had heard of our new role but not the details. I took out my Colt. "I need a silencer for this. If it works then I want it for my men too."

"I have heard of them but I am not certain where we get one from. Let's go and see Harry the Gun and ask him." He turned to his Corporal, "Jack, take over eh?"

Harry the Gun was the Sergeant Armourer. Like Daddy he had been a Sergeant in the commandos and, like Daddy, had been wounded in a raid in France. He knew his job and, more importantly, he knew how

209

we did our job. After we had explained he said, "I have heard of them and seen them. You know, sir, that they affect the range of the gun."

"I had worked that out Sergeant but if we have to use them it will be in the dark and the range will be short anyway. We just need silence."

"It will never be totally silent but leave it with me and I will see what I can make. When do you want them sir?"

"As soon as you can make one but by the middle of May would be handy."

We left him to it. Daddy was a wise old bird. He lit his pipe as we walked back from the range and the armourer's workshop. "You are away again soon then eh, sir?"

"It looks like it."

"Anything special you need sir?"

"Any chance of oilskins? We will be at sea a fair bit."

"I'll get that sorted for you."

By the time I had returned to the office the Major was there. "Right Tom, let's go down and meet Lieutenant Jorgenson and his crew."

We now had a car for Major Foster's use. I suspect Admiral Mountbatten had arranged that. He seemed like a chap to get things done. We did not head to Falmouth but north towards the Carrick Roads and Restronguet Creek. There, close to the Carnon River, we saw the E-Boat. It was tied up to a small, recently made jetty. We parked the car beneath the trees and headed for it. I saw that they had rigged camouflage nets above it so that it was hidden from aeroplanes. The crew were busy working. I could see some stripping and cleaning the guns while three men were in the water, at the stern, attending to some problem or other. The damage I had seen when we left her had been repaired and she looked, to all intents and purposes like a ship of the German Navy.

The sailor who was sitting cross legged working on a magazine for the 20mm saw us and jumped to his feet. He had a huge grin on his face. He held out his hand, "Ah you must be Major Foster and the chap who captured this wee beastie. I am Alan Jorgenson formerly of the Royal Norwegian Navy and I am the captain of this little pirate ship!"

210

I liked him immediately but found it disconcerting to hear him speak with a posh Scottish accent. He saw my expression. "Norwegian father and Scottish mother. And then my father was stationed in Berlin at the embassy while I was growing up so I speak German." He spread his arms, "Perfect for this little job eh?" He wiped his oily hands on a piece of cloth. "Come on let's give you the tour." He nodded to me. Looks a little different from last week eh?"

"It certainly does. When those 110s attacked us, I thought we were swimming home."

"They are a tough ship. And they are faster than anything we have. We can reach almost forty knots!" We were passing the torpedo tubes. He patted them. "We won't be using torpedoes and so we will not need to carry them. That will save quite a bit of weight. It means that we should be able to out run the German E-Boats. We have stripped out everything we don't need to make her a lean mean fighting machine."

A young officer approached, "Captain we have finished at the stern. The rudder is moving better."

"Good, "This is my other officer, Midshipman Graham Jennings."

"Morning sirs."

"Morning."

He scurried off. "Young but keen as mustard and he can speak a bit of German and a bit of French. They will more than make up for any nautical shortcomings. I have a really experienced crew. We pinched most of them from the MTBs, MGBs and MLs you have been using."

"Leslie!"

Bill Leslie's head appeared from the bridge. "Sir?"

"This is my senior rating, Leading Seaman Bill Leslie."

"I know Bill. We have served together before."

Bill grinned, "We have both been promoted then sir but yours is a little higher than mine."

Alan seemed happy about the happenstance. "Excellent. This is going to work out I think."

We finished the tour and met the whole crew. I recognised some of the faces but the engine room crew were all unknown. There were men who knew diesel engines. We sat in the small mess. The Major wanted to make sure that the lieutenant and his midshipman understood what the job entailed.

"The navy is a little jealous of this ship. They want it for themselves. It is only because of Admiral Mountbatten's intervention that we have it. It is vital that we look after it. Some boffins will be down tomorrow to fit a Type 79Y radar set. It should give you an edge."

Lieutenant Jorgenson groaned, "The trouble is, sir, we have to have wires and masts. We had got rid of the mast to improve our speed."

"It is a trade-off, lieutenant. You may lose speed but you will have forty miles of warning."

I knew a little about radar from my Dad. "If you ask the boffins when they come there may be a way to stow it when the array is not needed."

"Good idea."

Major Foster continued, "Now the first mission is set for the last week in May. You will be taking Lieutenant Harsker and his men to Dieppe. You will drop them and then pick them up again two days later. The two of you will be responsible for deciding the pickup and drop off point. That way security will be tight."

"What about our aeroplanes and ships, sir? We don't want to be hit by them."

"That is where the radar will come in. You will spot any danger and can radio them before you see them. We will, of course, tell coastal command of your existence and they will be informed to be judicious when engaging E-Boats. Your lookouts and signallers will need to be on the ball."

"Righto sir."

"We want this first mission to be a complete success. It will convince the navy that we can put this boat to better uses and it will make our landings more effective. I shall leave you chaps to get to know each other. I will send the car back for you, Harsker."

"Thank you, sir."

When he had gone Lieutenant Jorgenson took out a pipe. "He seems a nice chap but I am glad he has gone. Senior officers looking over my shoulder always makes me nervous."

"Major Foster isn't like most senior officers. He is a good chap. You can tell him and ask him anything. He is not pompous at all."

"Good. When do your chaps arrive then?"

"A couple of days. They were given a leave after the St. Nazaire raid."

"Excellent. Then by the time we have set up this radar and collected our stores we should be ready."

I nodded, "I have checked the maps. We will have to head for the north Cornwall coastline to find similar terrain to Dieppe."

"They were my thoughts too. We will try a couple of landings in daylight and then at night. I am worried about the depth at the bows. I don't want to risk grounding us."

"It does ride higher than an ML. We will just have to see. We will be using radios. That will affect the way we land. Can't have them getting soaked, can we?"

By the time the car came for me I was quite happy about the ship and the crew. Despite his cavalier attitude Lieutenant Jorgenson was level headed. We would be putting our lives in his hands and I was happy about that.

Chapter 18

When my men returned from leave we were thrown into a maelstrom of activity. I allocated the new roles and my two radio operators were whisked away to train on the Type 18 Mark III radio. Sergeant Poulson organised the new equipment while I spent hours with Major Foster going over what the Admiral wanted from us. We had to identify the guns, the wire, the garrison and the beach approaches. It was a tall order for our first operation.

Red Dean was waiting for me as I came out of the first meeting, "Here you are sir!" He handed me a cardboard box.

"What is in here, Sergeant Major?"

"Every map I could lay my hands on." I picked out a petrol company's map. It was pre-war. He shrugged, "I thought that the towns wouldn't change and they have the roads on. The others I managed to requisition."

"That is excellent."

Major Foster came out of his office, "Has the Sergeant Major told you his news, Lieutenant?"

"I was just about to, sir. I have been appointed to this camp as training officer. My days of going behind the lines are over. My gimpy leg stops that. Me and Daddy Grant will stay here as permanent residents." He grinned, "Mrs Bailey is letting me have Bert Grimsdale's old room. She is a good cook, you know."

"I know. Has she forgiven you yet then?"

"Forgiven me?"

"You know when we brought the E-boat back?"

"Water under the bridge. We are the best of friends now."

I was happy. She would have company which would not be going into harm's way and Reg would have someone his own age with whom to talk. It almost made me believe in some sort of higher being ordaining our lives.

214

It did not take long for us to be ready for sea. When we reached the S-88 I saw that they had fitted the radar array. It did not look as bad as I had expected. Lieutenant Jorgenson stood at the top of the gangplank. "Welcome to the 'Lucky Lady'." I cocked my head to one side. "The lads thought she should have a name and S-88 didn't seem to do justice to our venture. If you and your lads go aft Leading Seaman Leslie will get them squared away."

When they had gone Alan pointed to the array. "We compromised. We haven't got the range we should have. This just covers thirty miles from the boat but it doesn't get in the way and doesn't spoil our profile. We have to fool Jerry, you know."

"It looks fine."

"And we can get it down in a hurry if we have to."

Bill appeared, "All squared away, sir."

"Right let's see what this little beauty will do then."

We went sedately down the Carrick roads and we passed the entrance to the harbour at Falmouth. We headed gently along the coast towards Land's End. From there on it was a wild coast. We flew the white ensign from our stern. As an added precaution, we had informed Coastal Command of our route. As soon as we passed Land's End and headed north east Alan opened her up. Even I was taken aback by the acceleration.

He grinned at me, "Faster than when you had her?" I nodded. "It needed a good service and the fuel the Germans used was piss poor. In fact, our engineer thought it was German piss! We have good fuel, a retuned engine and we cleared the weed from the hull. We are getting ten knots more than when you sailed her."

We soon found the spot we had decided was similar to Dieppe. There was a tiny fishing port at Porth. Although smaller than Dieppe, the land to the east and west were similar to that at Dieppe. We sailed in close to inspect the depth. I noticed a seaman at the bows. He had an old lead weight with grease around it. He dropped it into the water to ascertain the depth. It had been a method used since the days of sailing ships. Although old fashioned, it worked. Our draught was four feet ten inches. That was too deep for Fletcher and Crowe. The radio they carried would be under water.

"Right, Tom. We will experiment here. Have one of your lads at the bows with Smith the man with the lead."

"Hewitt, go to the bow and be ready to jump into the sea on my command."

The Norwegian Lieutenant shrugged. "If we ground her we all go over the side to free her but we have to know the grounding point." He cupped his hands, "Smith, call out the depth. Let me know when it is five feet!"

He edged us in.

Smith shouted, "Five feet, sir."

"Let's push a little further eh? And again, Smith."

"Four feet six."

We went a little further and felt a judder; we had touched bottom. He backed out enough so that we had movement. He nodded to me. I shouted, "In you go Hewitt!"

He jumped in and I saw that the water came up to his waist. That was no good. The radio might be damaged. I went forrard. "Scouse, come with me." My radio operator came to the bows. "Could you get out of the way Smith I want to try something." He obliged. "Right Scouse when we land we have to get off at the sharp end! Your radio will get wet."

"I could carry it in front of me sir and hold it over my head."

"That is a good idea but let's try this. Run along the deck and see how far you can get from the boat." I turned, "Sergeant Poulson, chuck me a Bergen!" When it arrived, I gave the Bergen to Fletcher. "Try it with this."

He held it before him and ran. He jumped high and landed some eight feet from the bows. He stumbled a little but kept his balance. Hewitt helped him to steady himself. I saw that the water came to his knees and the Bergen remained dry.

"That is the way we will do it. Crowe will go before you, Scouse, and steady you in case you fall."

216

With that problem solved we perfected our landing technique. I went in first followed by Sergeant Poulson. The last three were the two men with the radio and Lance Sergeant Gowland, now returned and fit. When we had done it ten times in daylight we waited until dark and did it five more times.

As we headed back through the dark, we were well pleased. We knew we could land and we were a well-oiled team. The sailors and my commandos got on well. We worked hard each day getting to the ship, the landing and, most importantly, each other. Three days later we felt we were ready to go. Major Foster gave us the go ahead. Before we left he told us that the Canadians would be the troops making the assault but that there would be paratroopers with them.

We slipped out of our berth in the early afternoon. We would sail along the coast and make the dash for Dieppe after dark. We would conserve fuel during daylight hours but make better time at night. The liaison set up by my father meant that we had air support during daylight. At night, there would be a flight of Bristol Blenheims close at hand but we would need to summon them by radio. We would not be alone.

The two teams had gelled well. As we headed along the coast I joined Alan and Leading Seaman Leslie who was the coxswain. Bill smiled, "You know sir, she feels like she is desperate to run. This tootling along at thirty knots makes her seem like an old lady. She is keen to run."

Alan Jorgenson nodded, "I know what you mean. Don't worry, Killick, we will let her have her head tonight."

"That's grand, sir."

"Alan, our radios only have a range of ten miles. We should never be more than a mile or so from the coast but if you are out to sea..."

"Don't worry. After we drop you back off then we will head for Newhaven and lie up there during the day. We will be on station the moment it is dark. I guarantee that we will be within five miles of you at all times."

"Good."

We had planned on one night to explore the southern side. Alan would pick us up and then drop us at the northern side the second night. It meant we did not have to risk crossing the town. I remembered when we had raided close to Calais and lost two men when we had had to go into the outskirts. We would not need to do that this time.

When the order came to darken ship, we went below to prepare for our raid. The men repacked their Bergens so that nothing was omitted. They put in their food and camouflage nets at the bottom of the bags. They would be the least necessary. Then the grenades, toggle ropes, bolas and spare ammunition. Finally, they put in their maps. I had had the men make their own copies of the maps of the area. They needed to know the roads and main features. They would all amend their own maps when we found emplacements, wires, mine field, sentries and machine gun posts. We had lost too many men when we had attacked St. Nazaire and that was before the attack had even begun. Everything else went on their webbing belts. I was the only one with the silencer on the Colt. I was the experiment. We had tried it on the range and it appeared to work. There was just the slightest of puffs when I used it. I also had a second holster for my Luger. I risked losing it from my battledress.

The last thing we did was to black up. We all checked each other's bags. Fletcher did not have a Bergen. He carried the radio. Crow had doubled up with his equipment. The two of them were the heaviest laden of any of us. Lowe and Gowland had the demolition charges although we had no plans to use them. They were for emergencies only.

There was a voice pipe in the cabin and I heard Bill Leslie's voice. "Thirty minutes from landfall."

"Lights out lads."

We turned out the lights and slipped up on deck. I glanced in at the shelter they had erected around the radar. "Anything?"

"No, sir, quiet as the grave."

I returned to the bridge. I saw that we had slowed down as we approached the French coast. Aerial photography had identified a huge gun emplacement at the top of the cliffs by Vasterival. We would begin our search to the east of the guns close to Quiberville and then head

218

towards the edge of Dieppe. When we had explored the western side of the town we would hide up for the day in the woods which lay just a mile from the town. We had contemplated doing it one night but it was too risky. We might rush things. This way we could give one report to Alan and if the second half of the operation ended in failure the message would still get back to base.

We moved to the huge foredeck and waited. Alan slowed the ship down as much as he dared and Bill edged it in. The leadsman did not shout but when his hand went up we knew that we had arrived. I slipped over the side and the water came up to my waist. I rushed to the shore and carried on across the sand. Kneeling I cocked my Thompson and scanned ahead of me. The cliffs rose to my left, dark and menacing. I saw two pill boxes guarding the entrance to the beach where the River Saane flowed. I slipped my Thompson over my shoulder and took out my silenced Colt. I waved Sergeant Poulson forward and we ran to the pillbox on our left. I saw no machine gun snout protruding from its mouth and I slipped around the back. It was, mercifully, empty. Even in the dark the concrete looked bright. This was a newly built defence. We had been lucky; they had yet to man it.

I stepped out and saw that we had all landed. The E-Boat could be barely seen as the captain took it back to Newhaven. We moved along the bank of the Saane. We saw no one. After half a mile or so I turned to head up the slope towards the hamlet of Blancmesnil. The houses were silent. I doubted that they were occupied; the Germans would not risk civilians this close to their guns. Once we had passed them I halted. The guns were to the left of us. I spread the men out in a sweep line and we headed through the woods toward the guns. Unlike the pillboxes, these would be defended. That I knew for certain.

It was a well defended site. I saw a flak tower and some way behind it the gun emplacements. I led my handful of men along the line of defences, using the tree cover and the ditch alongside the road. We had to find a way down to the beach for that was where we would be picked up by Lieutenant Jorgenson. The guns were huge and there were six of them. They would make mincemeat of any ship foolish enough to

219

attack the town. I smelled smoke and dropped to the ground. Two Germans walked along the rear of the guns. They were chatting about a bar in Dieppe which had friendly girls who were happy to collaborate with German soldiers. They were looking forward to their day off the next day. They passed us and headed along the far side of the guns.

I gambled that they would take longer to patrol the perimeter than it would take us to find the beach. A good commando was always ready to find his way out of trouble as fast as he got into it. As the ground descended I saw a barn which looked abandoned. It was on the edge of the woods. I stored that information and we went down the gully which led to the beach. There were obstacles at the beach. They were intended to deter, rather than to stop. We could get passed them whenever we chose. We quickly returned to the barn and then headed towards Dieppe.

The woods gave us cover and we moved quickly. I was acutely aware of the time. We had been right to use two nights to complete the work. Although we needed to check out the cliffs the town was the priority. I decided I would explore the cliffs during daylight. We stuck to the road which twisted down the slope towards the hamlet of Pourville-sur-mer. This was almost on the edge of Dieppe. By my estimate we were but a mile from the port. Thankfully the Germans had not defended Pourville-sur-mer. That was worrying. They would only do that if they thought this western flank was secure.

I left the road. Suddenly we came upon a double ring of barbed wire. It had no gaps. For us it was not a problem; we laid our Bergens across it and walked over the path we had made. For an attacking force, it would be a barrier which would slow them up and allow the Germans to cut down any attackers.

Once passed the obstacle we moved cautiously through the woods and over the scrubby heath land. Even in the dark we recognised the castle of Dieppe. Although it had medieval stone walls it would not stand up to pounding by bombers. However, I could see, even in the black of night, a flag fluttering from its top. The Germans were using it. I guessed it would be a control centre. I halted the patrol. I pointed to Sergeant Poulson and then to my right. He nodded and took Hewitt and Groves with him. I pointed to Lance Sergeant Gowland and pointed to my left. He tapped Groves and they headed away into the night.

I led the rest towards the town. We were moving across fields and so had to watch our footing. I heard a movement as we approached a hedgerow and I held up my hand to halt us. I wriggled beneath the hedge and saw that we were just thirty yards from the German defences and they looked to be formidable. Even in the dark I saw that they had many flak guns on the cliff top and it bristled with machine guns. This was the strong point. I consigned the picture to my memory and then led my men back to the rendezvous point. We waited for half an hour for the others to join us. This was the worrying time. We would know they had been discovered if we heard gun fire. They appeared simultaneously. I saw that we had an hour before dawn. Already the sky was becoming lighter.

I turned and led them back through the woods towards Pourville-sur-mer. We crossed the barbed wire, this time at a different point. I hoped our route would not be noticed. To my horror I saw movement ahead. There were people up and about. Farmers were heading for cow byres and others were moving around in their homes; I saw the lights and smelled the smoke. We skirted the hamlet. It ate up valuable dark and we had to move both swiftly and silently until we were beyond the houses. We had half a mile to go and a road to cross but the sun had made it lighter. We had little choice. I chose a section of the road which twisted above and below us. One by one we darted across and made the safety of the trees and scrub. I waved Sergeant Poulson forward to find a camp for the day. Once more we had been lucky.

Polly was experienced enough to find the perfect place for us to lie up. It was a dell in a wood. There were plenty of bushes and low stubby trees around to break up the profile of the camp we would erect. We were far enough from a path to avoid casual visitors. If someone found us they would be looking for us. Harry and George scouted the perimeter while the rest of us used our netting to make us even harder to spot.

I took out my maps and marked on them all that I had seen. When the perimeter was established I waved over my NCOs. "Mark on my map what you found and then copy my information on to yours."

I went to detail the sentries. We would need two on watch at all times. The rest of the section ate, drank and then made a nest. We had a long day in May to wait. When I returned to my two NCOs they had finished.

"The guns don't look daunting but the town is a fortress, sir."

I nodded, "I will take Hewitt out this afternoon. He is the quietest of the men and he can use a bola. I am keen to scout the cliffs and see if I can see the seaward defences against infantry. We will get our heads down now. Polly, you take charge."

"Right sir."

I found Hewitt. He was using branches to make a hide. "You get your head down now. No guard duty for you. We will have a Recce this afternoon."

"Right sir."

I took out my net and rolling in it, settled myself under an elder bush. I was asleep instantly.

My internal body clock awoke me. Even without looking at my watch the sun told me that it was afternoon. I rolled from my netting and immediately packed it. We had to be ready to move quickly if danger threatened. I saw George and Scouse on watch. I joined them and ate some rations and drank some water. "Report."

"Quite as the grave, sir. A flight of 190s flew over and that has been about it. I think they were just watching the coast. We have heard a little bit of noise from the guns. I heard a klaxon and I am guessing they were practising."

"Right. I will wake Hewitt. I want to see what the cliff is like and to get a little closer to the guns. If we are discovered tell Poulson to take charge and get the men back to the boat. If we are spotted or captured then abort the second part of the operation."

"Right sir." He paused, "But if you could manage it, don't get caught eh sir? Mrs Bailey would blame us!"

I shook Hewitt awake. "Get some food and water. When you are ready fetch your bola and your Colt. We are going for a Recce."

"I am ready now, sir!"

"There is no rush. Food, water, pee, then you are ready!"

"Sir."

I went to my Bergen and took out my binoculars. They would come in handy.

Despite my words he rushed his food. I waved him forward and we headed towards the cliffs. We went right to Gorge de Moutiers. This was a narrow gully which led to the beach. It struck me as an easy way down to the shore. As we made our way towards the cliffs we used every piece of cover we could. I could do this with the two of us but the whole section would have been a liability. We saw no one. I went to the cliffs first. We crawled the last thirty yards so that we were not silhouetted against the sky. It was depressing when we reached the edge. The cliffs were sheer. They could be scaled but it would take a great deal of time and require the highest levels of skill. We back off and returned to the gorge.

I saw the open sea. This was the back passage to the guns. We made our way down. Sand had blown in and it was soft. That appeared to be the only obstacle. Then I saw the barbed wire at the end. That was my first warning. I looked carefully and, as we scanned the beach I saw the real danger. The beach had been mined. There was no warning sign but the wind had whipped the sand from one of the mines close to the barrier and I saw the evil detonator sticking out of the sand. We could not use this beach.

We headed back up the gorge and along the cliff. I needed to reconnoitre the guns and their defences. I doubted that they would need to mine this approach as the cliffs were enough of an obstacle themselves but I had no doubt that they would have sentries there. We would need to be invisible. When we reached the cliffs, I saw that there was a piece of dead ground which would hide us from the guns. I spotted the German sentries before we entered the dead ground. I waited until they had finished one leg of their patrol and then we raced into the dead ground where we hid.

After a moment, we moved quickly along the safe piece of ground. I had spied a rocky formation which would afford us some cover and

223

allow us to examine the guns closer. When we reached it I slowly raised my head. We were beyond the sentries. I used the binoculars to sweep the defences. Although, apparently unoccupied, I saw a line of pill boxes below the massive 150mm guns. I moved the glasses up to the guns and saw that they were manned. There were some of the crew enjoying a smoke outside them. Behind them I saw the barracks. I guessed that the numbers of guns would necessitate a regiment. In addition, they would have guards. This would take many men to assault.

I returned to Hewitt and we made our way along the cliffs. A movement arrested me. I saw the lighthouse. It was manned. More than that there were Germans all over it. I used the glasses and saw that they were using this as the fire director for the guns. If that could be knocked out then the guns would be less effective. It was a bonus. Aeroplanes could take this out. We had seen enough.

When we reached the dead ground, I stopped and sent Hewitt to keep watch. There was still light and I wanted to amend my map. That way if anything happened to me Hewitt and the others would have a record of what we had seen. It did not take me long. When we reached the edge of the dead ground we waited for the sentries to move off before hurrying back to the camp. The sun was already beginning to set. I had taken too long. We had to be at the pickup point as soon after dark as possible.

We crossed the road. There was a culvert beneath it taking the stream down to the gorge. We were almost at the camp now. As we neared the woods I stopped. Something was not right. The woods smelled differently. We had come back a different way to the way we had gone and there were broken branches on the bushes. We had not done that. There was someone in the woods. The odds were, it was Germans. I took out my Colt and Hewitt did the same. I shook my head and pointed to his bola. He nodded. We moved slowly along the trail. I could see where the men had gone. I heard, in the distance, the sound of voices. Although very faint they were English voices. If I could hear them then the Germans we were following certainly would. We had been found!

Chapter 19

There were three of them; three inquisitive German soldiers. I spotted their grey uniforms. There was a sergeant and two others. The sergeant had a submachine gun and the other two had rifles. Even as we approached I saw them raising their weapons. I tapped Hewitt's arm and pointed to the man on the left. I raised my Colt and then I shouted in German, "What are you three idiots doing?" I used my best sergeant's voice and, even as they turned to see who was shouting at them I shot the Sergeant between the eyes and the man next to him in the chest. Hewitt's bola had stunned the third who lay on the floor. Hewitt ran to him and drew his dagger across the man's throat.

Sergeant Poulson and my section ran towards us. I put my fingers to my lips. I ran back to the camp and grabbed my Bergen. We had to move and move quickly. The others followed suit. I went to Scouse. I whispered, "Tell the boat we need them now!"

I led Sergeant Poulson and Hewitt. "Hewitt take the Sergeant to the culvert. Sergeant Poulson, hide the bodies in the culvert and wait for us there. I will come with Scouse and Groves."

When I reached my two signallers Scouse was speaking quietly, "Scouse to Wacker, Scouse to Wacker, over."

His voice sounded inordinately loud to me but it was necessary. There was silence. Then the radio crackled, "Wacker to Scouse, on station, go ahead, over."

"Scouse to Wacker, pick up now. Repeat pick up now! Over."

"Understood, over."

The two of them were packing the radio the instant they heard the word '*over*'.

I led them to the road. It had been a happenstance that meant that the radio operator on the 'Lucky Lady' was also from Liverpool and was known as Wacker. The codenames would fool any German while the accents would be impenetrable.

When I reached the section waiting at the culvert there was no sign of the bodies. I led them down the road to the beach. The obstacles there reminded me of the ones we had seen at the gorge. Were there mines here too? I signalled for a defensive perimeter and then I used my Bergen to bridge the wire barrier. Once over I dropped to my hands and knees. There was soft dry sand for thirty yards. That would be where the mines were; if there were any. I used my dagger and my bare hand. I swept the sand in an arc on either side of me and then prodded with my dagger. I moved twelve inches forward each time I tested the sand. After ten yards, I knew there were no mines but it would be stupid to stop the search. Eventually I reached the water and turned. I waved the others forward. They walked down the swept sand. Sergeant Poulson, who was tail end Charlie, used the stock of his Thompson to sweep away our foot prints. When they reached me, we peered into the dark. There was no sign of the E-Boat. We were precariously placed now at the edge of the sea. A sharp-eyed sentry might spot us.

Then I heard, against the sound of the surf and the wind, the sound of the diesels. I began to wade into the water. Scouse had the radio held high above him and he followed me. The dark shape of the E-Boat's bow loomed up out of the black. Scouse reached up and the radio was plucked from his hands. We scrambled up after it and a few minutes later we began to back out. We all went below decks. We had much to do and little time to do it.

I took out my map. This was the master one. Sergeant Poulson took out his and I copied my details on to the second one. A hand came with some hot cocoa and sandwiches. I felt the motion as we headed out to sea. Alan Jorgenson came below decks. I handed him Sergeant Poulson's map. "The defences are marked on here. We had a bit of bother before we came away. We had to kill three guards."

"Then we abort the operation!"

I shook my head, "We have to complete the mission. There were minefields, wire and pill boxes that we couldn't see from the aerial photographs. There will be as many on the north section you can bet. We stick to the plan Alan, my call."

He nodded, "You live life to the full I will say that."

"When we call for you we may have to be brief. If we say 'Everton' then come and get us as quick as you can."

He frowned, "Everton?"

"Scouse and Wacker are both Liverpool fans. They hate Everton."

He nodded. "Eat. We land you in fifteen minutes. We scouted out the landing site before we came for you. There is a gully to the west of Berneval-le-Grande. It didn't look mined."

I shook my head as I chewed the sandwich. "They are not marking them as mined. We found a minefield at Gorge les Moutiers and there were no signs."

"Sneaky bastards!" He turned to go, "Best come up when you have finished."

The others were all eating too. Sergeant Poulson came over to me, "Sorry about that, sir. Hewitt told me the Germans heard us talking."

"It is a lesson learned, Sergeant and it didn't hurt us but next time just use hand signals eh?" He was improving all the time but one mistake was all it took to get you killed.

I felt much better with something hot inside me. I made my way up to the deck. I saw that we were closing with the coast quite rapidly. The beach and the gorge were quite clearly visible against the darker cliffs. I felt more confident about our landfall this time. The radio had not been damaged the first time and I was hopeful that this time we would be even quicker. As soon as the leadsman dropped his arm I leapt into the sea. My trousers were still wet from our embarkation. It was a very narrow beach. I was at the cliffs in six strides. My reloaded Colt was out and ready to be used. There was no one in sight: I smelled no smoke and heard no voices. It was only when I looked at my men racing behind me that I realised I hadn't checked for mines. I suspect the narrow beach meant they thought it was unnecessary. The dry part of the sand was less than two paces deep. I saw that there were footprints in the gully. That suggested people had walked on it. It would not be mined.

I waved the men forward and we headed up the gully. Aerial photography had identified a radar station to the north of us close to

227

Berneval-le-Grande. That would need checking out first. There was also a battery and I guessed it was not far from where we were. After forty paces, I stopped. I saw a trail leading from the gully. I took a chance and followed it. It climbed up the bank towards the battery which I assumed was to the right of me. I dropped to all fours when I saw the guns poking out. I turned left and headed down towards the cliff.

Once again there was a patch of dead ground. I had worked out that this had been created when they had built the emplacements. They had excavated the ground to protect the guns. I decided to move along this and approach the radar station from the side of the battery. I was taking a chance I knew but it allowed us to see more in a short space of time. We were lucky. Half way along the path, which still appeared to be hidden from the guns, I stopped. Waving Sergeant Poulson and the section forward I took out my binoculars and crept up the slope. My uniform, hat and blacking made me invisible but I was just twenty yards from the line of the sentries' patrol. I was able to confirm that there were three 170mm guns and four 150mm. There were even more here than on the other side of Dieppe.

I rejoined my men and we approached the Freja radar station. We had attacked enough of these to know that they were manned at all times and so we skirted it. I led my men due east. We had to explore this side of Dieppe. Once again, we came to a road and houses. We smelled the smoke and heard voices in the houses. These were inhabited. Our rubber soled shoes came to our rescue again. We crossed the road silently and ran down a lane between two houses. I was close enough to smell the garlic soup and Gauloise. They were French. Once we had left the gardens behind I took us through the woods to skirt Le Petit Berneval. I avoided the tempting road. If there were soldiers at Le Petit Berneval then they might well use the road to go to the larger Berneval-le-Grande and the batteries.

It took us longer to cross the fields but we found ourselves close to the hamlet of Belleville-sur-mer. Once we had passed it I took another chance and we ran the last mile to the outskirts of Dieppe. There was more wire. Without scouting it I knew that this would ring the town.

The only way through would be at roads and they would have checkpoints. The photographs had not spotted it. We used our Bergens to cross it. I sent my sergeants away to search left and right and I led the rest of the section towards Dieppe. Almost as soon as we had moved towards the town I saw the anti-aircraft batteries which ringed this side of the town. We had to keep ducking and hiding to avoid the Germans who manned them. After a fretful hour, I led us back to the wire. We crossed it and awaited the others. Sergeant Poulson returned with his men and then we waited for Harry and Groves. They seemed to take for ages.

We were looking towards Dieppe and almost failed to see the two Germans walking along the road which led to a crossing of the wire some half a mile from us. I waved my arm and every commando found shelter. I took out my Colt. I thought they would pass and we would be safe but two things coincided to stop them. First one of them saw the flattened wire. By morning it would have sprung back but we had just crossed it. I heard one of them say, "Someone has crossed here."

"Probably a poacher. The woods are full of game birds."

"The Lieutenant said to report anything out of the ordinary."

"That means we have to go all the way back to the battery."

"It is our duty."

"I have a duty to my stomach and it involves beer!"

It was at that moment that Gowland and Groves loomed up out of the dark. I saw the two Germans react and I fired one bullet. Sergeant Poulson leapt up and grabbing the second one by his helmet so that he could not cry out and slit his throat. Gowland and Groves rejoined us. There was no convenient culvert here. I signalled for the bodies to be picked up and we headed back towards the cliffs. This was a disaster. I glanced at my watch. Dawn was two hours away. If we stayed here during the day then the five men we had killed would be missed and there would be a hue and cry. However, the 'Lucky Lady' would be well on her way back to England. Now we would have to hide these bodies and then go to ground.

I realised, as we hurried over the fields that there were few woods and trees on this side of the town. We kept heading towards the gully. We had to be close to that and ready to embark. If we had done this the other way around we would have more chance of survival. As we neared the road which led to the gully I saw there were woods on both sides. They were not as extensive as we might have wished. We would have little choice over our camp and we would not be able to get much rest; half of us would have to be on watch. I led us in nonetheless.

We found a small clearing and the bushes at the sides afforded some protection. I pointed to the bodies. Take their ammunition, grenades and any papers. Then bury them."

I took out my map and began to jot down what we had discovered. This side was easier for us to attack and the guns here were potentially more dangerous. I think the section realised our predicament for they camouflaged the camp so well that I was certain we would not be spotted. Dawn was just breaking when they had finished burying the bodies and disguising our presence. I waved over Polly. "Have the men work in pairs. One sleeps, one watches. I will stay awake. Make sure they have plenty to drink. We need them alert and ready to move."

Sergeant Poulson nodded and went to tell the others. I took my own advice and drank sparingly from my canteen. We had embarked in relative peace the previous night. I hoped we would do the same again but I had to prepare for a hot embarkation. I decided to use the demolitions. We would use the German grenades as a trip wire booby trap and the charges close to the entrance to the gully.

Sergeant Poulson came back. He said, quietly, "What is the plan sir?"

"Roughly the same one we came up with before. We wait until dark and we leave but we need a contingency plan. We lay booby traps with grenades along the road to the gully. At the gully, we use charges. We may have to leave hot."

"I'll tell the lads. When do we lay them?"

"Not until we know that there is a hue and cry. Those two Germans last night were on their way to town. They won't be noticed until ten or so and then they will look. The other three are a bigger problem. They will have missed them by last night at the latest and be searching on the yonder side of Dieppe."

It was noon before we knew they were hunting us. The Fieseler Storch began to make circles high in the air above us. I recognised that he was flying a pattern up and down the coast. After an hour, he descended to a lower height. You could easily see movement from the slow-moving spotter aircraft. This was a test of our skills at camouflage. At two he left, probably to refuel. The gully and the trees afforded us cover but we would have to move down to the beach sometime. We had to slow down pursuit. Our new, temporary camp was the obvious place to lay booby traps as well as the narrow road down the gully.

As soon as he had gone I summoned my sergeants. "Have the grenade booby traps laid at the entrance to the woods, close to where we came in and then the charges by the gully. Don't arm the demolition charges yet."

"Right sir. They might not have seen us."

"I don't think they have. If they had then there would have been Stukas here already but they are looking for us. Best be ready."

I went to Fletcher, "We may well have to use the emergency codeword. If we are discovered then, no matter what time of day it is, send 'Everton'."

"Right sir. But it won't come to that will it? I mean they have no idea we are here."

"They wouldn't have sent up the search aeroplane if they weren't looking for us. We have some hope that they will search the other side first but if we have to move then run like you have never done before."

By four the charges and grenades were in place. Normally it would have taken a quarter of the time but my men had to lay them so that they were not easily seen. It was made harder when the Storch returned an hour after it had left. It flew much lower this time and seemed to be concentrating on the cliff top.

Sergeant Poulson returned. "All the charges are ready, sir. I left Groves at the edge of the wood as a sentry."

"Good thinking. I should have thought of that."

He shook his head, "If you don't mind me saying so, sir, you lead from the front too much. Don't you trust us?"

"Of course, I do. This is the first operation; it has to go well!" He nodded. "Make sure that everyone is ready to go as quickly as we can and tell the lads to use grenades before their guns if we are attacked. I don't want to make it easy for them to find us."

Each minute closer to dusk gave me hope. Those hopes were shattered as it drew closer to seven o'clock. The sun was lower in the sky, a warm red glow above the horizon but there was no way that it was dusk. Groves raced in, "Sir, Jerries. A couple of truckloads of them. They have dogs and they are heading in this direction."

"Fletcher send the code word. Groves stay with him; get down to the beach when the signal is acknowledged. Sergeant Poulson, I want a skirmish line. Set some booby traps here where we camped. They will find this quickly enough. Then get the men to the beach. Leave one man to show us where the booby trap is. Harry, come with me."

As we ran I said, "Get ready with your grenades. Wait for my command."

I drew my Colt. The silencer would help. We waited just fifty yards from our camp. I wanted them to find it. Sergeant Poulson would make it a death trap. I heard the dogs barking. I drew my Luger. We knelt behind two of the slightly larger trees. The four German Shepherds made straight for me. I fired both pistols at the same time. Two dogs fell immediately and the other two swerved to come for me. I managed to hit one with a bullet from my Luger but the other leapt at me and fastened his teeth around my left hand. I hit it hard with my Colt and it fell stunned. I fired a bullet into its head. I holstered my Luger. My left hand was bleeding too much to be able to grip it.

At that moment, there was a double explosion as the booby traps at the end of the wood went off. I heard shouts and then a German voice urged his men forward. I had seven bullets left in my magazine. I had to make them count. I fired at the young officer who was leading his men on. He fell with a surprised look on his face. They were too far away for

232

a grenade and so, as his men gathered around his body I fired the last six bullets in their direction. Three fell and the other two dived to the ground. They began to fire blindly in our direction. I waved Harry away and then, after holstering my Colt I pulled the pin from a grenade and placed a convenient rock on the grenade.

I turned and ran. Harry was waiting for me at the camp where Hewitt also stood. "Go right sir."

As I moved in the direction indicated I heard my grenade go off. One of them had tripped over the rock. Then I heard another booby trap explode. I joined the two of them in our former camp. "Throw a grenade as high as you can and then run to the beach."

I saw the Germans as we lobbed the grenades. They fired again but by that time we had left and were running down the slope towards the gully. There were more screams as the grenades exploded in the air showering the Germans with shrapnel. I hoped we were making them cautious. I saw that the sun was setting now. There were low clouds which made it darker. In ten minutes, it would be dusk. I yelled. "Ten minutes on the timer!" I heard a ripple of explosions as the last of the camp booby traps were triggered.

We reached the road and I saw Germans coming down the road. I pulled my Thompson round, cocked it and emptied the magazine in their direction. As I reloaded Hewitt and Harry emptied theirs. It takes a brave man to face three Tommy guns and they dived for cover. We had bought another few minutes.

I saw Sergeant Poulson kneeling by the side of the gully. He stood as we approached. "Ten minutes, sir!" He fired his Thompson up the track as we burst on to the beach.

I looked out at the darkening sea. There was no sign of the 'Lucky Lady'. "Right lads get ready for a swim. Sergeant Poulson has set the timer for ten minutes. We leave in three." I shouldered my Thomson and took out my Luger. "Backs to the sea."

"Sir, what about the radio?" Scouse still gripped his precious machine.

"Drop it by the charges and then run!"

233

My men were working as pairs, one firing and the other running. I doubted that we would hit anything but so long as it slowed them down that was all that I wanted. I had to rely on the Royal Navy. I hoped they would not let us down. I felt the water at the back of my knees as Fletcher joined us. He grinned. "I hope they don't take the radio out of my pay, sir."

"We will have a whip round if they do." I glanced behind me. The sea was empty. "How much longer Sergeant?"

"Two minutes!"

"Everybody, into the sea and swim."

"What about the Bergens sir?"

"They have air in them. They will help you float." That was the theory but I was not certain about the practice.

Once the water came up to my waist it became harder to move and I heard more firing from behind us. George Lowe shouted, "Sir, they are setting up a heavy machine gun!"

"Poulson! How long?"

"Any second sir!"

"Everybody underwater and hold your breath!" I dropped my head beneath the waves. It was remarkably quiet and cool. I began to count in my head. I reached ten when there was a concussion above us and I felt a wave of hot air. I broke the surface and looked behind us. I could see bodies and wounded men staggering around. We had stopped them but we had got no closer to home. I wondered if we would have to swim home.

The heads of my men broke surface and they looked around. Sergeant Poulson said, "What now, sir."

"We swim!"

"To England?"

"If that's what it takes Scouse, yes, but it is in the direction of the 'Lucky Lady'. Keep your ears open."

We swam backwards just using our legs. It was easier that way. We were laden down and water washed over us but we did not sink, not completely anyway. We could see the shore receding. The tide must have been on its way out and was taking us out to sea. It was getting on to dark now and I doubted that the Germans would be able to spot us.

Suddenly my ears caught the throb of diesel engines. It drew closer. Was it a real German or was it S-88? A rope snaked out and a friendly voice said, "Grab hold sir! Sorry we are late."

Chapter 20

It took some time because we were all sodden and soaked but as soon as we were all on board the ship edged back out to sea. The Midshipman who had pulled me on board said, "There is another German E-boat out there, sir. The captain didn't want them to see us so we headed further south. That is why we were late."

"You got here, Middy, that is the important thing."

He noticed my hand, "Sir, you hand is a mess."

Hewitt said, "Leave him with me, sir. I have a kit in my bag."

"Take him down below Private, it is going to get a little busy up here."

Once we were below decks I took off my Bergen and my battle dress. One of the ratings gave us blankets. I found I was shaking. It was not fear but it was the cold. Hewitt said, "Sir, we should get all your wet things off."

"Hewitt, if you think I am going to go around stark naked with just a blanket around my shoulders you can think again."

He began to clean up my hand. It looked far worse than it was. There was a lot of blood and the dog's teeth had punctured the skin in a number of places but with the blood wiped away and antiseptic applied he was satisfied enough to bandage me. He put my arm in a sling. I did not need it but it made him happy. I took the mug of tea and went on deck to speak with the lieutenant.

He nodded towards my arm, "What happened?"

"A dog!"

He laughed, "At least they don't carry guns." He nodded towards the radar shack. "Jerry is still out there. We have the signal books that were on board when you captured her. I just hope they haven't changed them. I don't want to go racing west; it would look suspicious. We have been picking up signals about British commandos. Every vessel is searching for you. If it is any consolation they think there are at least fifty of you. They are searching all over Dieppe for you." He pointed to the sky. "We heard night fighters overheard. You have really annoyed them."

"Yes, but the trouble is this will just tighten up their defences. They had mined one of the gullies. I can see the same happening to the others."

"If you are going to make an omelette you have to crack eggs." He suddenly seemed to understand what I meant, "You think you should have aborted after the first one."

I nodded, "Yes."

"Well the damage was done by then anyway. Once they found those dead Germans they would either think it was the resistance or commandos. At least the locals won't suffer for this."

Wacker suddenly came out of the radio cabin, "Sir, just had a message from a German trawler he wants to come and check us out. He is suspicious. I have used all the codes but he doesn't recognise which flotilla we are from."

"Keep bluffing him, Hanson." Turning to me he said, "I have an idea, get your men on deck. Keep the blankets draped around their shoulders but have them ready to take cover if this goes pear shaped. Let's try to make a mug out of this German captain."

"Right." I think I knew what he intended. I went to the cabin. "Right lads; the captain wants Jerry to think we have been captured. Come on deck with your blankets and look hang dog but have a grenade and your Colts to hand."

I took the silencer from my Colt and refitted a magazine. As we reached the deck Lieutenant Jorgenson said, "Sit on the fo'c'sle. Try to look as though you are prisoners. When they get close I will tell them that I have captured you and intend to take you to Boulogne. Hopefully they will let us head that way and we can nip back to Newhaven."

It was a gamble but it felt like it might work. "Right lads, sit back to back and spread out. They think there are fifty of us."

Because we had radar Lieutenant Jorgenson was able to track their approach, even in the dark. There was no sign of Royal Navy white. The crew all had navy blue tops and would pass for Germans. The German flag fluttered above us. Lieutenant Jorgenson had stuck a thin cigar in his mouth and he looked every inch a German. His blond hair was the final argument.

He said, quietly, "They are half a mile away. We now talk in German." Apart from Bill Leslie and a couple of others, most of the crew had a smattering of German. There were three who spoke it fluently.

I heard the trawler's engine as it approached. Alan had his idling. The trawler captain was suspicious. He had his 37mm gun manned and it and the machine guns covered us. Alan took his megaphone and stood next to the bridge. "Good evening Captain. You see I have captured some of the Tommies." He pointed to the east of us. "I found them in the water over there. I was searching for more. I only have a few. I do not know where the others are."

The German captain said, "I do not know your boat. Which flotilla are you?"

Alan shrugged, "I am afraid I cannot tell you for we are on a mission for the Abwehr. It was pure luck that we heard the request for help to capture these gangsters." I smiled to myself. It was the phrase Hitler used about us. I think it was because we carried Tommy guns. "We are heading for Boulogne. I will hand them over to the Gestapo there."

It was a convincing story and Alan's piratical look made it more believable. I saw the gun crews relax. The trawler captain, however, edged his ship a little closer to us. It was broadside on. "I do not want to delay you. I am senior captain here. I will transfer the prisoners and you can be on your way. You will not need to deviate from your course."

"It is not a problem. We are a fast boat."

"I will decide what is a problem and what is not. I command in these waters and I will take the prisoners back to Dieppe!" I noticed the Alan's gun crews had surreptitiously closed up on their guns. Alan shrugged and said, "Very well. I will just tell the leader of these commandos what we are doing." He turned to me and nodded. Even as I stood and threw off my blanket he shouted, "Fire!"

I pulled the pin on my grenade and threw it at the crew of the 37mm and then I drew my Colt and fired at the trawler captain who stood exposed. I fired four bullets and he was thrown backwards. The grenade exploded behind the gun shield. It scythed through the crew and we were protected from the shrapnel by the metal guard around their gun. The E-Boats machine guns and my men's Colts cut through the crew. One of Alan's crew threw a timed charge towards the stern of the trawler where her depth charges were kept.

Alan shouted, "Hold on! Full speed coxswain." It was lucky he said what he did for we were thrown to one side by that savage manoeuvre. I barely managed to grab a rope with my good hand before we leapt away. As we turned there was an enormous explosion as the charges went off. The stern began to slip into the sea and then the depth charges at the stern all went off and the whole trawler was thrown into the air as it was destroyed by its own depth charges. We were showered with debris. As Bill brought the E-Boat back onto a straight course. I saw that the trawler and its crew had disappeared as though it had never been.

"And now lads, we have pushed our luck enough. Time to go home!"

We turned and headed due west. We would make Falmouth by dawn. Even as we headed west the message was being transmitted to the Hurricanes and they would be on station when dawn broke. I lay back on the deck. Alan was right, we had ridden our luck but I had learned that he too, like me, was a risk taker. It had paid off. The Germans would have no idea what happened to their trawler and they would continue to search for us.

It was mid-morning when we reached Falmouth. We had not been able to maintain full speed as one of the engines had suffered a malfunction but it did not bother us. We were all alive and we had achieved what we had set out to achieve. I knew we had not been perfect but we did not live in a perfect world and accidents would happen.

Major Foster was waiting for us as we edged into Carrick Roads and our little base. He had with him a pair of intelligence officers. I had

239

my maps already to hand for I knew what they wanted. "Sergeant Poulson, take charge of the section and my bag. I have a feeling that I am needed."

"But sir, your hand! You need to go to hospital."

"I think Hewitt did a good job. I will be fine. Take tomorrow off too, Sergeant. I think we have earned a rest."

I was right. No sooner had the E-Boat been tied up than Major Foster said, "Well done, Tom. I am afraid these chaps need to debrief you as soon as possible."

He saw my sling and looked concerned. "Don't worry sir. Just a dog bite."

We were driven to headquarters in Falmouth where I was grilled and questioned until three o'clock in the afternoon. As I suspected they were less than happy with the fact that we had been discovered. I knew what it meant. However, the maps and the intelligence mollified them and they left with a grudging nod of thanks.

"You know, Tom, some of these chaps need to do what you do and then they would appreciate you more."

"We don't need their appreciation sir. We are just doing our job."

"And you do it damn well. There is no one better at going behind enemy lines."

I laughed, "And I guess that means that it will not be long before we are asked to make another little trip across the Channel."

"Perhaps."

"Then in that case I am pleased that *'Lucky Lady'* needs repairs. It buys just a little time!"

"And speaking of luck, let's have your hand seen to before your luck runs out."

After the hospital, he dropped me off at Mrs Bailey's. The others had all eaten. As I went through to the kitchen I saw Reg Dean with his arms around Mrs Bailey. They both saw me. Reg nodded and Mrs Bailey's hand went to her mouth. "Eeh whatever has happened to you Lieutenant?"

"I was bitten, Mrs Bailey, by a dog."

240

Reg said, "A German Shepherd?" I nodded. He grinned and said, "A wound inflicted by an enemy. You could be due another medal, sir!"

When we both began laughing Mrs Bailey shook her head, "Soldiers! Who can understand them?"

The End

Glossary

Abwehr- German Intelligence

Butchers- Look (Cockney slang Butcher's Hook- Look)

Butties- sandwiches (slang)

Chah- tea (slang)

Comforter- the lining for the helmet; a sort of woollen hat

Corned dog- Corned Beef (slang)

Fruit salad- medal ribbons (slang)

Gash- spare (slang)

Gauloise- French cigarette

Gib- Gibraltar (slang)

Glasshouse- Military prison

Goon- Guard in a POW camp (slang)- comes from a 1930s Popeye cartoon

Jankers- field punishment

Jimmy the One- First Lieutenant on a warship

MGB- Motor Gun Boat

MTB- Motor Torpedo Boat

ML- Motor Launch

Killick- leading hand (Navy) (slang)

Oik- worthless person (slang)

Oppo/oppos- pals/comrades (slang)

Pom-pom- Quick Firing 2lb (40mm) Maxim cannon

Pongo (es)- soldier (slang)

Potato mashers- German Hand Grenades (slang)

QM- Quarter Master (stores)

Recce- Reconnoitre (slang)

SBA- Sick Bay Attendant

Schnellboote -German for E-boat (literally fast boat)

Scragging - roughing someone up (slang)

Scrumpy- farm cider

SP- Starting price (slang)- what's going on
Sprogs- children or young soldiers (slang)
Squaddy- ordinary soldier (slang)
Stag- sentry duty (slang)
Stand your corner- get a round of drinks in (slang)
Subbie- Sub-lieutenant (slang)
Tatties- potatoes (slang)
Tommy (Atkins)- Ordinary British soldier
Two penn'orth- two pennies worth (slang for opinion)
WVS- Women's Voluntary Service

Maps

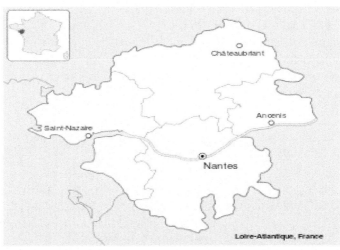

Maps courtesy of Wikipedia- The layout of St. Nazaire docks showing Normandie Dock

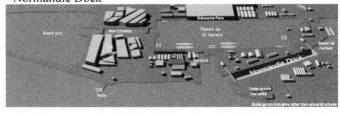

244

Historical note

The first person I would like to thank for this particular book and series is my Dad. He was in the Royal Navy but served in Combined Operations. He was at Dieppe, D-Day and Walcheren. His boat: LCA 523 was the one which took in the French Commandos on D-Day. He was proud that his ships had taken in Bill Millens and Lord Lovat. I wish that, before he died I had learned more in detail about life in Combined Operations but like many heroes he was reluctant to speak of the war. He is the character in the book called Bill Leslie. I went back in 1994, with my Dad to Sword beach and he took me through that day on June 6th 1944. We even found the grave of his cousin George Hogan who died on D-Day. As far as I know we were the only members of the family ever to do so. Sadly, that was Dad's only visit but we planted forget-me-nots on the grave of George.

I would also like to thank Roger who is my railway expert. The train Tom and the Major catch from Paddington to Oswestry ran until 1961. The details of the livery, the compartments and the engine are all, hopefully accurate. I would certainly not argue with Roger!

I used a number of books in the research. The list is at the end of this historical section. However, the best book, by far, was the actual Commando handbook which was reprinted in 2012. All of the details about hand to hand, explosives, esprit de corps etc were taken directly from it. The advice about salt, oatmeal and water is taken from the book. It even says that taking too much salt is not a bad thing! I shall use the book as a Bible for the rest of the series. The Commandos were expected to find their own accommodation. Some even saved the money for lodgings and slept rough. That did not mean that standards of discipline and presentation were neglected; they were not.

The 1st Loyal Lancashire existed as a regiment. They were in the BEF and they were the rear-guard. All the rest is the work of the author's imagination. The use of booby traps using grenades was common. The details of the German potato masher grenade are also accurate. The Germans used the grenade as an early warning system by hanging them from fences so that an intruder would move the grenade and it would explode. The Mills bomb had first been used in the Great War. It threw shrapnel for up to one hundred yards. When thrown the thrower had to take cover too. However, my Uncle Norman, who survived Dunkirk was demonstrating a grenade with an instructor kneeling next to him. It was a faulty grenade and exploded in my uncle's hand. Both he and the Sergeant survived. My uncle just lost his hand. I am guessing that my uncle's hand prevented the grenade fragmenting as much as it was intended. Rifle grenades were used from 1915 onwards and enabled a grenade to be thrown much further than by hand

During the retreat the British tank, the Matilda was superior to the German Panzers. It was slow but it was so heavily armoured that it could only be stopped by using the 88 anti-aircraft guns. Had there been more of them and had they been used in greater numbers then who knows what the outcome might have been. What they did succeed in doing, however, was making the German High Command believe that we had more tanks than they actually encountered. The Germans thought that the 17 Matildas they fought were many times that number. They halted at Arras for reinforcements. That enabled the Navy to take off over 300,000 men from the beaches.

Although we view Dunkirk as a disaster now, at the time it was seen as a setback. An invasion force set off to reinforce the French a week after Dunkirk. It was recalled. Equally there were many units cut off behind enemy lines. The Highland Division was one such force. 10,000 men were captured. The fate of many of those captured in the early days of the war was to be sent to work in factories making weapons which would be used against England.

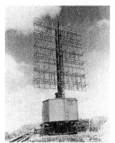

Freya, the German Radar.

Germany had radar stations and they were accurate. They also had large naval guns at Cape Gris Nez as well as railway guns. They made the Channel dangerous although they only actually sank a handful of ships during the whole of the war. They did however make Southend and Kent dangerous places to live.

Commando dagger

The first Commando raids were a shambles. Churchill himself took action and appointed Sir Roger Keyes to bring some order to what the Germans called thugs and killers. Major Foster and his troop reflect that change.

The parachute training for Commandos was taken from this link http://www.bbc.co.uk/history/ww2peopleswar/stories/72/a3530972.shtml . Thank you to Thomas Davies. The Number 2 Commandos were trained as a battalion and became the Airborne Division eventually. The SOE also trained at Ringway but they were secreted away at an Edwardian House, Bowden. As a vaguely related fact 43 out of 57 SOE agents sent to France between June 1942 and Autumn 1943 were captured, 36 were executed!

The details about the Commando equipment are also accurate. They were issued with American weapons although some did use the Lee Enfield. When large numbers attacked the Lofoten Islands they used

247

regular army issue. The Commandos appeared in dribs and drabs but 1940 was the year when they began their training. It was Lord Lovat who gave them a home in Scotland but that was not until 1941. I wanted my hero, Tom, to begin to fight early. His adventures will continue throughout the war.

The raid on German Headquarters is based on an attempt by Number 3 Commando to kill General Erwin Rommel. In a real-life version of *'The Eagle Has Landed'* they almost succeeded. They went in by lorry. Commandos were used extensively in the early desert war but, sadly, many of them perished in Greece and Cyprus and Crete. Of 800 sent to Crete only 200 returned to Egypt. Churchill also compounded his mistake of supporting Greece by sending all 300 British tanks to the Western Desert and the Balkans. The map shows the area where Tom and the others fled. The Green Howards were not in that part of the desert at that time. The Germans did begin to reinforce their allies at the start of 1941.

Motor launch Courtesy of Wikipedia

Motor Gun Boat Courtesy of Wikipedia

Short Sunderland

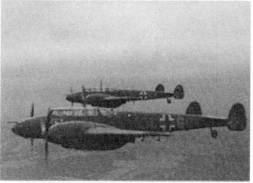

Messerschmitt 110s over France

Fieseler Fi 156 Storch

The St. Nazaire Raid was an incredible story of bravery and skill. The 5 Victoria Crosses which were awarded are testament to the bravery and the skill with which the ship was guided, at night, to strike its tiny target perfectly is astounding. Tom and his section are an amalgam of the actions of a larger number of Commandos. Their actions prevented the Germans from using the only Atlantic dry dock capable of repairing the Tirpitz which spent the rest of the war in a Norwegian Fjord. Had the Commandos and the Royal Navy not done what they did then the Atlantic convoys would have been at risk and the war might have ended differently. HMS Sturgeon was used to guide the flotilla of ships into the Loire estuary. The "Lancastria" was sunk during the evacuation in 1940. Over 4000 men died, and it was the greatest single loss of life in British maritime history. The wreck was left in the Loire estuary.

S class submarine HMS Sturgeon. The same class as the 'Sunfish'.
Courtesy of Wikipedia.
The S Class had a crew of 39 officers and men.

The Campbelltown being converted

The Campbelltown just before she exploded.
Photographs courtesy of Wikipedia

S-160 Courtesy of Wikipedia

The E-Boats were far superior to the early MTBs and Motor
Launches. It was not until the Fairmile boats were developed that the tide
swung in the favour of the Royal Navy. Some MTBs were fitted with
depth charges. Bill's improvisation is the sort of thing Combined
Operations did. It could have ended in disaster but in this case, it did not.
There were stories of captured E-Boats being used by covert forces in
World War II. I took the inspiration from S-160 which was used to land
agents in the Low Countries and, after the war, was used against the
Soviet Bloc. They were very fast, powerful and sturdy ships.

Reference Books used

- The Commando Pocket Manual 1949-45- Christopher
  Westhorp
- The Second World War Miscellany- Norman Ferguson
- Army Commandos 1940-45- Mike Chappell
- Military Slang- Lee Pemberton
- World War II- Donald Sommerville
- St Nazaire 1942-Ken Ford
- Dieppe 1942- Ken Ford

- The Historical Atlas of World War II-Swanston and Swanston
- The Battle of Britain- Hough and Richards
- The Hardest Day- Price

Griff Hosker November 2015

Other books

by

Griff Hosker

If you enjoyed reading this book, then why not read another one by the author?

Ancient History

The Sword of Cartimandua Series (Germania and Britannia 50A.D. – 128 A.D.)

Ulpius Felix- Roman Warrior (prequel)
Book 1 The Sword of Cartimandua
Book 2 The Horse Warriors
Book 3 Invasion Caledonia
Book 4 Roman Retreat
Book 5 Revolt of the Red Witch
Book 6 Druid's Gold
Book 7 Trajan's Hunters
Book 8 The Last Frontier
Book 9 Hero of Rome
Book 10 Roman Hawk
Book 11 Roman Treachery
Book 12 Roman Wall
Book 13 Roman Courage

The Aelfraed Series (Britain and Byzantium 1050 A.D. - 1085 A.D.

Book 1 Housecarl
Book 2 Outlaw

Book 3 Varangian

The Wolf Warrior series (Britain in the late 6th Century)
Book 1 Saxon Dawn
Book 2 Saxon Revenge
Book 3 Saxon England
Book 4 Saxon Blood
Book 5 Saxon Slayer
Book 6 Saxon Slaughter
Book 7 Saxon Bane
Book 8 Saxon Fall: Rise of the Warlord
Book 9 Saxon Throne

The Dragon Heart Series
Book 1 Viking Slave
Book 2 Viking Warrior
Book 3 Viking Jarl
Book 4 Viking Kingdom
Book 5 Viking Wolf
Book 6 Viking War
Book 7 Viking Sword
Book 8 Viking Wrath
Book 9 Viking Raid
Book 10 Viking Legend
Book 11 Viking Vengeance
Book 12 Viking Dragon
Book 13 Viking Treasure
Book 14 Viking Enemy
Book 15 Viking Witch
Bool 16 Viking Blood
Book 17 Viking Weregeld
Book 18 Viking Storm
Book 19 Viking Warband
Book 20 Viking Shadow

The Norman Genesis Series
Rolf
Horseman
The Battle for a Home
Revenge of the Franks
The Land of the Northmen
Ragnvald Hrolfsson
Brothers in Blood
Lord of Rouen

The Anarchy Series England 1120-1180
English Knight
Knight of the Empress
Northern Knight
Baron of the North
Earl
King Henry's Champion
The King is Dead
Warlord of the North
Enemy at the Gate
Warlord's War
Kingmaker
Henry II
Crusader
The Welsh Marches
Irish War
Poisonous Plots

Border Knight 1182-1300
Sword for Hire
Return of the Knight
Baron's War

Modern History
The Napoleonic Horseman Series
Book 1 Chasseur a Cheval
Book 2 Napoleon's Guard
Book 3 British Light Dragoon
Book 4 Soldier Spy
Book 5 1808: The Road to Corunna
Waterloo

The Lucky Jack American Civil War series
Rebel Raiders
Confederate Rangers
The Road to Gettysburg

The British Ace Series
1914
1915 Fokker Scourge
1916 Angels over the Somme
1917 Eagles Fall
1918 We will remember them
From Arctic Snow to Desert Sand
Wings over Persia

Combined Operations series 1940-1945
Commando
Raider
Behind Enemy Lines
Dieppe
Toehold in Europe
Sword Beach
Breakout
The Battle for Antwerp
King Tiger
Beyond the Rhine

Other Books
Carnage at Cannes (a thriller)
Great Granny's Ghost (Aimed at 9-14-year-old young people)
Adventure at 63-Backpacking to Istanbul

For more information on all of the books then please visit the author's web site at http://www.griffhosker.com where there is a link to contact him.

Printed in Great Britain
by Amazon